Jackie's heart stopped. She had heard it! No animal could have made that sound. Only a human footstep could make such a breaking clamor. Raising the gun, she started a crouching walk toward the door that led out on the veranda where Graham worked outside. Leaning up against the large glass door, she listened carefully. Her hand started shaking again.

There might be one man out there . . . there might be several! Whatever. She didn't want to be caught inside the cabin with an attacker. She had to get outside where the assailant couldn't corner her. Probably the man already knew there was only one woman in the house, and that made her a prime target for attack. Jackie's mouth went dry, and for a moment she thought she might faint.

Lying on her stomach, Jackie reached up to make sure the doorknob was still unlocked. The knob wouldn't turn! Gingerly, she ran her hand down the side until she felt the small lock release. With a flip of her thumb, she popped the lock open. Taking a long, deep breath of air, Jackie jumped up, swung the door open and dashed outside.

TAGGED

ROBERT L. WISE

THE
TRIBULATION
SURVIVAL
SERIES

WARNER
Faith

NEW YORK   BOSTON   NASHVILLE

Scriptures are taken from the REVISED STANDARD VERSION of the Bible. Copyright © 1949, 1952, 1971, 1973 by the Division of Christian Education of the National Council of the Churches of Christ in the U.S.A. Used by permission.

Warner Faith

Time Warner Book Group
1271 Avenue of the Americas, New York, NY 10020

Visit our Web site at www.twbookmark.com.

The Warner Faith name and logo are registered trademarks of Warner Books.

Printed in the United States of America

First Warner Books printing: September 2004
10 9 8 7 6 5 4 3 2 1

Library of Congress Cataloging-in-Publication Data
Wise, Robert L.
    Tagged / Robert L. Wise
        p. cm. — (The tribulation survival series)
    ISBN 0-446-69164-X
    1. Rapture (Christian eschatology)—Fiction. 2. Electronic surveillance—Fiction. 3. End of the world—Fiction. 4. Chicago (Ill.)—Fiction. I. Title. II. Series.

    PS3573.I797T34 2004
    813'.54—dc22   2004010405

*To the countless number
of Christians
who endured terrrible trials
in the face of
overwhelming circumstances*

ACKNOWLEDGMENTS

My deepest thanks to David Howlett and Dr. Fred Pike for their kind input and insights. In addition, Steve Wilburn's editorial assistance and wise insights are gratefully appreciated, as is the work of my good friend and agent Greg Johnson. Finally, my excellent secretary Rhonda Whittacre always goes the extra mile, and does all things well.

CONFUSION ABOUNDS | I

The sun became black as sackcloth,
the full moon became like blood,
and the stars of the sky fell to the earth
as the fig tree sheds its winter fruit when
shaken by a gale.

REVELATION 6:12–13

CHAPTER 1

May 1, 2023

THE FOREST REMAINED QUIET except for the occasional sound of a deer breaking through the underbrush. A fresh scent of damp pine needles filled the air. In a few weeks spring would break out across the Lewis and Clark National Forest, sending new growth through the virgin landscape, but today the dead grass and dried plants still wore the look of winter. The tall pines reached toward the blue sky while their branches extended across the needle-covered sloping terrain. Not many people ventured into the back corners of the area seventy miles from Great Falls, Montana, but the beauty of the untouched land always left its mark on anyone hiking into the pristine wilderness. Because the leaves of the aspens had not yet broken out, the emptiness made it easier to see through the branches.

Two Cheyenne tribesmen had returned to the area where their people had traveled in an earlier century. Life in town had gotten crazy, and they needed a break from the strange events that seemed to pop up every day. Joe White Owl and Archie Big Bear had the eyes of ancient warriors for reading the paths and hidden trails in the backcountry. Having grown up on the edge of the national forest, they had traveled the back paths many times in search of rabbits and other game. As they grew to young adults, their climbing skills became as keen as a mountain goat's, equipping them to scramble along the treacherous edges of the bluffs.

White Owl led the way down the side of a steep cliff that dropped at least sixty feet to the floor of the canyon beneath them. Joe hesitated just as he was reaching for the next handhold. The dusty wall of rock shook slightly and unnerved him.

"What was that?" Joe grunted.

"The ground shook!" Archie Big Bear said. "It never did that before."

"In my whole lifetime!" White Owl shouted back. "I don't know what's going on. Be careful!"

The two men slowly worked their way farther down the stone wall. Halfway to the bottom the entire cliff shook once more, sending small rocks flying past the two climbers. Joe grabbed a small pine tree growing between two boulders and hung on for dear life. Although the rumbling lasted only a few seconds, it felt like an eternity.

"I've never been in an earthquake," Joe shouted. "But this feels close enough."

"You bet," Archie called back. "We've stumbled onto something. I want out of here!"

Both men hunkered down into the side of the cliff to catch their breath, hoping that whatever was shaking the earth would quickly pass. Nothing any longer felt predictable. Their hands turned clammy.

"Look!" Big Bear pointed to the normally placid terrain below. "Check that out!"

In the canyon beneath them, a small geyser abruptly spewed steaming hot water from the cracks in the rocks. They could see splotches of residue dotting the terrain, creating a yellowish tint across the top of the huge boulders. Nearby, the land dipped, and a boiling mud pool bubbled up from the depression in the earth, splashing churning black mud everywhere.

"Wow!" Joe squinted. "Strange sights down there."

"Never seen anything like it around here," Archie answered. "Not in this valley."

"Like you said back in town, the whole world's gone crazy. Attacks happen everywhere. Millions of people disappear overnight. Politicians promise answers, but we don't get any. We come out here to escape and only find more craziness."

"We ought to get out of this area. Worse may yet come."

"We're closer to the bottom," Joe reasoned. "I think it would be quicker to go on down and get off this wall."

"My hand's starting to get warm," Archie said. "Feel the sand."

White Owl sniffed the air. "Yeah. Strange smells, too." He inhaled again. "Could be sulfur. Why would there be the smell of sulfur out here in the forest?"

Abruptly the ground shook violently, nearly sending both men flying. They hung on fiercely, fearing the plunge would kill them.

"The dirt is walking!" Archie screamed. "We can't stay here."

"Listen." Joe pressed his ear even harder into the cliff

where he rested his head. "Funny noises! The earth is rumbling."

"This place is turning into Mount Saint Helens," Big Bear shouted. "Remember Devils Tower in Wyoming? They say it came from hot ground."

"I think we should get back to town," White Owl insisted. "We need to report what's going on to somebody." He started to hurry down the steep incline. "Everything else has gone nuts. Who can say what's going on out here."

With a terrible rumble, the ground resumed shaking. Off in the distance they heard a violent explosion, and the dirt slipped out from under both men. Dust filled their eyes and noses. Directly below, trees buckled and tumbled forward. Cracking sounds of branches breaking filled the air while the smell of smoke became more intense.

"My God!" Joe screamed. "There's an eruption over there by that waterspout! Smoke and fire are coming up! Even the trees are shaking. It's coming this way."

"I'm falling!" Archie screamed. "Everything's breaking loose!"

Joe White Owl felt the scrub pine he was holding start to break loose. "I can't hold on!" he cried. "The ground's slipping away." The agile man tumbled backward, bouncing off the wall of the cliff.

A shower of spewing, boiling water shot straight toward them. Joe futilely grabbed for a rock, a branch, anything that would stop his fall. Beneath him the earth split open, the newly formed crevice heaving clouds of black smoke through the trees.

Turbulent boiling mud splattered brown stains over the green pines. The roar became deafening, drowning out Joe White Owl's screams. With one more violent jerk, the earth hurled both men into the fiery pit, which bubbled up in a pyroclastic flow of molten magma. Rocks tumbled in behind them, and then the earth suddenly crunched back together. Steaming hot water and boiling mud calmed. The rumbling noise ceased, and silence fell over the valley. Nothing moved. Death now rested at the bottom.

The smoke and fire had stopped . . . *for the moment.*

CHAPTER 2

June 2, 2023

GRAHAM PECK pulled back the curtain and peered out the window of his family's summer home overlooking Mohawksin Lake. Virtually no one knew about this cabin—purchased six years earlier in Wisconsin—but they couldn't take security for granted. Staring suspiciously, he studied the thick grove of trees to make sure no one was spying on them. Picking up a small pair of binoculars, he examined the forest, looking carefully for any hint of movement along the edge of the trees. Only after a couple of minutes was he satisfied.

"Anyone out there?" Jackie Peck asked cautiously.

Even in jeans and a sweatshirt, her oblong, angular face and brilliant brunette hair gave the thirty-nine-year-old mother the look of a model. Her tall, poised appearance imparted an air of dignity even out in the woods of northern Wisconsin. "I trust no one's crawled in during the night."

Graham smiled. "Not yet. After six months of hiding, we're still safe. If Bridges' men knew about this cabin, they would have caught us last Christmas."

His mention of Mayor Frank Bridges flooded Graham's mind with memories of their awful escape from Illinois. Bridges had ordered his men to storm the Pecks' home after killing Graham's secretary, Sarah Cates. Graham was forced to take Adah Honi and Eldad Rafaeli, two new Jewish friends, with his family when they fled at midnight to avoid the ominous and ubiquitous electronic surveillance. At the moment when Jake Pemrose had nearly caught them, Graham pushed the red button on a small metal device Sarah Cates had lifted from Pemrose's office. Apparently the nanorobots hidden in the security implant on Pemrose's forehead were excited by the signal from Graham's device and attacked him, causing a fatal car wreck. At that moment the Pecks had fully realized how dangerous their predicament was.

"Fortunately we never let anyone know about our summer home," Jackie said. "You were too embroiled in Chicago politics. Being an assistant to Mayor Frank Bridges made you a public entity. We had to have a getaway to escape from the world and the media. I thank God we kept the hideout a family secret."

"*Hideout*'s the right word." Graham sat down at the long, rustic breakfast table. "This log cabin's been our security blanket from capture, but I have to admit, not seeing anyone except our family is beginning to wear thin."

"We see Adah Honi and Eldad Rafaeli every day. The Israelis have certainly taught us volumes about the Bible during these days. No boredom there."

"Sure, I love and appreciate them. But I once hated being inundated by those noisy, demanding voices at work. Now, I miss them."

Jackie laughed. "Hey! We're alive, and even that wicked mayor of Chicago hasn't caught up with us. Borden Camber Carson's right-hand man can't find us, and we should thank God."

Graham grinned. "Don't think I'm not grateful. We managed to crawl out from under a surveillance system of monumental proportions. Not having those beastly security markings on our foreheads kept the police from being able to find us when we sneaked out of Arlington Heights. I thank God every day we've been able to avoid being located."

Jackie reached over and took Graham's hand. "We're only a few miles from the Canadian border. Do you think we'd be safer out of America?"

"I think about that possibility a great deal of the time." Graham took a deep breath. "We could claim political asylum, but running north doesn't feel right today. I think we need to stay put. We've been able to buy groceries in the village. When we want to venture farther out, Rhinelander is close, and it's much larger. For the moment, I think we should stay where we are."

Jackie watched the early morning sunlight drift through the cracks in the curtains. She stood and opened the long white drapes. "Look! There's a deer not fifty feet away!"

The magnificent buck walked in slow steps across the slope of their property, completely unaware they were looking down on him. Graham smiled. "Wow! What a beauty."

"Boom," Jackie said quietly. "One shot from up here, and you'd have tagged a deer."

"Interesting word," Graham said. "*Tagged.* You know, we are like that deer. The mayor and security people from across the state of Illinois are a virtual army of hunters armed with computers, every kind of electronic surveillance equipment, nanorobots, guns. They are trying to tag our family. It's like a big children's game of 'tag and you're out.'"

Jackie abruptly hugged her husband. "You're frightening me."

"The fact that we haven't done anything doesn't make any difference. Bridges is trying to run us down, to trap us, to make us the victims, the losers—except if we get tagged, we are out *forever!*"

"I'm getting shivers down my back." Jackie bit her lip. "Do you think Bridges' thugs could escalate the chase? Use some sort of national police force?"

"We're peanuts to anybody but Bridges . . . and Carson. State lines make a difference, but . . ." Graham stopped. "Don't worry, Jackie." He patted her hand. "Who'd want to catch us? We can trust God for our safety."

CHAPTER 3

MATTHEW PECK came up from the bottom floor of the family's summer home and found his parents still sitting at the long wooden table. Graham's striking dark eyes were as bright as ever and his brown hair had not changed, but nineteen-year-old Matt thought his six-foot-tall father looked unusually worn and tired. His normally round face seemed more narrow and pale.

"Good morning, son," Graham said. "You're up for the day?"

"Yeah," Matt said. "Mary and George haven't stirred, but little Jeff will come bounding up the steps any minute."

"Adah and Eldad awake?" Jackie asked.

"I didn't check their rooms, but I think they are both still asleep." Matt glanced out the window. "What a beautiful June day! Glorious, brilliant sunlight!"

"A big buck wandered by just a bit ago," Graham said, "but I didn't see any signs of attackers moving in on us."

Matt raised an eyebrow. "That's good news."

"Your father was telling me that he has started

missing those mobs of people he used to hate," Jackie said. "Isn't that a hoot?"

"Dad missing the rabble packing the metro trains? Now that's a kicker!"

"Both of you are telling me that you're not getting a little stir-crazy sitting in this house day after day?" Graham said.

"I didn't want to mention it," Matt told his father, "but every now and then I feel like the walls are closing in on me. Sure, the cabin gets a little tight."

"I simply have no idea how difficult this struggle is going to be," Graham said. "How long are we going to sit out here camouflaged in the trees?"

"*Boker tov,*" Adah Honi said from the basement steps. "I see the family has awakened before me this day."

"Ah, Adah," Graham said. "Good morning."

"I trust you slept well," Jackie said.

"Yes. Our discussion last night went into the wee hours of the morning. I slept soundly."

"Maybe, you can help us with a question I have," Graham said. "How long do you think this time of world-wide struggle is going to last?"

The Jewish woman pushed her thick black hair to one side and looked out the window. Her finely chiseled profile offered a majestic countenance against the beaming sunlight. She seemed lost in thought.

"Tough question?" Jackie finally said.

"No," Adah replied. "I am simply thinking about what I should say." She turned away from the window. "In some ways the matter is simple. In other ways, it is complicated."

"I don't understand," Matt said.

"There are many biblical interpreters who believe the Tribulation will last for seven years," Adah began. "Of course, the Rapture occurred on Avi 9, the date in our Jewish calendar when everything catastrophic happened to Israel. Using the prophetic insights of chapter 9 in the book of Daniel as well as chapter 13 in Revelation, we can surmise the possibility of seven years." Adah smiled. "But remember, numbers often stand for ideas in the Scripture, and seven is an extremely important number in Israel. Creation took seven days. There are seven candlesticks in a menorah in Revelation, as well as seven seals and seven trumpets. The Holy Land has seven different names. Ezekiel chapter 36 promises seven great blessings of the Lord for Israel. The Bible goes on and on. See what I mean?"

Graham shook his head. "No, I don't understand."

"Seven is a number for fullness, completion, wholeness," Adah said. "Like seven days completing a week, it is a symbol for the fulfillment of God's Word, of spiritual perfection." She shrugged. "Seven is used as no other number in the Scripture. It comes from the Hebrew root *savah*, meaning 'to be satisfied or have enough of.' Maybe it simply tells us that the Tribulation will be over when God's work is done, when His plan is fulfilled."

"Then we won't know when the end will come!" Graham complained.

Adah smiled. "Maybe not on a calendar, but we will be challenged to trust God all the more."

"You're playing a game with us," Graham argued.

"No," Adad said. "I am being very honest."

"Hey!" Matt noticed that the sunlight had started to fade. *Sunlight shouldn't be diminishing at this hour of the day*, he thought. "Look!" He took a couple of steps toward the window. No question about it; the sun was disappearing. "Something strange is going on."

Jackie stood up. "What's happening?"

Graham looked out the window. "Shadows are falling like nighttime." He pointed across the landscape. "How can that be happening at this hour of the morning?"

Matthew watched the shadows darken and the sunlight quickly disappear. "I've never seen such a strange sight."

"The book of Revelation says that the sun will turn black during the Great Tribulation." Adah pointed toward the disappearing sun in the sky. "We are seeing it happen."

"It's an eclipse," Jackie said. "Isn't it?" She hesitated, and the worry sounded in her voice. "I didn't know one was predicted." Jackie swallowed hard. "I—I think I'm getting frightened."

"The world is descending into the shadows," Graham mumbled. "We are living in a time of darkness. Adah is right. No one can know for certain what is ahead, but I fear it will be a day of night."

CHAPTER 4

FOR SEVERAL YEARS, the U.S. government maintained a hush-hush facility for nanotechnology experimentation. South of Chicago, the University of Illinois operated the secret research facility in Urbana. Interstate highway 57 traffic zoomed past the entrance without anyone even suspecting the university's Microfabrication Research Laboratory was hidden underground. No one knew more about the cutting-edge work with nanorobots than the thirty-two-year-old scientist currently conducting an experiment.

Pulling a small laser flashlight from the pocket of his long white lab coat, the brilliant young doctor flashed the intense beam on the specimens several times. The penetrating light swept across the tabletop and reflected off a petri dish inches away from his hand. Flipping off the laser, the nanotechnologist quickly returned to the microscope. Intense silence hovered around the researcher while he stared into the microscope, studying the strange sight unfolding before his eyes.

Dr. Allen Newton mumbled and groaned while he peered through the lens for several minutes. Something was obviously wrong. At that moment, the lab's door abruptly swung open and another scientist walked in.

Because Dr. Paul Gillette was exceptionally good at obtaining funding for the expensive projects, he had been chairman of the research project and head of the lab for a number of years. Gillette had a nose for sniffing out how best to worm the required large sums out of Congress without overplaying his hand. However, Gillette remained a scientist, seldom mixing socially with more than a couple of close friends. Always keeping a sharp eye on Newton's work, he studied Allen for a second and immediately realized something was wrong.

After a quick exchange, Gillette looked into Allen's microscope and studied the strange creatures floating through the saline solution. At a length of one 100-billionth of a meter, the nanorobots were more than just extremely small mechanical creations. They were pronged living bombs. With their grotesque shapes and serrated teeth, a few of the creatures resembled repulsive monsters that might swim in the depths of the ocean. And their probing eyes left the scientific observer with the unnerving sense of possibly being observed himself. The ugly microscopic creatures wiggled and zoomed through the solution as if they were off on a thousand important missions—or on journeys directed by their own hidden inner sensors.

Gillette carefully observed the nanorobots for several moments, but he didn't like what he saw. Rather than miniature computers, they looked more like landing craft from the moon or guided missiles searching for a human heart to attack . . . maybe his! Even though these man-made creatures were important to his obtaining federal funding, they made his skin crawl.

Paul Gillette and Allen Newton were the absolute

authorities on the nanorobots. Having first designed the gadgets for national security purposes, their laboratory had been chosen by the president of the United States to provide nanorobots for use in markings on people's foreheads—an instant security technique devised after terrorist attacks exploded from public concern into a national issue. Dr. Allen Newton had devised a plan that allowed, with only one brush of a cotton swab, the nanorobots to be placed on a person's forehead, putting them in instant contact with a computer in a central police observation location. When attack or death was threatened, patrol units were instantly dispatched to the individual in danger. At least the idea sounded good.

Starting with identification nanorobots, Allen had gone on to perfect the devices so they had the capacity to work inside the human body, and could send back photographs of everything from the inside of teeth and heart valves to livers. But now he had discovered something strangely different. The gizmos seemed to have developed the ability to think for themselves!

When Allen Newton studied the gadgets speeding through the saline solution, he realized they had developed the unique capacity to seek independent direction and function divergently from how they were programmed to act. Because the doors to new and unexplored areas were being pushed open, the nanorobots' independence alarmed him. Having worked in organic morphology and the molecular arrangement of nanorobots, Dr. Newton knew the potential for these creatures, but he had also discovered that light affected them strangely, creating unpredictable behavior and often making them act like infuriated attacking bees or wasps. A sudden flash of light could send them into erratic responses.

As Dr. Gillette studied the gizmos under Allen's microscope, he began to realize just how bizarre their behavior could become. Allen had found a problem . . . a *big* problem.

Dr. Newton picked up an intense bright light and flashed it on the nanorobots in the solution. As he did so, the beam also struck a petri dish filled with samples of the miniature robots. Reaching across the table to pick up a pipette, Allen's foot slipped, sending him sprawling across the table. His hand struck the petri dish and it shattered, spraying glass over the tabletop and shooting sharp slivers of glass into Allen's hand.

Allen Newton screamed as pain shot up his arm. Grabbing a towel, Gillette wrapped it around the slashed laceration on Newton's hand, immediately realizing how serious the injury could be.

For a moment, Allen Newton looked across the tabletop at the broken dish and the splattered mess in stunned silence. He knew his hand had been cut deeply, but Newton didn't want medical attention. Still, he realized material from the petri dish might have gotten into the wound. Allen certainly didn't want any solution filled with nanorobots floating around in his bloodstream. Reluctantly agreeing to get medical help, he prepared to leave with Dr. Gillette.

As they started toward the door, Newton began to feel

dizzy, and his vision blurred. Surely the cut couldn't have affected him so dramatically? But as he tried to walk, his sense of stability started to fade. Instead of strong, steady steps, he staggered. Allen's knees buckled, and Gillette grabbed him to keep Allen from falling.

Dr. Gillette stared at the hideous transformation occurring before his eyes. Color was fading from the face of his strong, virile colleague. Newton's eyes widened and turned red. The young man gasped for air and mumbled that he feared the nanorobot-filled suspension material might have seeped into his bloodstream. The flash of light could have activated them, turning these strange machines into frenzied attackers.

Dr. Gillette tried to help Allen toward the door, but the young man found it impossible to take another step. His eyes widened farther, and a small stream of blood erupted from his right eye, making him look like he was weeping tears of blood.

Finally collapsing into Gillette's arms, Newton sank listlessly to the floor. Never closing his eyelids, the man's eyes took on a glassy, empty stare. Gillette frantically searched for his friend's pulse but found none. Staring in disbelief and shock, Paul Gillette realized Dr. Allen Newton was dead.

CHAPTER 5

O N THE OTHER SIDE of the world, the sun's sudden darkening was observed at a later hour locally than in Wisconsin. The entire country of Turkey had been caught with the same unexpected blackness in the sky that fell over America. Hassan Jawhar Rashid stood at the window of his massive petroleum offices in Istanbul, looking up at the opaque sky. Darkness had settled over the ancient city, and the streets were filled with alarmed citizens screaming in the streets.

"What is it?" Rashid's assistant asked timidly.

"*What?*" Rashid turned around slowly and looked at his assistant with disdain. "What do you think?"

Abu Shad was not easily frightened, but today he looked anxious. "I've never seen the sun go out and the streets fall dark at midday. No one expected an eclipse. The sight frightens me."

"Expecting the world to end?"

Abu Shad shook his head but didn't speak.

"Come now. You're as bad as those morons running around in the streets in total panic. Social unrest, wars around the world, and the moon turning red, plus this current blackout, and they think it all signals the end of time." Rashid shrugged. "It's not!"

"Then what has happened?" Abu Shad pushed.

"An unexpected asteroid spun out of its orbit and

veered across the orbit of the earth." Hassan spoke rapidly with an annoyed tone in his voice. "The so-called eclipse is nothing more than celestial junk blocking the sun from shining on the earth. It will be finished shortly."

Abu Shad looked relieved. "Thank you, sir. You always understand these things."

"The meeting is about to begin, Abu. Make sure the room is ready, and stay close to me. This is an important meeting."

The secretary bowed and hurried out of the room.

"Fools!" Rashid murmured to himself. "They never pay attention to astrological reports until something like this unanticipated asteroid flies by. My God! I am surrounded by idiots and fools."

Before marching out of the office, Rashid always stepped in front of the mirror to check his appearance. Hassan's black eyes carefully studied his impeccable white coat. The usual Nehru jacket with the high collar still looked freshly pressed. White contrasted favorably with his meticulously cut and combed blue-black hair. Rashid's dark skin gave him a Mediterranean appearance, allowing him to pass for any nationality from an Italian to a Turk. The truth was, he carefully guarded the enigma of his nationality and racial origins. No one knew exactly where he came from.

Starting from humble origins, Hassan had quickly realized his extraordinary intelligence and uncanny ability to read people's faces and detect the secrets hidden in their eyes. He seldom missed perceiving when someone lied or tried to deceive him. Even a minute blink was read with clear understanding. Using his ability and building on every opportunity that crossed his path, he began as an oil field worker and built through the acquisition of smaller companies what eventually became the Royal Arab Petroleum empire, a worldwide industry with the capacity to control oil prices everywhere on the globe.

During the early years, he used the name Borden Camber Carson to conceal his identity and allow himself to work unobserved behind the scenes. Having two names served his purposes well. By cloaking his appearance, Rashid had been able to keep the world from knowing what he looked like until he was ready to strike for even higher gain. And that was what he was about these days. Much higher gain.

In the last several years, Hassan Jawhar Rashid had developed a new interest in politics. He sensed this was the perfect time for a ruthless but clever manipulator to work his way to a position of power, literally dominating the international scene. He had money and power, but nothing like what he might acquire when he controlled nations with the skill of a sideshow puppeteer. And he was a ruthless, clever manipulator.

"Good afternoon, gentlemen." Hassan Rashid walked briskly into the large conference room. "Something has your attention?"

The diplomats staring out the windows turned around quickly and hurried toward their chairs.

"You seem to be, shall I say, *fascinated* with the darkness of the sun . . . as the rabble in the streets are right now."

"Mister Prime Minister," one of the men at the end of the table said, "we are sure you are aware that across the world this eclipse has created great concern. We were wondering . . ."

Rashid cut him off. "Cut the crap. Let us get down to business. This celestial twitch will be gone shortly, and the sun will come back out. We have more pressing matters to attend to."

The diplomat's mouth dropped open and he looked shocked, but he said nothing more.

"You recently brought to my attention an issue of concern with my personal security," Rashid continued. "Since I have gained international prominence, I can understand the need for greater security, but I sensed a particular personal interest in the report. Please clarify the issues for me."

"You will soon be returning to the United Nations," the secretary of commerce observed, "and traveling around America. Our fear is your vulnerability on such a trip."

Rashid thought for a moment. Yes, he had every intention of undercutting the authority of the United Nations and replacing their control. But how did that leave him unusually exposed?

"Our sources have identified a new movement taking shape in America," the commerce secretary continued. "A backlash of resentment over the rise in crime and the loss of morality is threatening to produce vigilantes who run around the countryside with guns hidden in their cars and trucks. Since the so-called Rapture, fear is rampant in the streets. These self-appointed watchdogs are a threat."

Rashid blinked several times. He'd not heard of such a thing, and he didn't like the suggestion. "Get serious," he clipped.

"I am, sir. Americans have a strange history of an intense love affair with guns. Their Constitution guarantees them the right to carry weapons anywhere. Remember the role of guns when that Jack Ruby nutcase killed Lee Harvey Oswald after Oswald shot Kennedy? Americans kill each other all the time."

Rashid was seldom surprised. With incredibly fast reading ability and a photographic memory, he didn't miss much, but this idea caught him by surprise. "What would you suggest?"

"I believe too much is at stake at this time in our history to treat your security with anything less than total concern. We must stop spontaneous exchanges when there is a large crowd. We must keep you covered with a shield of protection because guns are instantaneous and deadly."

Rashid was not sure how to respond. He had not even thought about the possibility of an assassination. Actually he felt invincible. "I must think about this aspect of my next trip to the United States. Give me some time. Next question."

The discussion continued, but Rashid was distracted. He had to decide how important it was to appear as a "man of the people," in touch with everyone, rather than becoming a remote, aloof figure. Of course, he preferred the latter, but personal contact to achieve his immediate goals might be needed. Perhaps he ought to discuss the matter with Frank Bridges, the mayor of Chicago. Bridges had floated in under his umbrella of power and was controllable, and a politician should give him a good feel of how to handle the issue. If Bridges was anything, he was a politician!

CHAPTER 6

BY EVENING, the blackness that had settled over the world cleared in Tomahawk, Wisconsin. Normal illumination had returned in the area of the Pecks' cabin when the nightly news came on television. The CBS anchorman delivered the evening review of events to the American public at a quick, clipped pace. "Tonight the world is recovering from an eclipse of the sun. The asteroid that created the problem has fortunately moved away from its near collision with the planet. Affected by the earth's field of gravity, the asteroid spun around the world until it broke free and went hurtling back into outer space. During the period of parallel orbits, the world existed in near total darkness because the sun became black. If the object had gotten any closer, a collision might have occurred that would have literally destroyed our planet."

"I'd say that's about as disturbing as the news gets," Graham said to his family.

Adah Honi and Eldad Rafaeli, their two Jewish friends, nodded in agreement.

"You know," Matthew said thoughtfully, "we've become so disconnected from the world that we really don't know what's going on in many other places. Maybe we ought to venture beyond the Tomahawk area. The town's so small, it offers nothing but groceries. Rhinelander's not that far away, and it's got far more people."

"Yeah," Graham agreed. "Good point. I'd like to get a larger perspective on that eclipse."

"But the Scripture it confirms," Adah added. "No coincidences there. It is absolutely amazing."

"Those strange events terrify me," Jackie said. "I suppose this experience is another one of the ways God is attempting to get the world's attention, but it's frightening."

Adah turned to Eldad, who had come to America from Israel. "What would you say about such an unexpected sign?"

Eldad squinted and pursed his lips. "Let me see," he said slowly. Eldad had worked for years in the Pil Tobacco factory in Rosh-Ha'Ayin, near Tel Aviv. "Rabbi Akibba from Prague once told the story of a sudden freeze that fell in the middle of the summer." Puffs of white hair shot out from the sides of his otherwise bald head and shook when he spoke. "One day it is as hot as August, and the next day a pond in the middle of the pasture is frozen as solid as if it was the coldest part in winter. His students ask, 'Why would the Holy One, bless His name, do such a thing?' Do you know what Rabbi Akibba said?"

"N-o-o-o," six-year-old Jeff said with wide-open eyes.

"Tell us!" George demanded in his high eight-year-old voice.

Teenage Mary rolled her eyes indifferently as if she could care less, but she leaned forward slightly to hear what the Israeli said.

"If the blessed One of Israel can't get your attention when it's cold, then He will certainly get it when it is hot!" Rafaeli roared. He shook his finger in the air like a professor lecturing in a class. "The Holy One who created the universe will use nature anyway He chooses to make His point! Is that not what has happened yesterday?"

"Good point!" Graham muttered. "Anything is possible."

"*Really?*" Mary said with more than a hint of disgust.

"I worry about the people who have been marked on their foreheads," Matthew said. "They are really in danger. Dad's foresight kept our family out of that loop, but we've already seen how dangerous nanorobots can be. If he hadn't pushed the red button while we were escaping from Illinois, Jake Pemrose might have killed all of us during that wild chase."

"I have been thinking about this strange mark on people's foreheads," Adah said. "Of course, the Scripture speaks of the mark of the beast, but I think there is even more we should be aware of." The Israeli woman picked up a Bible. "Let me read a strange portion of Revelation." She thumbed through the back of her little black Bible. "I think this is most interesting. 'And out of the smoke locusts came down upon the earth and were given power like that of scorpions of the earth. They were told not to harm the grass of the earth or any plant or tree, but only those people who did not have the seal of God on their foreheads.' Isn't this amazing?"

"Are you suggesting that the Bible predicted nanorobots?" Jackie said skeptically.

"No, no," Adah said. "*Predicted* is too strong a word, but I find in Scripture that there are amazing similarities of thought. Sometimes the Scripture speaks in general terms, using ancient analogies that we must interpret. Certainly the apostle John wouldn't have any idea what a nanorobot might be, but this apostle of Christ was on to something with those strange locusts he described. Perhaps, he is painting a picture that today we must interpret in our own special way."

"Locusts make a startling analogy for what nanorobots look like," Matt said. "I saw pictures of those minute things in some of my college classes. A scorpion isn't a bad image either."

"Yes, I will read some more." Adah continued, "'The locusts looked like horses prepared for battle. On their heads they wore something like crowns of gold, and their faces resembled human faces. Their hair was like women's hair, and their teeth were like lions' teeth.' Fascinating, isn't it?"

"That may not be a prediction," Graham said, "but it's close enough for me."

"I should add this portion," Adah said. "The section ends with this explanation: 'They had as king over them the angel of the Abyss, whose name in Hebrew is Abaddon, and in Greek, Apollyon.'" She stopped. "In English those words mean 'the destroyer.'"

"However one concludes these passages fit into a biblical scheme of things, the truth is that the destroyer, the angel from the Abyss, is hard at work in the world today," Graham said. "Our job is to make sure the force doesn't land here."

"Indeed!" Eldad said. "We must offer no shelter in your home to Apollyon."

CHAPTER 7

THE SUDDEN *SNAP* ECHOED through the kitchen with the sharpness of an attacker breaking through the door. Jackie jerked away from the sink and stared over her shoulder. The sound of a branch breaking or the crackling of pine needles sent shivers down her spine these days. Her heart started to pound. Maybe the noise was a deer, maybe nothing. But the unexpected noise frightened her.

Creeping away from the kitchen sink, she inched along the front wall of the cabin until she stood next to the curtains on the picture window. Gingerly, she peeked around the curtains, but saw nothing. Even though the forest appeared empty, she kept looking. Jackie grew up in a family where camping in the trees and nature trails hadn't been a part of her world. She lived far more on the indoor side of the world. Concerts, art museums, lectures; the sort of things most kids dreaded, she had been weaned on. When Graham came up with the idea of buying a cabin "up north," the idea hadn't sat well with her, but she didn't say anything because she knew secret outings would be good for the family and she would adjust. Jackie didn't like the possibility of a bear's wandering by (which never happened), but she did enjoy seeing deer (which happened frequently). It was the occasional "noises" that set her off, but this seemed far more than an *occasional* noise.

Boom! The loud thumping nose ricocheted through the cabin, coming from somewhere on the other side of the bedroom wall. No animal ever caused a reverberation with such a solid thud. Only a man's foot could create such a booming noise. Instantly, she remembered Graham had taken the children and their Jewish friends into town for groceries. The realization of their absence was more than unnerving. Jackie was *completely alone.*

She grabbed a butcher knife from the kitchen drawer and dropped below window level. Days had passed since they had seen anyone around their place, and the chances were high the intruder wasn't a friend.

Crawling on her hands and knees, Jackie scooted across the living room floor and inched into the bedroom. The second-story windows would allow her to look down on anyone prowling around the side of the house the noise had come from. At that moment she heard another sound. Quieter, but equally terrifying—the crunching of pine needles under an adult foot . . . right below the window.

Clutching the knife with an iron grip, Jackie pressed against the wall and slowly inched up to peek out the window. With her head barely showing, she stared through the windowpane. If a deer had been there, the animal would still be standing by the house, but there wasn't anything; not a squirrel, not a rabbit—*nothing*. Jackie choked. A cold, frightening sensation crawled across her mind. Graham had warned her that it was possible for their adversaries to catch them off guard electronically and sneak up on the house. If that happened, they must be prepared to protect themselves to the death. These assailants had already proved themselves to be killers, and no chances could be taken.

Dropping below the windowsill, Jackie crawled across the floor and into the closet. Shortly after they arrived in Wisconsin, Graham had purchased a pistol and a rifle that he kept concealed in the closet. When the family debated whether it was appropriate to have guns, Eldad Rafaeli argued the Scripture supported self-protection. Not to defend themselves was paramount to surrendering to murderers. Today she wasn't worrying about that debate. Jackie wanted a gun!

She quickly found the holster containing a 9mm pistol that Graham had hidden behind one of the shoe racks. He had always instructed that the clip stay loaded because time could be a factor. Jackie yanked the pistol out of the leather holster and slowly, cautiously, pulled back the slide, chambering a live round. Her hand shook so badly she feared accidentally firing the weapon. Jackie pulled her finger off the trigger and tried to catch her breath, but her furiously pounding heart made it difficult. Turning around, she started crawling back across the floor. Leaning against the bed, Jackie tried to pull her thoughts together, but the all-absorbing panic swallowed her. Graham always said she overreacted. Well, she wouldn't admit it, but he was right. Noises always got bigger inside her head than they were to her ears. Maybe she was only being overly sensitive to some normal sound. She took another deep breath and lowered the gun.

A *crack* echoed from the other side of the house.

Jackie's heart stopped. She had heard it! No animal could have made that sound; only a human could make such a noise. Raising the gun, she started a crouching walk toward the door that led out to the veranda. Leaning up against the large glass door, she listened carefully. Her hand started shaking again.

There might be one man out there . . . there might be several! Whatever. She didn't want to be caught inside the cabin by an attacker. She had to get outside where the assailant couldn't corner her. The man probably already knew there was only one woman in the house, and that made her a prime target for attack. Jackie's mouth went dry, and for a moment she thought she might faint.

Lying on her stomach, Jackie reached up to make sure the door was still unlocked. The door wouldn't move! Gingerly, she ran her hand down the side until she felt the small lock release. With a flip of her thumb, she popped open the lock. Taking a long, deep breath of air, Jackie jumped up, pulled the door open, and dashed outside.

"I'm going to kill you!" she screamed. "Blow your ugly head off!" Aiming the gun at the trees, she fired madly in every direction until the chamber clicked, signaling it was empty. The roaring blasts echoed through the trees.

Jackie suddenly realized she not only didn't have any more bullets, but she'd left the knife on the floor in the closet. Once more her hand started shaking.

Jackie listened intently and thought she might have heard someone running on the other side of the house, but she couldn't be certain. For five minutes she waited for another noise, but none came. Finally, she crouched down next to the house and waited with her gun outstretched, ready for an instant response, even though the gun remained empty. She was too exhausted to move.

Nothing. Nothing at all followed.

An hour later, Jackie heard the family car winding its way down the gravel road to their house. For the first time, she lowered the depleted gun and carefully eased her cramped finger off the trigger. She wanted to cry in sheer relief. Should she tell them her story and risk being laughed at?

There was no choice. She had to. That sound wasn't her imagination.

CHAPTER 8

THE MORNING AFTER the eclipse, Graham sat on the veranda and thought about their discussion the day before and Jackie's fears that someone was lurking outside. Graham knew his wife had a tendency to overreact, but then again, maybe she didn't. It gave him something important to ponder. Regardless, Matthew had been right. The family needed to move from beyond the narrow confines of the summer cabin. After months of seclusion, getting back in touch with the larger world might prove profitable. Possibly a larger circle of contacts would allay some of Jackie's fears. Undoubtedly, the intensity of the search by the mayor and his cronies had eased. After all, who was he that they should so relentlessly pursue him and his family?

Jackie often got emotional and overstated the issues. After all, the Peck family had been virtually invisible, and Frank Bridges surely had bigger fish to fry these days. Since the petroleum magnate and politician, Borden Carson, was pushing Bridges for some sort of national office, the mayor probably had lost interest in chasing Graham. And Carson couldn't have any interest in him.

A cold wind swept across the porch and sent a shiver down his spine. It was spring, but it could still get chilly out in the woods. For a fleeting moment, Graham thought maybe the weather was sending him a warning, but he dismissed the idea.

He thought again about Adah Honi's discovery that Borden Camber Carson's anglo name, and the Arabic name Hassan Jawhar Rashid, each had six letters that when put together stood for the biblical number 666 of the Antichrist. Her insight had changed Graham's point of view about everything. He certainly didn't like the charismatic leader, but Peck hadn't dreamed he could have the influence and significance that the Scripture attributed to the Antichrist. Carson, or Rashid, had grown explosively, beyond any presuppositions about evil Graham might have.

A highly intelligent man, Graham Peck had always been unusually creative and innovative. His inventive talents had propelled him to the top of the political world. While he actually preferred to stand in the shadows, most Chicagoans had known he was Bridges' right-hand man, and probably his backroom brains. In the last several years, Chicago had climbed the ratings ladder in its standing in national politics, surpassing even New York City and Los Angeles with the big-league politicos. Whoever stood on this ladder couldn't help but become well known in a wide circle, and Graham had placed a foot in that circle.

Those days had vanished like a mirage on a hot highway. What Graham had once believed was "normal" everyday life had completely disappeared. Never religious, the murder of Maria Peck, Graham's mother, radically shifted the family's ultimate commitments. Matt's involvement with a secret group at Northwestern University had brought them into contact with an emerging form of what had once been called Christian faith. Everyone except his daughter, Mary, had been deeply affected by this new biblical faith, and that was one of the reasons Graham got into so much trouble with Bridges and the front office. He could no longer go along with their schemes and manipulations, and if there was anything the mayor's political circle didn't want, it was people asking moral, ethical questions.

The passing months had not lessened Graham's grief over his mother's death. The discovery that her shooting was one part of Bridges' diabolical plans to test Graham's loyalty infuriated him. It also kept him aware of how deadly the intentions of Bridges and Carson remained. These men weren't playing games, and they'd do whatever was necessary to achieve their purposes.

Maria's influence on Graham's life remained constant even after her death. While the family hadn't gone to church, she had tried to instill positive values and enduring hopes in his life. A good woman, Maria's major interest unequivocally had been her family. Graham, Jackie, and the three children remained the singular focus of her dreams. Her untimely death had ripped away the barriers the Peck family used to negate the Christian message and forced them to seek the truth about the meaning of life and death. From this grim scene had come the spiritual discoveries that sent the Pecks down a very different road . . . except for Mary. She remained closed to the family's new faith.

When Matt brought Adah Honi and Eldad Rafaeli home from college, a needed dimension had been added to their spiritual lives. Much older than college students, the two Israeli immigrants brought a knowledge of the Old Testament that turned into a graduate education for the Peck family. Forced to leave with the Pecks when Bridges' men closed in on the meeting of Christians in Graham's home, the two Jews became the family's tutors, vastly widening their knowledge of the entire Bible.

But months had passed. Possibly the seasons *really had* changed things. Jackie's fears aside, Graham was certain the pursuit was more lax. Going beyond the narrow perimeters of the town of Tomahawk would certainly prove good for the children, and the family might learn some important insights about what was happening outside. Yes, a trip to Rhinelander was definitely a good idea.

CHAPTER 9

THE MAYOR OF CHICAGO stood in his large conference room, watching his advisers gathered around the table. Since Jake Pemrose's death, Bridges had lost two of the most important cogs in his political machinery. Pemrose had always been his most trusted confidant, and Graham Peck his most insightful strategist. He was minus two badly needed associates as the political struggles intensified. Borden Camber Carson had hurled him into the fray up to his neck, and he required the best brains available. The "best" wasn't out there. These days the supply of talent was proving to be highly limited.

Bridges knew political chips had been falling his way, but he couldn't chance doing anything that might offend Carson. Meachem had to take over responsibilities to minimize any fuss over Pemrose's death. The mayor had been forced to do top-drawer business with Al Meachem, Jack Stratton, and Bill Marks because they already knew most of his backroom secrets, and they were all that was left of Bridges' inner circle. While appearing far more sinister than either Peck or Pemrose, Meachem had stepped into the role of Bridges' right-hand man. Bill Marks didn't say much, but Bridges knew he could count on him. The mayor needed these men sitting around the table to function on a more professional level.

"I expect each of you to fulfill your tasks with exquisite skill," Bridges said. Wearing maroon suspenders clipped to his khaki pants, the dark-haired mayor had on his usual polo shirt and was maintaining a laid-back appearance, which meant he wasn't expecting any television appearances today. "You must perform at the highest possible level."

"We always do," Meachem said casually. His long, narrow face and deep-set eyes gave him a hardened appearance. "What's the problem?"

Bridges didn't like Meachem's predictably glib responses. "You've got to become more uptown, more sophisticated," he said forcefully. "Quit sounding like you stepped out of some side-street bar, Al."

Meachem didn't say anything but frowned. The other two men stared straight ahead.

"I'll be having another holographic conversation with Carson shortly, and I need each of you to both look and sound like you're capable of exceptional responsibility. Am I clear?"

"Certainly," Meachem's voice had shifted into a professional journalistic sound. "We'll give you nothing but the best, boss."

"Good!" Bridges said. "And don't call me boss. Make it 'Your Honor.' Let's keep comments on a high level." He put his hands behind his back while he paced. "I want to know what each of you has discovered about this recent so-called reactionary movement. I understand we have a resurrection of neo-patriots running around with guns and attacking like criminals, while claiming they are on a mission from God. What's going on?"

"I think the reports are vastly overstated," Meachem said. "I don't see any movements forming. A few people have gotten up on the strange side of the bed, but no real problems have followed."

"I'd second what Al just said," Jack Stratton added. "Certainly we've got some terrified citizens because crime and violence are so frequent, and no small number of folks are starting to believe the loss of religion created the mayhem." He shrugged. "You've got to expect some form of a backlash. The real problem is confusion in the streets."

Bill Marks said nothing.

Bridges rubbed his chin. "How big a backlash are we talking here?"

"Citizens always had guns stashed under their mattresses," Bill Marks said. "They're getting more obvious these days. Too many thugs are roaming the streets. So many attacks make them nervous."

Bridges listened and didn't like what he was hearing. "You realize a bunch of wild-eyed reactionaries could upset my apple cart? I can't afford to have arbitrary shooters taking potshots at public officials."

"I don't see these losers shooting at people like us," Meachem said. "They're more likely to be pluggin' some drug-crazed punk roaming the alleys. That ain't all bad."

"How organized is this movement?" Bridges persisted.

"I wouldn't even call it a movement," Meachem repeated. "We're talking about the fact that today we've got more crooks than we do cops. It's a police problem. Up the ante on the number of armed cops we keep on the street, and the vigilantes will disappear. It's that simple."

"I see," Bridges said thoughtfully. He didn't like their cavalier attitude and knew these men were telling him what they thought he wanted to hear. Peck never did that, and his challenges often saved the day. This circle of advisers was second-rate, and he needed to keep them away from the holographic transmissions from Carter when possible. "Anyone got anything to add?"

Most shook their heads, but Bill Marks held up his hand.

"We should underscore that there are strong reasons for people to be upset. When the curfew is enforced, and the criminals remain on the streets, people have good reason to complain. Don't forget that fear is a powerful motivator."

"Okay, let's move on to another subject," Bridges said. "I have some concern over the budget. Income and spending are down, and we need to review the numbers."

The door abruptly opened and the mayor's secretary rushed in. "I'm sorry to interrupt you, sir, but I just received an emergency phone call from Max Andrews, your supervisor of police," Connie Reeves said. "I think you should take it now."

Frank Bridges studied the woman's face. Knowing her as intimately as he did, it was easy to read when she was serious and the situation demanded immediate attention. Connie's eyes said, *Now!*

"Excuse me, gentlemen." The mayor walked quickly out of the room. "What's happened?" he snapped.

"Talk to him." Connie shoved the telephone into his hand.

"Bridges here."

"You need to get down to the station house on Fifth Street as quick as you can," Max Andrews said. "We've had a terrible shoot-out with six policemen killed. A bunch of local apartment dwellers hit them at the station house. Shot 'em dead!"

"Why?"

"I don't know. The only report I have was these neighborhood creeps came in blasting away and screaming 'conspirators.' They all got away except for one man shot going out the front door."

"*An attack?*" Bridges' voice elevated. "An attack by regular citizens?"

"I'm afraid so."

CHAPTER 10

HAVING CHANGED his casual clothing, Mayor Frank Bridges' expensive navy blue suit now carefully concealed his bulging paunch. Because his conversations on the holographic transmitter with Borden Camber Carson were three-dimensional and in color, he always attempted to present an impeccable appearance. Inevitably, Bridges looked as elegant as anyone working in Chicago's Magnificent Mile.

"Sit down in the chair behind me," Bridges told Meachem. "I want you to look like a tower of security, but keep your mouth shut. Say nothing unless Carson speaks to you. Understand?"

Meachem nodded his head solemnly.

"Bill, you stand against the door," the mayor told Bill Marks. "Keep beyond the range of observation and watch quietly."

Bill Marks walked to the closed door and silently stood, watching the holographic process unfold.

"I have no idea what we'll be talking about today, but you need to be seen and not heard. I want Carson to think of you as primarily providing my security."

Meachem said nothing, but nodded.

Bridges reached to the control box on the corner of his desk and pushed several buttons. Immediately a wall panel slid open, revealing a large black unit that looked like the giant base of a blender. The machine made a low whirring sound and began to project a powerful beam of light upward. After a few moments, the light took on a greenish glow, and a form slowly began to take shape in the center of the light beam.

Bridges stiffened to appear more erect and cast a glance at Meachem, who was staring hypnotically at the beam of light forming into the shape of a man. Bridges looked back at the green light that was now taking the form of Borden Camber Carson.

Carson appeared to be sitting in a large leather chair in his usual white Nehru jacket. On top of his head seemed to be a turban, but as it took on a more defined form, his face became clearly lined with thick black hair. Frozen in place, Carson's eyes began to move, and the diamond ring he wore on his pinky finger started to sparkle. While coming from the other side of the world, the prime minister of Turkey appeared to be sitting in the mayor's office as if he had just walked in the front door.

"Your Honor." Frank Bridges stood up.

"Good afternoon, Frank." Carson extended his hand with the palm turned up. "I trust you have Chicago under control today."

"Our pressing problems seem to be receding, and we haven't had any terrorist attacks in some time."

Carson raised an eyebrow and smiled knowingly. "And why are we not surprised?"

"We are moving into a quieter period," Bridges continued. "It's been six months since the election, and nothing catastrophic has shaken the economy. I'm hopeful we won't be faced with any monumental decisions."

"You will be," Carson quipped. "Matters will be moving quickly in the near future."

"I see."

"I want you to be prepared for some important information that will be coming your way shortly. We have now linked the data coming through your country into the international computer system I am operating in Rome. Of course, the security devices on people's foreheads feed into this matrix. My agents tell me we have access to any possibilities for terrorist or subversive activities. Implementing key words, we have made this system highly sensitive to words like *bombs, guns, espionage, attacks,* that sort of thing. We can run down coded remarks in a matter of seconds. You can see where this is going."

Bridges nodded. "Yes, your intentions are clear."

"Good." Carson turned his attention to Meachem. "I see you have a new assistant sitting with us."

"Al Meachem has been providing security. He is one of my advisers."

"Good afternoon, Mr. Meachem." Carter's eyes narrowed. "You are an expert in security?"

Meachem nodded his head but said nothing.

"Security is one of the issues I want to talk about," Carson continued, not taking his eyes off Meachem's face. "I will be coming to your country soon to speak at the United Nations. Security has become an increasing concern."

"Your face is everywhere," the mayor said. "Where you were once a mystery man, today this entire city and state recognizes you. It's the same in the East and the West."

"I am told your country has been producing a bumper crop of terrorists who might be interested in shooting me." Carson barely paused, looking at Bridges with the casualness of having just asked him for the room temperature.

Bridges blinked several times. It wasn't the question he was expecting or wanted. "I know of no one who would want to shoot you, sir. Since you enacted oil agreements favorable to our area, you're more of a hero."

"I've been misinformed about vigilantes shooting people. My advisers tell me citizens are angry over the lawless condition in the country."

Carson's question was too specific. Bridges couldn't afford to be evasive, especially with Meachem and Marks listening. "We've had some of that activity, yes, but I'm not concerned for a man of your stature. You should feel safe."

Carson started drumming the desk with his fingertips. "*Safe* is a peculiar word, my friend. Easy to attribute to someone else. Would you use that word to cover your political situation?"

Bridges relaxed. He could safely and enthusiastically answer that question. He didn't worry about his personal security and felt safe when walking down the streets.

"How would you answer me, Frank?"

"I can honestly tell you that I don't give those concerns even a thought. I'd walk down any street in Chicago in a second. Sure, we've had a few shooting incidents and riots on the streets, but I don't take them personally. Nothing new about crime in Chicago. My associates tell me they are aimed at knocking out criminals and thugs lurking in the backstreets. You and I could walk down the street arm in arm, and you'd feel completely secure."

Carson said nothing but studied Bridges' face with the same intensity he had focused on Meachem. "I appreciate your candor."

"Ah . . . I . . . do have a slightly different question, sir. Earlier we talked about the possibility of my running for the presidency. Isn't that an issue we should address at this time?"

"I have recently made new plans," Carson said with no hesitation, "and I have a more important position for you to fill."

Bridges felt his jaw drop slightly. He tried to catch his breath without being obvious, but Carson's words stung. *More important?*

"Matters are unfolding even faster than someone in your strategic position could be aware of." Carson kept talking with a smile on his face. "Before long, the American president will be even less of a factor than he is today, Frank. We will shortly begin a campaign to discredit your central government. America is currently struggling with chaos. I want to increase the national sense of confusion, and we will do this by making the president appear incompetent. I will need your assistance in this effort."

Bridges tried not to frown. "I—I don't know how I could make an impact in such an effort."

"We do! I will be unfolding these details in the next few days. In the meantime, I want to appoint you as my top American assistant. You will be in charge of the intelligence efforts we have in this country. Sitting in that secret service chair is the equivalent of sheer power."

"*Head of intelligence?*" Bridges squinted.

"Exactly! For the moment we will not release this to the press, but in a short while the news will be a worldwide headline story."

Bridges gritted his teeth. He wasn't sure how to respond. The idea sounded good, but the position was certainly far less powerful than he considered the president of the United States to be. "I see," he concluded.

"We have one detail we must get out of the way," Carson said. "Have you captured Graham Peck?" he asked bluntly.

Bridges swallowed hard. He felt like a prizefighter knocked into the corner, only to discover the opponent was using a baseball bat instead of padded gloves. "No."

Carson kept smiling. "I am concerned about this man because he has seen so much of our operation. He could still hit the papers with a story of long-range consequence." Carson leaned forward and stared intensely at Bridges. "I want him found *immediately.*"

"We haven't been slack in looking for him," the mayor answered. "No one has written Graham Peck off."

"You have surveillance around his house?" Carson pushed.

"We did up until a month ago, but there's been no one touching the place in months and—"

"Get the police out there!" Carson abruptly shouted. "Don't leave any rock unturned. Find him!" The smile vanished as he hit the table with a clenched fist. "*Now!*"

"Yes sir," Bridges mumbled. His halting affirmation was all the mayor could say. Bridges felt a strange combination of humiliation and exaltation that left him completely in Carson's hands.

CHAPTER 11

MUCH LARGER THAN a simple house in the forest, the Pecks' summer home had extra bedrooms that turned out to be more than adequate for Adah Honi and Eldad Rafaeli. Remoteness remained beyond the top of their list of outstanding attributes of the sanctuary in the woods. On a pleasant Friday evening, the Peck family sat around their long wooden table adjacent to the kitchen, eating supper.

"I've been thinking about our talk the other day," Graham said. "Matt made the suggestion that we ought to think about going into Rhinelander. I believe it would be good for us to widen our circle of contacts."

"But what about the noises I heard outside?" Jackie objected.

"Ah, we haven't heard a thing," Mary taunted. "I think the sounds were all in your head."

"I beg your pardon!" Jackie leaned forward to speak directly into her daughter's face. Mary stared down at her plate and didn't say any more.

"Not to discount your mother's experience," Graham said, "I think it would be emotionally stabilizing for all of us to see some new faces. It would be for me."

"What makes you think Jackie didn't hear thugs sent from Bridges' office?" Adah Honi asked.

"I couldn't say for certain she didn't," Graham said. "But if his vigilantes found us, they would have attacked by now, and I don't think that sort of hoodlum would have run away."

"Indeed!" Eldad said. "But extra eyes would help! I will make it my job to be for us a special watchdog. I can roam around through the trees and watch while you are gone. You will find me a skilled soldier."

"Eldad will be our new police dog!" Jeff said. "He'll catch the bad guys."

The family chuckled and returned to eating supper. In twenty minutes they were finished.

Eldad pushed back from the table. "There once was a rabbi in Prague," he began, "who was asked if he should protect himself." He scratched his head. "The rabbi said—"

Adah cut him off. "Thank you, Eldad. I don't think we need any more rabbi stories today." She patted his hand. "What do you think the news is tonight?" Adah asked. "Maybe we should listen?"

"George!" Jackie called to her eight-year-old son. "Turn on the television."

George flipped on the remote control, and the Wisconsin evening news report appeared, followed by the weather forecast.

"I wonder what is happening in the rest of the world?" Adah said.

"Hang on," Graham answered. "The national news will be on in a few moments." He returned to clearing the table. "George, turn up the volume."

"Another round of terrorist activity has shaken Israel," the announcer began. "Recent negotiations sponsored by Borden Camber Carson, or Hassan Jawhar Rashid as he is known in the Middle East, promise to guarantee Israel's security, but these attackers seem to have come out of nowhere. No one is certain of the source, but ten Israelis were killed and fifty more wounded in the latest suicide attack aboard a bus in downtown Jerusalem."

Adah gasped. "The Holy One, blessed be His name, please help us! Look, Eldad!"

The older man shook his head. "The Evil One never ceases to chase us." Eldad's voice filled with sadness. "The world always sees the Jews as its target."

"I had hoped Israel was more secure," Graham said. "This attack is serious business."

Jackie finished wiping her hands and laid down the towel. "A new round of attacks in Israel certainly won't help peace in the world."

The announcer interviewed the president of the

United States for his response as well as the American ambassador in Israel. Each man condemned the strike.

"What can any of them say?" Adah asked. "Of course, they deplore the violence!"

"And back in this country," the announcer continued, "an unexpected harsh response came from the mayor of Chicago. Frank Bridges issued a statement just moments ago."

Intense quietness settled over the Peck household. Jackie hurried toward the television set and even Mary listened intently.

The face of Frank Bridges filled the screen. "After careful consultation with my advisers both here and in Israel, I must condemn the weak response of the president of the United States," Bridges began. "He has not grasped how potentially dangerous this latest round of terrorist attacks is. Washington cannot sit idly by and allow another Jewish-Arab war to explode in our faces."

Graham's eyes narrowed. What was Bridges attempting to do? He knew Bridges' style like the back of his hand.

"We must have a stronger hand at the wheel," Bridges continued. "The United States can no longer allow tragedies to unfold and make only vague condemnations. If the president doesn't have the ability to respond forcefully, then we need to look to other sources for direction and purpose."

"Bridges is attacking the president," Graham said out loud. "That's what this nonsense is about."

"What do you mean?" Adah asked.

"Bridges didn't come up with this statement on his own," Graham said. "You're hearing Camber Carson's words rolling out of the mayor's mouth. Other reasons exist for this attack."

"You think Bridges is really after the president for some other reason?" Matt asked.

"If Carson is pushing him, you'll hear Bridges sounding like a cross between George Washington and Teddy Roosevelt," Graham said. "Don't worry. Carson's people know how to build a castle on top of a foundation of confusion. Bridges isn't about to let this opportunity to create chaos pass."

"What does that mean for us?" Jackie asked.

"It's all the more reason for us to get out of seclusion and find out what the wider world is thinking. We need to take a trip into Rhinelander."

CHAPTER 12

MONTHS OF LIVING in close quarters had pushed the family into a new experience of relationships. In the past, the Pecks had lived at such a fast pace, they seldom saw one another long enough to develop any depth of conversation. Jeff and George lived in their own children's world. Having become a high and mighty teenager, Mary tried to avoid the family. But their emotional distances dissolved when they were only a few feet from each other day and night.

Graham had gained a more personal respect for his children and found their opinions to be better than he expected. Even rebellious Mary often had insightful ideas that added to the drift of conversation. She had been forced to talk more directly to her parents even with her hesitancies and resentments.

All in all, the long sequestered time in the trees had produced good results. Jackie's rapidly developing spiritual life had increased Graham's already significant respect for his wife. Adah and Eldad's teaching had helped deepen their relationship, and their time together had become more meaningful. While the threat of discovery hung over their heads, Graham had to conclude the last few months had been one of the richest times in his life.

The little boys kept their noses pressed against the windows while the exuberant Peck family zoomed down the highway toward Rhinelander. The trip was virtually their first outing in seven months beyond a narrow five-mile ring around their cabin. While Rhinelander wasn't a city, they still felt as though a world tour had begun.

After a slow drive through Rhinelander, the family got out of the car and walked down the town's main street. No one appeared to pay attention to them.

"I wish Eldad had come with us," little Jeff said. "I like him."

"He likes you, too," Adah said. "But Eldad wants to make sure no one finds us. He is an excellent soldier."

"Really?" Matt said. "A *genuine* soldier?"

"You see," Adah began, "in Israel, every person must

learn to shoot a gun and know how to protect themselves. Attacks could happen at any moment."

"How horrible. Obviously the country needs relief to ease people's fears," Jackie said.

"You must remember how urgent the problem is," Adah said. "We have spent decades worrying about a war exploding at any moment. Eldad learned to be a soldier after he emigrated from Russia. He is a clever man."

"I still wish he'd come with us," Jeff said.

"Hey!" Jackie pointed to a local restaurant. "We haven't eaten in a joint like that since we left Chicago. Let's do it."

"You're on!" Graham said. "How about a big piece of pie?"

A worn red sign across the large plate-glass window advertised "Betty's Café." Delicious smells floated out the front door and sweetened the thoroughly used appearance of the old place. Through the window they could see some people sitting inside. The family picked up their pace and hurried in. A few customers were seated across the restaurant, with one woman by herself in a corner reading a menu. The Pecks found a table and sat down.

"Feels excellent to me," Matt said. "Not like Northwestern University, but maybe even better!"

"See," Graham said. "I told you that getting out of the cabin would be good for us."

"I'm hungry," George announced and grabbed a menu out of Mary's hands.

"Give me that!" Mary whacked him with her hand.

"Stop it!" Graham demanded. "Have you children forgotten how to act in public?"

Mary leered at George and took back the menu. "No!" she answered insolently. "My brother's a jerk."

"Both of you straighten up," Graham demanded.

"Look," Adah said quietly. "Notice that woman over there in the corner booth."

"Why?" Jackie asked.

"She's different from the rest of the people," Adah said. "The woman appears more self-contained, happier. Her face looks far more relaxed and at ease."

"Why do you think she's unusual?" Matt asked.

"I'm not sure yet," Adah said. "We must observe her further."

The waitress took the woman's order and then came over to write down the Peck family's wishes. Dressed with an apron around her waist, the distant waitress seemed almost insolent, but the family took her in stride. Ten minutes later the waitress brought out the order of the woman in the booth.

"Look at that!" Graham said under his breath.

"I can't believe my eyes," Jackie answered. "It looks like that lady is praying before she eats."

"She is!" Matt said. "I can't even remember the last time I saw someone praying in public."

The woman opened her eyes, picked up a fork, and started eating without any awareness that the family across the room was studying her as if she were a science project.

"This is no accident," Adah concluded. "I think we've found a new Christian!"

"We've got to make contact," Graham whispered urgently.

"We certainly can't say anything in here," Jackie said and glanced around the room. "Who knows what these local residents are into?"

"We have not come here by mistake," Adah said. "This is God's timing."

"But I don't know how we can talk to her without getting ourselves in trouble," Graham concluded. "We'll have to think about it carefully."

CHAPTER 13

GRAHAM STUDIED the unusual woman, who wore a dark blue dress, as she walked over to pay her bill. He definitely wanted to talk to her. When the insolent waitress responded in a harsh and abrupt manner, the woman kept smiling and wished her a good day. The waitress looked surprised and went back to hauling out the food. The woman in the blue dress left.

"We've got to follow her," Matt said.

"That's exactly what I was thinking," Graham answered quietly. "We can stay behind her some distance and watch where she goes."

"I'll leave right now while you pay our bill," Matt said. He slid out of the seat and took off.

"You think Matthew will get in trouble?" little Jeff asked in his most serious six-year-old voice.

"Who's going to nab him?" Mary retorted. "The *boogeyman?*"

"Mary," Jackie said, "we don't need you making smart remarks every time someone speaks."

Mary rolled her eyes.

"I'll go over and stand by the counter," Graham said. "That'll hurry the waitress up with our bill." He got up and walked across the restaurant. No one looked at him. In fact, no one was talking to anybody else. The family's chatter prevented him from realizing how silent the place actually was.

The waitress came out of the kitchen and saw him standing by the front counter. A disgusted look crossed her face, but she came over to the cash register. "You folks in a rush?"

Graham forced a smile. "No, just enjoying your town."

"Rhinelander? You got to be kidding."

"Looks nice to me."

"Humph!" The waitress snorted. "Okay, you owe the amount written on the check." She shoved the paper tab across the top of the counter.

"I imagine you get lots of tourists through here." Graham dug in his pocket for the plastic card he used for money.

"Did once upon a time," the waitress said. "Nowdays people are too frightened to venture this far north very often. Mostly just the locals eat here."

"I see." Graham pushed the plastic card forward. "Did you watch the news last night?"

"No!" the waitress growled. "I got enough trouble without piling on that nonsense." She looked suspiciously at Graham. "What are you people anyway? The Gallup pollsters?"

Graham didn't like the look in her eye. The waitress's face had a mean twist, and he didn't want to start any problems. "Just asking."

The woman looked at him with a mind-your-own-business glance and ran his card through the machine. She didn't say anything and handed back the card.

Graham pulled his cap down lower on his forehead and walked away. Obviously conversation wasn't big around this café. He walked outside to wait for the family.

"Wow!" Jackie said as she came out the front door. "I could hear that waitress clear over in our booth. Was she the poster child for the local Halloween event?"

"People don't seem too friendly," Adah added.

"Interesting," Graham said. "The town looks pleasant enough, but there seems to be significant distance between everyone."

"We better hurry to catch Matt," George urged and grabbed Jeff's hand.

"You're right!" Graham started walking quickly across the street. The family followed with Mary bringing up the rear, dragging her feet.

At the end of the next block Matt stood on the corner, waving and pointing to his left. He disappeared down the adjacent street.

"Got to hurry," Graham said.

"Hurry?" Mary groused. "We already look like morons chasing some woman we don't even know."

Jackie grabbed her arm. "What did I tell you back in that restaurant?"

"I'm just saying that we're out here on a wild-goose chase and this woman may—"

"Enough!" Jackie cut her off. "Keep up with us." She took the boys' hands and picked up her stride, leaving Mary behind her.

"Matthew has stopped," Adah said. "The woman is gone."

Graham could see his son standing quietly by a large tree in front of a plain brown house. Trying to look casual, Graham slowed to a more leisurely pace as he walked up to Matthew.

"Where'd she go?" Graham asked.

"The woman walked in the front door of that brown house directly behind me," Matthew said. "I don't think she even noticed me."

"Hmm." Graham looked at the house. "We know she's inside, but do I dare knock on the door?"

Jackie came hustling up with the two boys in hand. "What do we do next?"

Graham glanced at the house and then at the family. "I'm trying to decide if I dare walk up and knock on the door."

"See how she answers," Adah suggested. "I don't think you can know what to say until you hear her voice. If she's like the waitress, simply ask for someone's address."

"This is crazy," Mary complained. "She'll call the cops."

"No, she won't!" George shot back. "You always expect the worst."

"Children!" Jackie warned.

"Let's see what happens," Graham said. "You all stand here in plain sight, and I'll go knock on the door."

"Be careful, Graham!" Jackie said.

With hesitant steps, Graham walked to the front door. He took a deep breath and knocked. Nothing happened. He knocked again. Suddenly the door swung open.

"Yes?" the woman in the blue dress said. "Can I help you?"

CHAPTER 14

MAYOR FRANK BRIDGES paced impatiently around his office. Al Meachem should have returned by this time, and Bridges demanded punctuality. Connie Reeves came in.

"Where's Meachem?" Bridges snapped.

"Don't know," Connie answered. "Nobody's here but us, Frankie. You don't have to sound like you're tearing heads off today, especially mine."

"I told that jerk to get back here with the doctor from the nanotechology lab twenty minutes ago. It's not that far to drive from Urbana. I don't like delays."

"Indeed!" Connie kissed him on the cheek. "Don't worry, honey. Meachem will be here any minute."

"He better be!" Bridges snapped.

"Your wife called," Connie said, "but I said you were out."

The back door to the inner offices opened and the sound of men walking echoed down the hall. "That's Meachem," Connie said.

Bridges glared at the door, but the footsteps on the thick carpet were clearly coming toward his office.

Al Meachem walked in with a tall man behind him, wearing a black goatee and with his hair combed straight back. Bill Marks brought up the rear. "Sorry about the delay," Meachem said. "A truck overturned on Interstate 57."

Bridges ignored the comment. "You must be Dr. Paul Gillette, the head of the Microfabrication Research Laboratory." He extended his hand.

"Y—yes," Dr. Gillette said hesitantly. "I wasn't aware that you knew about our facilities." He glanced fearfully at Meachem. "I didn't expect your men to show up like they did or force me to come with them."

"Please forgive the intrusion," Bridges said warmly. "Many things are happening right now that are highly classified, but I can assure you that I am completely aware of your research." He motioned toward a chair. "Please sit down."

Gillette watched Meachem with a nervous look on his face, but the scientist sat down.

"I understand that Dr. Allen Newton recently died," the mayor began.

Gillette looked surprised. "His death was most unexpected."

"And deeply disappointing," Bridges said. "We all admired the bold research Newton was doing."

Gillette appeared to be totally uncertain of what to say next. "I wasn't aware the larger community knew of Allen's demise."

"They don't!" Bridges continued. "If you'll remember, Chicago was the first city in the country to use his nanorobots for security purposes. We applied them to people's foreheads. Consequently, I have followed everything Newton did."

"I see." Dr. Gillette rubbed his chin nervously and repeated himself. "I see."

"Good!" Bridges forced a smile. "We want you to continue the work Newton was doing with swarm intelligence. We have an immediate need for this application of the nanorobots."

"Swarm intelligence has the highest possible security rating." Gillette's eyes widened. "How could you know about these experiments?"

Bridges kept smiling, but his voice turned hard. "I know everything that is happening in your facility, and I also have the right to ask questions as well as request applications. Are we clear?"

Dr. Gillette glanced at Meachem again, and then looked at the mayor with uncertainty. "I haven't received authorization for such an inquiry," he said hesitantly.

Bridges reached across his desk and picked up a letter. "You'll find this document from the official responsible for your federal funding fully covers your questions." He shoved it into Gillette's hands. "Correct?"

Paul Gillette read the document carefully. Finally, he puckered his lip and nodded his head slowly. "I—I suppose it does."

"Good!" Bridges answered enthusiastically. "I want you to develop immediately a use for flying nanorobots that will have the capacity to identify a group of six persons. I intend for these devices to help me locate some . . . ah . . . escapees."

Gillette sank back in the chair. "I'm not sure I understand exactly what you intend."

"It's my understanding that Newton's work was creating a new approach where individual robots would come together and become interactive." Bridges smiled again. "You know what I mean, Paul. These tiny machines would coalesce and form, oh, let's say, a multifaceted lens, with the capacity to transmit their sightings back to our computers. I want to find six people together who don't have security markings on their foreheads. These nanorobots can accomplish that purpose."

Gillette pulled at his necktie. "Sir, you must understand that these devices are far from perfected. Sometimes they ah . . . spin . . . out of control."

"I don't care," Bridges snapped. "I want this product to operate in the way I have described."

"Please realize, our research can't respond to demands. We must work on a schedule." Gillette swallowed hard. "You see, Dr. Newton was killed while working on one of these experiments."

"You don't understand," Bridges said in a cold, calculating manner. "I can cut your funding off in a second!" He snapped his fingers. "You want the research lab in Urbana to be history?"

Dr. Gillette looked around the room at the solemn men, standing with arms crossed and staring with cold eyes. "Of course not," he answered.

"Then I'd suggest you get after the application I described," Bridges said. "Am I clear?"

Gillette nodded his head.

"I want to put this idea into gear immediately." Bridges started pacing back and forth again. "I realize you have some adjustments to make, but I intend this operation to be running in at the most ten days."

"Ten days!" Gillette's mouth dropped.

"*Am I clear?*"

Once again Gillette nodded.

"If you have any questions or problems, contact Mr. Meachem." Bridges pointed to his adviser. "He will talk with me."

"I—I can't promise you they'll be ready in ten days," Dr. Gillette babbled. "Dr. Newton's assistants cannot work as fast as h—he did."

Bridges ignored his excuse. "I will expect you to be expeditious." He suddenly extended his hand again. "Thank you for coming on such short notice, Doctor. Mr. Meachem will take you back to Urbana." He smiled and patted the scientist on the shoulder. "Have a nice trip."

Meachem, Gillette, and Marks left, with the scientist walking between Bridges' two assistants. Bridges stood immobile, watching them depart. A few moments later the sound of the back door closing sounded down the hall.

Connie Reeves walked in. "What do you think, Frankie?" the secretary said.

"I think between Meachem's strong-arm tactics and my threatening to yank his funds, we definitely got that little man's attention."

CHAPTER 15

"Yes?" the woman in the blue dress asked Graham Peck. "Can I help you?"

"Uh . . . I'm sorry to bother you." Graham said. The woman looked gentle and kind with no hint of animosity lurking in her eyes. "And please forgive me if I seem audacious, but my family noticed you at the restaurant." He pointed over his shoulder toward Jackie and the children. "I wondered if you would mind if I asked you a question."

The woman smiled. "No. Of course not."

"When your food was served, we noticed you bowed your head, and I assumed that maybe . . . you prayed?"

"Yes." The woman's face became much more serious. "I always thank God before I eat a meal."

"I don't know what the proper word to use is because so much has changed, but are you . . . a . . . Christian?"

The woman's smile broadened. "Yes, I am a believer in Jesus Christ."

Graham heaved a sigh of relief. "Praise God! *You are!*" He turned around and waved for the family to join him. "Yes!" he shouted. "She's a believer!"

"You must be more cautious," the woman said. "Many people in this town would not be pleased to hear what you just said." She pointed toward the front room. "Bring your family in quickly."

Jackie, Adah, and the children hurried up the steps and into the woman's house. They quickly learned her name was Alice Masterson and she had lived in Rhinelander for about five years, but her parents had lived there for decades. The Peck family and Adah introduced themselves, explaining they shared her newfound faith. Mary Peck hung back and didn't say anything.

"What an amazing consequence," Alice said. "God used my morning breakfast as an opportunity for me to witness in a way I would never have expected."

"How did you come to your new faith?" Graham asked. "During the last few months?"

"Actually, my parents were faithful believers and attended a church here in town," Alice explained. "Unfortunately, I didn't go to church and left the Christian faith to them. I was a highly indifferent young woman. Then one morning I went to their house, and discovered they had disappeared. It took me several weeks to realize what had happened. Then, I got serious about what I had ignored."

"Amazing," Jackie said. "Our story is different."

"Ah . . . we'll tell you all about it *another* day," Graham broke in. "Right now we wonder if their are any other Christians in this town?"

"Only a small group exists," Alice said. "After my parents vanished, I went back to studying the Bible and realized that I had missed the most important truths and insights in the world. I started memorizing the Scripture and began sharing with my friends in the neighborhood. Many of them didn't want to hear from me, but a few responded. In several months a circle of new believers evolved."

"Wonderful!" Jackie said. "What a great story."

"We've been meeting in the basement of the old church my parents once attended. It's boarded up, so we don't worry about intrusions that could happen otherwise."

"I understand," Graham said slowly. "From what we observed in the restaurant, people seem distant around here."

Alice nodded her head. "A long time ago this community was settled by German people migrating from the old country. Later Norwegians and Swedes moved in. They tended to keep to themselves, but with time the barriers came down and people mixed more freely." Alice shrugged. "Of course, recent events in the world canceled all that progress. Today, people have crawled back into those ancient shelters to protect themselves."

"This may seem like a strange question," Graham said. "But what are they most afraid of?"

Alice thought for a moment. "All those people disappearing freaked everyone out. Crime is so rampant that nobody trusts anything. I wouldn't walk these streets at night—someone might stick a shotgun out the window and shoot me. The gap between the rich and the poor has sent looters on a rampage."

"So, crime is the big problem?" Adah asked.

"Rhinelanders aren't used to war either," Alice added. "The world seems to be filled with nothing but endless strife. The people who don't have God in their lives are terrified. No one trusts the politicians. Most people quit watching television because the news frightened them."

Graham shot a glance at Jackie but said nothing.

"Shouldn't that make them open to learning about what you've found in the Bible?" Matthew asked.

"You'd think so!" Alice said. "But it hasn't! To the contrary, they feel people who pray in public and believe in God are nuts. I prayed in the restaurant because the Bible says I should, but I've always worried about doing that." She beamed. "Until today!"

"Alice," Jackie asked conscientiously, "do you think the people in your group that meets at the church would allow us to attend?"

Alice clapped. "They'd be thrilled!"

CHAPTER 16

STANDING ON THE VERANDA of his palatial home in Istanbul overlooking the Black Sea, Hassan Jawhar Rashid watched the seagulls flying over the water. Amassing great wealth in a short time had given him opportunities that most people could never have in six lifetimes. His unique approach of acquiring oil properties in Kuwait and then expanding his company into Iraq had netted billions of dollars before anyone realized the Royal Arab Petroleum Company was moving to take over petroleum assets in other countries. In those early days, he used the name Borden Camber Carson and kept his identity concealed. Even then he sensed a unique destiny that required caution, prudence, and the ability to work in a deceptive manner.

Hassan leaned over the granite rail that ran around the enormous deck of his massive home, which resembled a Byzantine castle more than a contemporary dwelling. The placid surface of the Black Sea lapped gently against the dock where he kept his yacht. Since casting anonymity aside, Rashid's bid for political power had accelerated even faster than goals he set for the petroleum industry. An unseen hand seemed to guide everything he did.

Along the way there had been a few women, but the affairs were casual and meaningless. Any relationships of significant depth would have been a deterrent to his purposes and couldn't be allowed. Rashid's dreams were hidden behind a mental shield and never exposed to anyone.

Turkey's Justice and Development Party, which had acquired power way back in 2002, dramatically promoted Rashid up the ladder. Old Tayyip Erdogan and his followers pushed him while the center-left Republican Party as well supported Rashid. The vast majority of the members in the 555-seat legislature enthusiastically endorsed Rashid's grab for control, and suddenly he was not only the prime minister of Turkey, his influence covered the entire region. The wars he initiated and won assured him of extraordinary power. Unknown to anyone but the immediate participants, Rashid was employing terrorists to attack Israel as a way of pressuring their cabinet to accept his proposed treaty.

During the early years when Rashid worked in the distant deserts, each night he studied, even by candlelight if necessary, reading the political ideals and philosophies of the great rulers of history. Even though he was amassing a financial and political empire, his eyes were on even higher goals. Rashid knew he had a rendezvous with destiny and suspected the rewards could be enormous. No head of state through the centuries had affected his thinking more than the political vision of Adolf Hitler.

Hitler had foreseen that any significant ruler of Germany must begin as a man of the people, a commoner, not an aristocrat. Such a ruler must seem to be an ordinary citizen. On the other hand, he actually had nothing to do with the masses. His own visions would lead him on a level far above the dreams of the people. Such a ruler would have nothing to do with the commoners. His public image and private performance would, by necessity, be two entirely different matters. In order to achieve personal goals, a powerful head of state must be ready to trample even his closest friends to death at a moment's notice. He must have a ruthless, hard heart, and Hitler certainly did. Rashid would do him one better.

Hassan had not seen any of these designs as evil, only necessities in his drive to the top. Actually, Rashid considered his goals to be good, solid achievements to bring renewed hope and purpose to the world, resulting in new solidarity for the world's people. This "good" was so significant that no one could be allowed to stand in its way. Should a deterrent appear, that individual would have to be eliminated *immediately*.

Rashid taught himself to master his emotions, allowing himself on occasion to weep like a child, while at a moment's notice he could switch directions and release his vilest feelings, lashing out like a whip. On some days he needed to appear tender; other times he must frighten people into obedience.

A crude side had always lurked in the recesses of Hassan Jawhar Rashid's mind, and he worked to keep the dark shadow under control. Not just profanity, but crude expletives could erupt unless he paid absolute attention to controling himself. In order to curb emotional explosions, Hassan's goal was to appear as a genteel, common man of exceptional ability. The objective required him to maintain the appearance of a man of refinement and dignity.

Behind the scenes of these decisions, his unusual religious experiences were kept hidden. He never spoke of the strange encounters that had awakened in him the compulsion to dominate the world. He settled for describing himself in terms of Friedrich Nietzsche's "superman," a genius above the law, a self-made god. Never mind that Nietzsche's dream existed for Germans or that the philosopher was insane the last eleven years of his life. Rashid would be one of the "lords of the earth" this Aryan thinker saw rising above the state and would not be bound by the morals of ordinary citizens. He would set his own directions and make up a peculiar set of ethics as was needed. Hassan Jawhar Rashid remained convinced he breathed a rarefied atmosphere reserved for only the mightiest, the most intelligent, the elite.

"Sorry to bother you, sire." Abu Shud appeared out of nowhere. "The secretary of state from the United States has arrived."

"Don't intrude!" Rashid barked. He didn't like to be interrupted when reflecting. "I will be there shortly. Have the fool wait in the lobby."

CHAPTER 17

THE EARLY JUNE SUN beamed across the forest, covering the mid-afternoon summer scene with exquisite splendor. The Pecks and Adah Honi had been in Rhinelander for a number of hours, but

Eldad Rafaeli had not moved from the secluded position he'd discovered on the side of the hill rising sharply above the Pecks' summer home. Hiding behind an outcropping of rocks, he could look down on the house and see anyone coming or going. He would immediately catch someone observing the property.

The years of struggle the Rafaeli family experienced while living in Russia had made him naturally suspicious. The town of Cherdyn, lying in the shadow of the Ural Mountains, had been the scene of many pogroms against the Jews. Ugly attacks and personal assaults had taught him never to close his eyes to the unexpected. After two decades of communist assaults, Eldad was the only member of his family left alive. When the opportunity came, he immediately immigrated to Israel.

Out of the corner of his eye, Eldad suddenly saw two men creeping through the trees. He hunkered down and watched between the space of two rocks. The men seemed to be circling behind the house and were not far below him.

Roughly dressed, they looked more like woodsmen. Their blue jeans were worn and dirty. Each man had on an old flannel shirt over a T-shirt. Hardly appearing to be any of the mayor of Chicago's crew, the two invaders looked more like deer hunters or fishermen.

Eldad had not anticipated anyone would come so close to his high perch, and he was forced to lie flat on the ground. Although the family had gone into town, he had not brought a weapon with him up the hill. The best he could do was watch the two men carefully creeping toward him. After several minutes, they stopped at the base of the rocks beneath him. He listened carefully.

"Yeah, sure that woman's in there?" the smaller of the two men said. "Could be somebody else hangin' around."

"Nah," the second man said. "From up here you can see how empty the house looks."

"That gal sure scared you off," the smaller man joked.

"She came runnin' out shootin' that gun! If I hadn't been on the other side of the house, she'd a had me!"

The two men leaned back against the rocks directly below Eldad and studied the house. For several moments they sat in complete quiet and said nothing.

"I tell ya, I don't see no one!" the smaller man grumbled.

"Yeah, but that's the way it was when I first spotted the house. I think the woman's livin' out here for some reason by herself." He nudged his friend. "Good lookin' babe, too."

"What you got in mind?" the smaller man asked with a scornful twist to his words.

"I'm hungry! Ain't had nothin' to eat in a while. I'd suspect we'd grab some food, then look for any money."

"And the woman?"

The man grinned. "We'll save her for last."

Eldad gritted his teeth. He'd seen men like these scummy characters in Russia. Ignorant fools, they had the capacity to kill and had to be stopped at once. He couldn't chance letting them get away. Glancing around the back of the rocks, he looked for a log, a rock, anything.

"I'd guess we'd best sneak up alongside the back of the house." The smaller man pointed straight ahead. "Then each of us can take a door. If we go crashin' in before she's had a chance to grab that gun, we'd be best off."

Inches below Eldad's foot a large rock lay on the ground. It was the only thing he could see. The limbs around him were either too large or small. He pulled up the rock and leaned over the edge of the boulder. With one swift thrust, he sent the rock down on top of the largest man's head. The dull thud echoed through the trees, sending the man crashing into a heap.

"What the—" The smaller man jumped to his feet and looked up.

Eldad leaped over the top of the rocks and landed on the man, knocking him back to the ground. With a wild fury, he swung and hit the bum in the side of the face. The thug groaned and rolled sideways, but Eldad stayed on him, pelting the man's back and stomach with hard blows.

"A-a-h!" the assailant screamed and rolled over. Blood was running out of his nose. "Stop it! I quit."

"Stop?" Eldad stood up. "You move and I'll smash your head."

"Okay!" The man rolled over on his knees. "Okay. You win."

"*Win!*" Eldad shrugged. "Humph! I'll teach you to sneak up on somebody else's cabin."

"Really?" The punk suddenly sat up and pulled a gun out of his coat. "Let's see who teaches who somethin'."

Before Eldad could move, the attacker stuck the gun straight out and fired three times. Each shot hit Eldad in the chest, knocking him backward to the ground.

"Got to get out of here!" The assailant ran back through the trees the way he had come.

Eldad lay on the ground, barely able to move. He could hear the man tearing through the forest, the sound of steps and breaking branches getting farther and farther away. He glanced out the side of his eye and saw the other figure lying several feet away, blood streaming down the side of his head.

Eldad's vision blurred, and he felt an overwhelming sense of light-headedness. Everything was turning white. He tried to catch his breath, but the pain was intense.

"Baruch atta Adoni," he groaned. *"Adoni . . . atta . . . e-echod . . ."*

Nothing more would come from his mouth. With his eyes staring wide open, Eldad Rafaeli left this world.

CHAPTER 18

NIGHT HAD NEARLY FALLEN by the time Matthew Peck found Eldad's body, along with the body of the assailant, at the bottom of the rock pile up the hill from the house. The children cried, and Mary completely lost her composure and panicked. No one had anticipated that such a terrible thing could happen. Months of relative quietness had lulled the entire family into believing they were beyond real danger.

Graham, Jackie, and Adah debated what to do next. If they contacted the police, their cover would be blown, which meant instant vulnerability. They had to weigh their options. Virtually no one in the United States knew Eldad, and the other man appeared to be little more than a bum cruising through the woods. His pockets were empty, and he carried no identification except a driver's license from Michigan. He was a long way from Saginaw and obviously up to nothing positive. The disappearance of both men would seem to draw little attention.

Jackie concluded she must have heard the bum behind the house a couple of days earlier. While he didn't say so, Graham realized he had too quickly and easily discounted her experience. Too many thugs and punks were on the prowl. Vagrants like this man now wandered everywhere. At the least, he didn't appear to be from the mayor's office.

Graham finally decided that it would be best to bury the man somewhere out in the forest, and then the family would give Eldad a proper burial. They could hide the driver's license in case it was needed later. Jackie and Adah reluctantly agreed. With Matthew helping him, he buried the assailant a long way from their property, covering the grave with pine needles to obscure all evidence.

"It won't be easy to bury Eldad," Graham told his son as they walked back to the house in the dark.

Matthew shook his head. "I could never have imagined this."

Graham put his arm around Matt's shoulder as they walked. "Obviously there was another man out there," he said quietly.

Matthew stopped. "What?"

"Eldad was shot, and the man we just buried didn't have a gun on him. Did you notice the footprints on the ground leading away from the place where we found Eldad?"

"No!" Matthew looked surprised. "No, I didn't see anything at all."

"I don't want you to tell anyone, but we're going to have to watch carefully. Probably the other attacker has disappeared, but possibly not. Regardless, we're going to have to keep our eyes open and be observant."

Matt nodded. "In one afternoon we've gone from tranquillity back into the maelstrom. The storm is churning again."

"I don't want your mother and Adah to worry about another attack any more than they naturally would. Let's keep this between us."

"Sure."

"Our trip today was fortunate. We've made contact with another group of Christians, but we don't want anyone to know about these deaths. We've got to make sure no one lets on."

"What do you think really happened up there?" Matt pointed toward the rocks where he had found Eldad's body.

"I don't know, son." Graham shook his head. "I'm guessing Eldad killed the man we buried with a large stone, and the other man who shot him escaped. I don't expect we'll hear from this criminal, but I can't tell. There may be a much larger picture here that I'm not seeing."

"I'll start sitting out in the trees and watch during the day," Matthew said.

"We'll have to work out some sort of system, but we must guard the house carefully."

The father and son walked through the trees until they came back out into the clearing where the cabin stood. They found the family sitting around the living room. No one was talking. George had slipped back into that distant, disconnected stare created by trauma. Jeff huddled in a corner of the room, drawn up in a tight ball. Mary's eyes were red, and all smugness had vanished.

"We took care of our job," Graham said. "Is everybody okay?"

Jackie shook her head. "I don't think we'll ever be okay again."

Graham nodded and looked at the Jewish woman. Adah sat on the floor, leaning against the wall with swollen eyes. She said nothing, but her face told a story of grief.

"I think we should finish burying Eldad tonight," Graham said. "I know it's late, but we dug a grave earlier and already placed Eldad there. I believe it would be better than waiting until the morning."

Jackie nodded her head solemnly.

"Adah, would you be able to do the service? I would think that everything should be said in Hebrew."

"Women don't say these things in Israel," Adah said. "The rabbis always say the words, but we don't have any rabbis, do we?" She stood up, assuming a dignity that fit her elegant profile. "I will cover my head." Adah reached for a black scarf. "It is our custom for each person to throw into the grave a handful of dirt. Can we all do this?"

The children nodded solemnly. Mary's eyes widened with fear, but she said yes. Adah reached for a Hebrew prayer book and motioned for the family to follow her. Like a solemn assembly marching down the hall, the family walked single file through the door with Graham bringing up the rear.

The wind had picked up and the night air felt cold. Even the trees seemed to be groaning in the breeze. The family walked fifty feet from the house and stood silently around the open grave.

"He was my friend," Jeff said and cried.

"And a brave man," George added stiffly.

"We will miss him dearly," Jackie mumbled.

"Eldad gave his life for us," Graham added.

Adah began reading the words, and the wind whirled about them as if adding its blessing.

CHAPTER 19

THREE DAYS AFTER ELDAD'S burial, another unexpected eclipse plunged the world into darkness. Intense blackness settled over Tomahawk at around 12:30. In a matter of minutes, midday became like the middle of night.

"Just as Revelation predicts," Adah said, "the sun has turned black. Scripture warns, 'Woe, woe, woe to the inhabitants of the earth.' The warnings are intensifying."

"I don't think we ought to turn on the lights for a while." Jackie said. "We would be easily identified in this darkness."

"I'm terrified," Mary wailed.

"Let's all keep our heads," Graham said. "If we're right, this sign will soon pass." He walked across the floor and turned on the television. "We can find out what the newscasters are saying."

"Probably not much," Jackie said.

"I'll bet they are as frightened as we are," Mary quipped.

"We interrupt this program for a news bulletin from New York City," the announcer broke in. The sitcom disappeared and the face of Stephen Sutton filled the screen.

"Reports of chaos are just now coming in from around the country as citizens are caught in the confusion of unexpected darkness," Sutton said in a clipped bass voice. "Apparently, another meteor has broken loose and created this current eclipse. Investigations are currently under way. Do not panic. We are not expecting anything worse than momentary darkness."

"Really?" Graham spoke back to the television. "You newspeople have no idea what any of this means."

"I repeat," Sutton said. "The phenomenon is only momentary, and the sunlight will return shortly. In the meantime, the president of the United States requests you turn on your lights and go about your business as if everything were normal."

"Normal?" Jackie laughed. "We're sitting out here in the woods miles from our Chicago home, which we can't return to because we'd be arrested—for doing nothing? That's normal? I'd call it chaos."

"Once begins the Tribulation," Adah said, "nothing is normal. That word has gone out the window. Abnormal is now the regular condition."

"You know," Graham said slowly, "Alice Masterson, the woman we met in town, said there would be a meeting tonight. I think this would be a good time to go back and see what the new Christians in Rhinelander have to say about today's blackout."

"I like that idea," Jackie said. "It's been hard to sit around here stewing in our grief over Eldad's death. We need to get some fresh air."

"Good!" Adah said. "Tonight we do this thing."

"Should we take the kids?" Jackie asked.

"Mary wouldn't go unless we dragged her, but she could babysit," Graham answered.

"Someone else might show up around here," Jackie mused.

Graham nodded. "Let's leave Matthew in the woods, watching the house to make sure there's no problems. He can take care of the kids."

"Okay," Jackie said, "I'd feel much better with that arrangement."

"It's settled!" Graham said in the darkness. "We'll try out the first meeting this evening."

CHAPTER 20

FOLLOWING ALICE MASTERSON'S instructions, Graham parked their car a block away from the church. Jackie and Adah walked with him around the corner. Just as Alice had said, the church's front door hadn't been opened in months, and pieces of plywood were nailed in front of the stained-glass windows of the sanctuary. The edifice looked completely deserted.

"She said to go around to the back to get in," Jackie said. "That door should be open."

"Here goes nothing!" Graham said. "Let's give it a try."

A long, narrow walkway led along the side of the church building. Flower beds had months ago sprouted weeds and contained only remnants of once beautiful plants. At the back of the church lay an abandoned playground with a slide and swings.

"What do you think?" Jackie asked.

"Looks like a perfect place to hide out I think," Adah answered. "Obviously no one ever comes here."

"I'll try the door." Graham turned the knob and found it unlocked. "First sign of life that we've hit. Looks dark inside."

"Go on down," Jackie urged.

"How brave of you to send me first," Graham jested. "I'll take the first step down if you ladies stay behind me." He walked down the steps.

At the bottom Graham stopped in surprise. In front of him stood a large fellowship hall, but there were no electric lights. Instead, candles had been set around the room, casting long shadows across the old asphalt-tile floor. In the back corner he could see a group of people sitting in a circle. It looked like maybe ten or twelve people had gathered.

"Ah, Mr. Peck!" Alice Masterson immediately stood up. "How wonderful of your family to come."

"Thank you." Graham nodded to the group and introduced Jackie and Adah. "We appreciate being able to visit you."

"I'd like you to meet some of my friends here in Rhinelander," Alice said and introduced the people sitting in the circle. "We were just about to open with prayer. Please join us."

"Sure," Graham said. "We'd like to."

The group prayed for a considerable time, with individual members offering intercessions for friends, relatives, the community, and the confusion sweeping across the country. The opening prayers were followed by Bible reading, and then Alice taught for a while.

Graham sensed the people watching them with oblique glances and subtle stares. No one had yet discovered Adah was Jewish, but the town's people sometimes stared at her. Their openness and warmth appeared somewhat tempered by their ethnic backgrounds and the disorder occurring everywhere. No one offered a name.

"Graham," Alice said and turned to the family, "I believe you've come here from Chicago?"

"Actually, we have a place over at Tomahawk and live there now." He smiled reassuringly at each person in the group. "I'm wondering how you feel about the eclipse tonight?"

After a brief pause, an older lady said, "I'd have been just as terrified as I was every time them motorcycle people come buzzin' through, except for Alice. She'd already taught about what the book of Revelation says about such things."

"I agree," a middle-aged man wearing overalls added. "I felt the same way months ago when the moon turned red. But we're probably the only people in town that didn't get all bent out of shape. Lots of folks sure turned strange."

For several minutes the conversation wandered on, with different people sharing humorous stories of what they had seen and heard during the darkness. Finally, Graham turned the conversation in another direction.

"You folks don't seem to be worried," Graham observed. "I'm surprised."

"Oh, there's plenty to worry about!" the older lady said. "It's simply that we know the Lord is in control and not us. Makes a heap of difference when you know whose hands are really on the controls."

A roar of motorcycle engines buzzed down the street in front of the church. The disquieting sound increased with loud popping and banging noises.

"Bolt the door!" The man in overalls jumped up and ran for the back door. "Get this place secured."

Bike wheels squawked, and it sounded like the bikes had gone around to the alley and were coming up behind the church.

"Everyone hide!" Alice commanded. "Get down and out of sight. Blow out the candles!"

The group scattered, with several people hiding under the long serving tables still sitting in the room. The older lady rushed for a closet. The man in overalls locked the back door and pushed a heavy piece of timber against the knob to secure the door from being forced open. Alice kept extinguishing candles.

"What's in there?" a man's voice echoed from the backyard.

"It's one of 'em churches! Let's break in and have a party," a rough voice answered. "Ain't used no more."

The men hammered on the back door and worked the knob, but the lock held.

"Break it open!" some man's voice growled.

The sound of men crashing against the door boomed around the room, but the timber didn't give.

"Can't get the damn thing open!"

"Think we can break in a window?"

"Ain't worth the effort. Let's go down the street. There's a bar open a block from here."

Graham could hear the men complaining, but in a few minutes the motorbikes roared back to life and drove off. The believers began crawling out of hiding.

"That's the third time we've had some wild batch of bikers try to break in," the man in overalls said. "Fortunately, we was ready."

"That group's been here before?" Graham asked.

"Hard to say," Alice replied. "Some of them come down from Duluth, and others ride over from Iron Mountain or even as far away as Traverse City or Manistee."

"Anyone ever come from Saginaw?" Graham asked.

"Never seen one of them," the man in overalls said, "but it's possible."

"Mobs of these unwashed crazies are crusin' all over the country these days," a woman said. "We just happen to be sitting here tonight."

"Yes, yes," the elderly lady added. "Don't make no difference where they come from, it's the fact that the Lord was with us that made the difference."

CHAPTER 21

HASSAN JAWHAR RASHID'S personal jet flew into New York City escorted by American fighters protecting the flight plan of the 747 as the huge plane came down over La Guardia airport. Surrounded by his personal bodyguards and Abu Shad, his secretary and aide, Rashid walked into the airport through a private entrance. Avoiding reporters, he walked straight to a waiting limousine. The long black Lincoln and a police squad surrounding the vehicle whisked him away from the airport toward the United Nations Building off FDR Drive.

"I have already summoned Frank Bridges and his people to meet me there," Rashid said. "When I arrive at the United Nations headquarters, I want to talk with him before the opening session begins. Make sure we are not interrupted and have complete privacy."

"Yes sir." Abu Shad scribbled on his electronic data pad. "Should I make the secretary general aware of this arrangement?"

"No. Bridges is already there and prepared to meet me. However, I want the room electronically swept for any surveillance equipment. That goes for Bridges and his associates as well."

Abu Shad nodded his head. "It will be done."

"I will make a speech that will rock the UN," Rashid continued in a cold voice. "You must be prepared for negative reactions, but they can be discarded because I am too strategically positioned to worry about what these monkey faces think of what I say. Their response is irrelevant."

"Naturally."

"In the last area of armed conflict, I brought Pakistan and India under my control. The oil flow to these countries is now dominated by Royal Arab Petroleum's wishes and how we handle delivery and production." Rashid chuckled. "Of course, millions died. Whether they liked it or not, both countries have buckled under to me."

"And Mexico and South America?"

Rashid's eyes became hard. "We still have work to do in this hemisphere. Don't worry. I'll soon have them in the palm of my hand as well."

The police motorcade zoomed past the Fifty-seventh Street exit and continued south. Abu Shad made a phone call to ensure the electronic security devices were in place and that the rooms and people had been checked.

"We'll be there in a moment," Abu Shad said. "Do you have any concern about security?"

"No!" Rashid snapped, and then paused. "Of course, some of our officials have concerns, but I think they are overreacting to the Americans' disturbed state of mind. After all, these people have lived with such affluence for so long that they can't handle change. We must not be swayed by their preoccupations."

"Yes sir," Abu Shad repeated.

"No, I am *not* concerned."

The motorcade swung off the freeway and into the private entrance to the United Nations Building. Reporters wearing badges of certification around their necks huddled on the walkways, trying to get pictures of Rashid. He only nodded back to them while maintaining his air of formality. The cavalcade pulled to a halt, and Rashid hurried inside where an elevator waited for him. The door closed and he shot up to the top floor.

"We will be there in a moment, sir," Abu Shad said. "Bridges' people should have been tested and the room prepared. You will be able to begin at once."

"Good! Time is of the essence."

CHAPTER 22

WEARING A REGAL SILK Armani suit, Rashid had carefully dressed for this formal occasion. The world would be watching, and he wanted to make sure he conveyed elegance of style as well as substance. He walked into the room reserved for his meeting with Bridges. Looking equally well groomed in a black suit with a red tie, the mayor of Chicago stood at attention, with Al Meachem and Jack Stratton standing on each side of him.

"Ah! Mr. Carson. It is an honor to have you in our country again." Bridges rushed forward and extended his hand. "Welcome, Your Honor. Welcome to America."

"Thank you, Frank," Rashid answered in a rich, elegant voice. "I appreciate your addressing me as Carson, but because of what I will be doing at the United Nations, we should use my Arabic name."

"Absolutely." Bridges beamed. "We'll make it Al-sayyid Rashid."

"Gentlemen, let us sit down." Rashid pointed to the chairs around the room, and stopped. "I notice you didn't bring Bill Marks with you today."

"No, he's here, but he's waiting outside," Bridges explained. "He's guarding the hallway beyond this room. You'll see him when you take the elevator down to the General Assembly."

Rashid smiled. "Yes," he said and sat down. "I am concerned to know how your work with intelligence has been progressing. Please deliver your report."

Bridges snapped his fingers, and Meachem laid a file in front of him. For ten minutes he spoke without stopping.

"You seem to have grasped the assignments I have given you quite well," Rashid said. "I am pleased with what you have accomplished. However, I understand this country continues to degenerate." He rubbed his hands together and the diamond pinky ring sparkled. "Is this a problem?"

"We have used unrest as a means to undermine the president of this country," Bridges answered. "During the recent international crisis, we made the front page of virtually every newspaper in this country, pointing out his inconsistencies."

"Excellent!" Rashid smiled. "And you have captured this Graham Peck? Right?"

Bridges no longer looked supremely confident. He took a deep breath. "Police surveillance has been reinstated around his home, and I am working on a new use of nanorobots to locate him and his family, but at this point we have not actually captured the man."

"*Actually?* I cannot tolerate delay on this front," Rashid snapped. "This man may seem insignificant to you, but this inconsequential ant is the one person out there with the capacity to expose our operation. *Do you understand?*"

"Of course." Bridges sounded embarrassed. "Please know that no effort is being spared to find Peck."

"It better not be," Rashid warned. "I don't care how you find him or capture him. I want this man *dead!*"

"Yes sir. We will locate him."

"Don't let there be any delays!"

"There won't be."

Rashid stood up with the irritated look still on his face. "Now I must make a speech that will shake the bricks out of the walls of this place," he announced coldly. "You must be prepared to stand behind me to reinforce that this is the decisive direction the world must take."

"Absolutely!" Bridges forced a smile. "I will be with you all the way."

"Good!" Rashid's glare shifted immediately to a broad smile. His voice again became soft with a soothing quality. "I will expect completed action on the Peck matter in the immediate future. Gentlemen, are you ready to accompany us down to the General Assembly?"

"Indeed." Bridges bowed. "We will follow you, sir."

Rashid marched confidently toward the door. Abu Shad opened it for him, allowing Hassan Rashid to start down the hall toward the elevator. Bill Marks stood on the other side of the door, a distance away from the rest of the guards. Rashid saw him and made eye contact.

Bill Marks smiled and bowed slightly. Suddenly, he straightened and swung a pistol out from behind him.

Holding his arms rigid, he aimed at Rashid's head and fired.

The impact of the bullet sent Rashid flying back into the adjacent wall. Marks fired again. Blood splattered over the wall. The prime minister of Turkey slid to the floor, bleeding profusely.

Marks turned his gun on Bridges, but Meachem knocked the mayor to the floor, and the shot struck a guard standing behind him. Before Bill Marks could fire a fourth time, a United Nations security guard shot him through the heart; he crumbled to the floor only feet from Rashid.

"He's killed him!" Bridges screamed. "Oh my God! Marks has killed Carson!"

DEATH LEASHED | II

*The beast that I saw was like a leopard,
its feet were like a bear's, and its mouth
was like a lion's mouth.
And to it the dragon gave his power
and his throne and great authority.*

REVELATION 13:2

CONFUSED REPORTS FLEW ACROSS the airwaves like the frantic heartbeat of a flee-ing deer as news of the shooting flashed around the globe. Carson's name had become a household word in virtually every country. While some feared his achieve-ments, many had come to see him as the only hope left for a world caught in continual strife. The news flashes about his near death condition only hyped the rampant fear flooding American towns.

Bill Marks's shots had struck Hassan Rashid in the head, but not killed him. The prime minister and oil magnate was rushed from the United Nations Building to the nearest hospital. Instant medical attention sustained him momentarily, but no one expected him to live through the day.

The incident propelled Frank Bridges' relationship with Rashid into headline news as well. While American government officials had suspected a significant link, the public had no idea how important Bridges had become in Carson's plans. When Bridges took charge immedi-ately after the shooting, it became obvious. Bridges even rushed to the hospital in the same ambulance with Car-son. It was now clear Frank Bridges had gained an inter-national prominence even the president of the United States had underestimated.

Bridges paced back and forth outside the emergency surgery room. Abu Shad and other members of the Turkey delegation stayed in another room. Bridges' white shirt was splattered with blood; the sleeve on his coat had been torn. With hair hanging down over his face, Frank Bridges looked more like the survivor of a Saturday night fight in a nearby bar than the mayor of one of the largest cities in America.

Al Meachem rushed into the room. "They're installing special biometric computer systems to ensure maximum security in this area of the hospital," he said. "They'll want a print of your thumb for digital fingerprinting as well as a voice sample for speech recognition. In addition to what was already in place, this should make this building the most secure in the world."

Bridges nodded. "Anything come in yet on Marks? I can't even begin to grasp what happened in his head. The man went nuts! How could he possibly do such a horrendous thing?"

"I don't know, boss . . . I mean Your Honor. None of us had any idea he was capable of assassination. Bill Marks avoided going through the electronic security check by hanging back and protecting the hallway. Marks didn't enter the room where Carson spoke with us so he didn't go through the security machines. He obviously knew exactly what he was doing. Bill sidestepped every device that would have picked up his gun. Because he came in with us, Marks was able to avoid normal detection at the entry door."

"I want the FBI, the CIA, whoever! I want every

agency under the sun on this case. We've got to find out what was going on with that idiot!"

Meachem nodded. "We're after it."

"And where's Dr. Paul Gillette? I want that expert on artificial life in here immediately!"

"Mr. Brain didn't like it, but we forced him into a private jet and he's on his way here at this moment. I can't promise when he'll arrive, but it will be soon."

"Okay! Okay. Just keep the pressure up." Bridges pulled Meachem closer to him. "Do you realize that our lives are on the line? If Carson dies, all our plans are *dead*!"

"I know, I know," Meachem mumbled. "We're doing everything possible."

"Don't stop!" Bridges growled.

Meachem saluted and rushed out. Bridges kept walking back and forth. Each tick of the clock made him more irritated. In no way could he understand how someone as close to him as Bill Marks could have been capable of an assassination attempt on the most powerful man in the world. Sure, Marks always hung back and said little, but he had been around the mayor's office forever. The man was privy to virtually everything going on and had never said one negative word. Marks always appeared to be a team player, a confidant, one of the boys. How could he have performed such a shocking act?

Bridges kept pacing. Beyond the doors he could hear the noise of news reporters jostling the security guards and demanding to get in, but they wouldn't get through. Whatever was left of Carson's life was in the balance, and those fools weren't about to have the opportunity to tip the delicate fulcrum on which survival hung.

The operating room door opened and the surgeon, Dr. James Silver, rushed out. "Rashid's barely alive," he told Bridges. "It doesn't get any worse than this."

"I wanted you to know that I'm flying in Dr. Paul Gillette from Chicago to help if needed."

Silver stopped. "You're talking about the expert in molecular engineering. The nanorobot guy?"

"Yes sir."

Silver's eyes widened. "Well, that's an interesting development. I know something about his work. We might need him before this is over."

"What do you mean? Level with me, Doctor!"

Silver cast a quick glance around the room to make sure no one was listening. "As you know, the first bullet hit Rashid in the head, but for some reason it didn't kill him. The second shot went through his right cheek and out the mouth, taking a couple of teeth with it. We have him on life support, ventilators, the works, but we don't know if he's even going to be functional."

"He's kept alive completely artificially at this time?"

"Exactly. We've got a call in to bring in a doctor who's worked with reverse engineering of the human brain. We want everybody we can get our hands on."

"To keep him alive?"

"Well, yes," Dr. Silver said. "We can do that for a limited amount of time. Maybe get him through part of the night, but we're concerned if he's going to have any brain function left when this is over."

CHAPTER 24

AL MEACHEM hustled Dr. Paul Gillette into the waiting room, where Frank Bridges waited for Dr. James Silver to make another appearance. Gillette's face looked pale and he appeared shaken. Meachem obviously wasn't on the list of Gillette's favorite people.

Bridges immediately stood and extended his hand. "Thank you for coming, Dr. Gillette. I'm sure you are aware of the seriousness of this situation."

"I don't see how I can be of any help!" Gillette looked angry. "I work in a very different field."

"Yes," the mayor said, "I am aware of the differences, but we believe you might be able to provide an important ingredient in saving Borden Carson's life. We need you to stand by, and you will be compensated for your time."

"I hope so!" Dr. Gillette crossed his arms over his chest and glanced nervously at Meachem.

Bridges took Meachem's arm and pulled him to the far end of the room. "Any problem with Mr. Brains over there?"

"He didn't want to come," Meachem said. "Our men virtually dragged him out to the airplane." He shot a glance at the doctor. "I don't think we'll have any problem now. He knows where the muscle is."

"Anything on Bill Marks?"

Meachem nodded. "Yeah. Several men were arrested outside the building hiding in cars along the street. We have determined they were extreme reactionary types and armed with guns. The information's being checked right now, but it appears they had a connection with Bill Marks. We've turned up a strong possibility that Marks had a secret tie with these people who hate everything the government has been doing lately."

"Oh, man! That's all I need!"

"Yeah, bizarre twist," Meachem said. "We're working the leads right now as hard as we can. We've also got people in Chicago trying to find Marks's wife. The woman has disappeared."

Bridges stared at Meachem. "She's gone? Nancy Marks left?"

"Yeah. May have been gone several days."

The door to the operating room opened again, and Dr. James Silver came back out. Bridges immediately grabbed the arm of his green scrubs.

"Dr. Gillette is here now," Frank Bridges said.

Silver stopped. "Excellent! Where is he?"

"Dr. Gillette! Come here!"

Gillette slowly walked across the waiting room floor. "Yes?"

"Dr. Silver is one of the doctors keeping Carson alive," Bridges explained quickly. "He may need your help."

"I've admired your work," Dr. Silver said and shook

hands with Dr. Gillette. "We may indeed need a person acquainted with molecular engineering."

Dr. Gillette nodded anxiously. "I am at your service."

"Some brain tissue was destroyed," Silver explained. "If it can't be replaced, there's no way to save this man."

"Tissue?" Gillette rubbed his chin. "Yes, I understand."

"You are an expert in such matters," Silver said. "Can you suggest any possibilities?"

Gillette nodded. "Some years ago I worked with xenotransplantation therapy. We were attempting to remove genes from a sugar called alpha-1-galactose that prompted human rejection of the immune tissue we had developed with pigs."

"Pigs!" Bridges exploded.

"Yes," Gillette said. "We mixed swine sperm with human DNA to transfer a gene causing the decay accelerating factor, or DAF. Our work was ultimately successful."

"What might this mean today?" Dr. Silver asked.

"As strange as it might sound to you, Mr. Bridges," Gillette said. "We were able to manipulate human genes with pig carriers, producing a transfer of tissue that could be used in developing animal organs for human usage. We dramatically eased the problem of people dying while waiting for an organ donor."

"What's this got to do with Carson?" Bridges objected.

"Our work at the Microfabrication Research Laboratory has moved on to brain tissue. I wouldn't have expected this result, but we may be able to help, Dr. Silver."

"Extremely interesting," Dr. Silver mused. "Fascinating."

"You must understand that's a significant danger," Gillette warned. "We are completely on the cutting edge. There's no guarantee. We could kill Carson."

"I understand," Dr. Silver said. "However, without this alternative, I don't think he'll live through the night."

"If you're willing to take the risk, then I can assist you," offered Dr. Gillette.

"This procedure must remain top secret," Silver warned. "I don't see any alternative but to try it. Please come back and talk with the neurosurgeons. Time is of the essence."

"Surely." Dr. Gillette fell in step with Dr. Silver, and they hurried back through the swinging doors.

"We may have saved Carson's life," Meachem said.

"And we may have finished him off," Bridges snapped. "Frightening! We can only watch."

CHAPTER 25

WITHIN AN HOUR Dr. Paul Gillette called the Microfabrication Research facilities and another private jet was dispatched with the tissue samples Gillette had requested. Even more reporters gathered outside the hospital. Cars slowed when they came down the street. The attention of the entire globe was focused on what was occurring behind the sealed doors of the fifth-floor operating room. As the hours dragged by, the frantic pace around the hospital picked up even more. Police kept the traffic moving, but the eyes of the world remained glued on this singular facility.

Near early evening, Al Meachem returned and found Bridges still sitting in the inner waiting area. "Boss," he said frantically, "I've got an update on Bill Marks." Meachem plopped down in the overstuffed chair next to the mayor of Chicago. "Our people in Chicago started running the data that came in on a radio-frequency identification device built into the tires on Marks's car. Basically, companies install those gadgets to help them update their inventories. The chips continue to transmit data unless they're removed."

"I didn't know we used anything like that."

"We don't. One of our men came up with the idea and started running it down through our computer system's link to Goodyear tires. Guess what?"

Bridges shook his head.

"We've identified the fact that during the last couple of months, Marks made trips every day to an old abandoned railway warehouse over in Cicero off Highway 56." Meachem grinned. "The place turned out to be a hideout for these extremist nut jobs. We raided it an hour ago."

"Yeah?" Bridges sat up in his chair. "Did you find Nancy Marks?"

"Sorry. We didn't get her, but we picked up files and a truckload of guns. It appears that Bill Marks was into this operation up to his neck. He'd been an inside man for the extremists for months."

Bridges took a deep breath. "My God! We ran a security check on him several times."

"Apparently, he passed because this sort of nonsense wasn't considered a problem back then. At best, that's all I can figure out now. Marks must have shifted ideologically somewhere along the way but kept his mouth shut. Maybe he was more afraid than he'd admit to any of us. Fear does weird stuff to people. It's possible all this activity with Carson pushed Bill over the edge." Meachem shrugged. "It's only a guess."

Bridges shook his head. "We'll know eventually." He stood up, looked out the window, and stared at the commotion going on in the street below. Intelligence had never been something Bridges lacked. His bright mind had propelled him through the political world at a pace not many could match, but he'd bottomed out in the last decade and seemed stuck in the Chicago mayor's chair. Nevertheless, the disappointment didn't keep him from thinking about a grab for the presidency someday. Unfortunately, nothing came together to push him on up the ladder . . . until Borden Camber Carson showed up.

It had been hard for Frank Bridges to call the man Hassan Rashid because he'd known him as Carson from the beginning. They'd met at a highly confidential meeting dealing with the petroleum needs of Chicago. The penetrating stare of the man and his incisive, biting mind had immediately grabbed Bridges' attention. Almost as if hypnotized by Carson, Bridges had immediately slipped under his spell. Before long, Frank Bridges did whatever Carson told him to do. Not that he was stupid or easily manipulated; Bridges had simply never seen anyone function with Carson's brilliance and decisiveness.

In time, Bridges had acquiesced to Carson so often that his life and career became radically tied to whatever the man decreed. If this oil magnate died during the operation, Bridges knew his world was destroyed. It wouldn't make any difference whether he found Graham Peck, Nancy Marks—anyone! Everything was on hold until the fate of Borden Camber Carson was decided.

"What time is it?" Bridges asked Meachem.

"My watch says seven o'clock."

"The operation may well take all night."

Meachem nodded. "Anything you want me to do?"

"Keep up the pressure to sort out what made Bill Marks tick. We may need the information later." Bridges paused. "And don't let up on finding his wife."

CHAPTER 26

WHEN FRANK BRIDGES AWOKE, he slowly realized he had slept through the night on the couch in the waiting room. He vaguely remembered watching the *Tonight Show* come on and then everything faded, but Bridges still felt drowsy and disconnected. He blinked several times. Something had awakened him. He looked up. A man was standing in front of him.

"Mr. Bridges?" Dr. James Silver said. "Sorry to awaken you."

"Oh!" Bridges jumped. "I apologize. I guess I drifted off to sleep."

"It was probably good you did. You may be surprised to learn it's seven in the morning."

Bridges cursed. "Didn't mean to sleep so long," he muttered more to himself than Silver. "Guess I was more exhausted than I realized."

"Yesterday was rough. You had to be tired."

"Yeah," Bridges grumbled and rubbed his eyes.

"We're about to hold a news conference, and I thought you'd want to attend."

"News conference?" Bridges ran his hands through his hair. "Carson? Oh my God! What's happened to Borden Carson?"

"We were surprised last night. With the material your man from the Microfabrication Research Laboratory provided, our research team was able to not only stop the bleeding, but to make repairs. We think Carson will live."

Bridges felt his mouth drop. "You're serious?"

"Yes, I am going to make that report to the public. To be completely frank, we're all rather surprised. When the ambulance brought Carson in, no one actually expected the man to live through the night, but there's been a resurgence of energy, and his vital signs are good."

Catching his breath, Bridges nodded his head vigorously. "Thank you! Thank you! I can't tell you how grateful I am for this." He shook Silver's hand. "Yes! Heaven knows this is wonderful news."

"I thought you might want to stand with me when I meet the press. We have a special room set up downstairs for the television cameras."

Bridges glanced at his bloodstained shirt and decided his appearance didn't make any difference today. In fact, the shirt might add a good touch for the cameras. He shook his head to get himself fully awake. "Thank you, Doctor. I'd be delighted."

"I'm ready to go if you are."

"Yes." Bridges stood up straight. "Carson's alive! I'm ready to report some good news for a change. Let's meet the press."

CHAPTER 27

STILL IN THEIR PAJAMAS, the Peck family sat around the television in their Tomahawk home, watching the special news conference being beamed around the world. Graham held his wife's hand, staring at the doctor march into the room before a bank of microphones. At his side, the mayor of Chicago stood at attention.

"There's Bridges!" Jackie pointed. "He looks like a truck ran over him."

"Sure does," Matthew said. "Look at those bloodstains all over his shirt!"

"Great PR," Graham said. "No accident in that look of a fellow warrior."

"I am happy to report that Mr. Hassan Rashid, the prime minister of Turkey, has survived yesterday's shooting," the doctor began. "The bullet hit Mr. Rashid in the forehead and went right between the hemispheres of his brain. I am delighted to report we were able to repair the damage and believe he will fully recover."

A collective sigh rose from the crowd. Instantly reporters began shouting questions, and the room broke into intense commotion.

Graham turned to his family. "Last night's news reports left me with the certainty that Rashid wouldn't live. Afraid he has survived."

"No surprise!" Adah said and opened her black Bible. "All night I have been praying about and studying what this strange turn in the road means. Much to my surprise, I discovered that I had missed an important passage."

"What'd you find?" George asked.

"Get your Bibles," Adah said. "Let's look together."

The family scurried around, each person grabbing a Bible except Mary. She sat in the corner with her arms across her legs, watching everyone else open a Bible. Even little Jeff scooted closer to George, looking over his shoulder.

"Look at the thirteenth chapter of Revelation," Adah directed. "It gives us a frightening picture of a beast, a terrible beast. Do you see it?"

"Sure," Matt said.

"Look at verse 3," Adah continued. "I will read. 'I saw one of his heads as if it had been mortally wounded, and his deadly wound was healed. And all the world marveled and followed the beast.' There—the shooting in New York City!"

"*Mortally wounded,*" Jackie mused. "That's what we've heard all night. A gunshot wound to the head is about as mortal as you can get."

"So, the Antichrist is far from dead," Graham said.

"Yes," Adah answered. "I am afraid so. Eldad would not have been surprised. I am so sorry that he's not here to receive this report."

"Our battle goes on," Matthew reflected glumly. "The war is not over."

"This I think is true," Adah continued. "Look at the next verse. 'So they worshiped the dragon who gave authority to the beast; and they worshiped the beast, saying, "Who is like the beast? Who is able to make war with him?"'" The result of this shooting will only increase the power of this frightening man."

"It's certainly increased Bridges' prestige in the world," Graham thought out loud. "I imagine he'll become an even more dangerous threat to the American president as well as to order in the world."

Adah nodded. "This man Frank Bridges may well turn out to be the false prophet in Revelation. The point is, through this shooting your enemy has grown."

"But I don't think he'd still be much interested in finding me," Graham said. "After all, I'm old news. I would imagine that Bridges has more work on his hands than he's got time to think about. I'm probably gone from his thoughts." Graham stopped. "Of course, Eldad will never be gone from our memory. I think about him every day."

"You think we can worry less about people seeing us in Rhinelander?" Jackie said.

"I would think so," Graham answered. "Let's get the rest of this story from the television broadcast."

"Mr. Rashid will be incommunicado for some time," the doctor's voice reported over the television set. "And we will keep the press advised of his progress, but today the world can breathe easier, as it appears Hassan Rashid will live."

"Breathe easier?" Jackie said. "I don't think so."

Adah shook her head. "No, no. The eternal conflict goes on."

Mary got up and walked sullenly out of the room.

CHAPTER 28

GATHERING HIS STAFF around him in a room the hospital provided, Frank Bridges pushed his inner circle for immediate action.

"Okay!" Bridges began. "You heard the television report, and it looks good. Carson is going to be out of whack for a while, but it looks like he's going to survive."

"But what about damage?" Jack Stratton asked. "Is he going to think right?"

"I don't know," Bridges answered, "and we won't know for probably a week. It's going to take time to get him back into gear. For the time being, we must assume he'll come out of this hospital in good condition."

"Amazing!" Al Meachem exclaimed. "Last night I thought it was all over."

"The whole world did," Bridges said. "I don't know how Carson survived, but apparently that bullet traveled one narrow line. Our boy's extremely fortunate."

"What next?" Meachem asked.

"I want a detailed report on what snapped inside Bill Marks's head," Bridges continued. "We've already pieced together quite a bit of information and identified a warehouse in Cicero where these extremists gathered. I simply can't understand how Marks got caught up with those people."

"We still haven't been able to find his wife," Meachem added. "She must have been in on this plot up to her eyeballs because she's been long gone for at least a week. She knew what was coming and left town."

"Anybody know anything about her?" Bridges asked.

"Actually, she was somewhat on the religious side," Stratton said. "Always into meditation, yoga, that sort of stuff. She was more likely to go completely crazy religiously than Bill."

"I don't want you to let up in your pursuit of Nancy Marks. Nail her as soon as you can get your hands on the woman."

"We won't let up, boss," Meachem said.

"Stop calling me *boss*," Bridges demanded. "Make it Your Honor."

"Yes sir."

"Assuming Carson comes back in one piece, I know he will want to know what's happened while he's been out this week. I think we can kiss that United Nations speech good-bye."

"Yeah," Stratton quipped. "He probably won't even remember he had anything to say."

"But what he told us to do will come back to him," Bridges continued. "This time I want to be ready with solid answers. One of them is that we've got to get our hands on Graham Peck. I don't care what it takes, we've got to find him. Increase security patrols around his Arlington Heights house. I still think he's hiding out in that area. If not, he's somewhere around Chicago."

"Chicago's a big place," Stratton added.

"Big, but it can be narrowed down," Bridges insisted. "Do it. Come up with a new plan. Find him!"

CHAPTER 29

TWO WEEKS HAD PASSED since the shooting of Carson, or Rashid, as the press had generally come to call him. The news media hyped his recovery through the roof. The fact he had survived a bullet in the head without any major loss of memory gripped the public's imagination. Details of the brain operation weren't leaked, but it was obvious something extraordinary had happened behind the closed operating room doors. Dr. Paul Gillette quietly disappeared back to his Illinois laboratory, while Dr. James Silver received constant recognition. The public remained fascinated with Rashid's capacity to endure as well as the technology that saved him.

After several nights of debating the question back and forth, the Pecks decided to look further at the Rhinelander schools. While it was only early July, they would probably still be living in the forest come fall, and the kids needed to be in school. If they could avoid detection, it would be far better for the kids to be back in a local school.

Graham decided a fake last name might hinder their identification or a possible slip of the tongue that could leak their location to someone in the Chicago area. They had already informed the Rhinelander Christian group that they would use a different name to avoid any problems with the school system because of their faith. The new believers seemed to think that was a good idea. Mary Peck refused to join in the discussion of local school possibilities. George and Jeff voted for a new last name of Kent to identify them with Clark Kent. Mary screamed at them that the name Kent was nonsense and she wouldn't have any part of it.

"Look, kids!" Graham finally intervened. "There are a billion 'Smiths' in the world. No one takes a second look at the name. From now on, around the local school you are George and Jeff Smith with an older sister named Mary Smith. Got it?"

The boys shook their heads, and Mary went charging out of the room like it was the dumbest idea in the world, but of course, she didn't have a better one.

Consequently, on this early afternoon Graham and Jackie Smith bumped down the dirt road toward town with George and Jeff in the backseat of the car.

"Remember," Graham warned, "we're simply investigating the school system. Be careful what you say, and for heaven's sake, don't call yourself *Peck*."

The boys agreed, and ten minutes later Graham turned down Rhinelander's main street. They could see the school a couple of blocks away. The old flat-roofed brick building appeared to have been built in the last century and didn't offer much of an appearance. Work needed to be done everywhere.

"Let's see what the principal says," Graham said to the family. "Possibly the inside is better than the outside."

"You boys go out and play while we talk," Jackie told George and Jeff. "The playground should have plenty to keep you busy. Just don't get in trouble."

"Hey, do we look like troublemakers?" George said.

"Yes," Jackie replied instantly. "Now keep your noses clean."

The car pulled into the parking lot and the family got out. George and Jeff ran for a large merry-go-round in the center of the playground while Graham and Jackie looked for the principal.

"The building looks rather dilapidated," Graham observed. "Walls need painting."

Jackie nodded. "Washing them wouldn't hurt anything."

Graham opened the door marked "Principal." An overweight, middle-aged man with glasses halfway down his nose sat hunched over a desk reading the morning paper.

"Excuse us," Graham said. "We wanted to inquire about your school system."

The man lowered the paper and looked up slowly. "I'm the principal. John Dune. What would you like to know?"

"We're thinking of putting our children in your school system," Graham said. "We wanted some idea of how things are going around here."

Dune folded the paper and stood up. "I suppose you're aware that we've been having considerable money problems, what with poor tax returns. The funds haven't been coming in, so the school suffers."

Graham bit his lip. "No, we weren't informed about that issue."

"We had similar problems back around the turn of the century," Dune said, "but this one is worse. We've had to cut teachers, and we now have around forty kids in every classroom." Dune shrugged. "Sure, it's bad, but we also have a limit on the number of textbooks, and that has caused the kids to share books. That's the only good thing that comes out of this problem. Kids have been forced to learn to be more flexible."

"You don't sound very promising, Mr. Dune," Graham said pointedly.

"I guess I could whitewash the facts some, but you'd hear this same information around town. I'm just being honest. We've got our problems."

George had just pushed Jeff down the school's slide when he noticed three boys emerging from behind the school building. They looked about the same age as himself, maybe older.

"Hi!" George yelled. "Come over and play with us."

The boys kept walking slowly, more like stalking prey than coming out to play. No one spoke.

"We're new here," George said. "Can you tell us anything about the school?"

No one answered. The three boys fanned out in a line and kept walking forward.

"Is this a good school?" Jeff asked.

"The question is, *are you good boys,*" the largest of the three said. "And I don't see no signs that ya are."

"Yeah," the second boy in the line chimed in, "and we don't like new kids. You look like a couple of little punks to me."

The third boy swung a long narrow board around from behind his back. "I think we ought to start you boys off with a good old-fashioned whippin' 'cause you didn't ask our permission to play out here."

The three boys charged George and Jeff. Before George could move, the board caught him across the chest. The largest of the three boys swung his fist and hit him square on the side of the face, knocking him to the ground.

Jeff screamed at the top of his lungs before the middle boy kicked him in the groin. He doubled up in a ball, unable even to moan.

Groaning in pain and dizzy, George rolled on the ground, trying to get free, but the largest of the boys leaped on him, his knees sinking into George's back. He heard Jeff start to scream and cry, but George couldn't get off the ground.

"Let's leave these two wimps with somethin' to remember us by," one of the attackers said. "How about smashing their noses in."

"No!" Jeff screamed. "Please don't!"

"Or kicking their teeth out," another boy said.

"Maybe we should cut 'em!" one assailant threatened.

George swung his feet with all his might and kicked the boy in the ankle, knocking him off balance.

"A-a-a-h!" the boy screamed in pain. "He smacked me!"

"Yeah? That little fink! Well, I'll kill him."

George heard the click of a knife opening above him. With a violent wrench of his body, he kicked straight up and knew his feet had caught the boy square in the stomach.

"O-o-o-h!" The boy with the knife heaved and tumbled backward.

George staggered to his feet, but he realized the boys couldn't be fought off. Out of the corner of his eye, he saw Jeff lying on the ground, crying. "Help!" George screamed at the top of his lungs. "Help us! Someone! Anyone!"

"You better holler!" The boy with the knife started getting to his feet. " 'Cause I'm gonna cut your heart out!"

"Stop it!" Graham Peck screamed, running from the front door of the school with the principal at his heels. "Stop this fighting, or I'll have the police on every one of you."

"Here comes ol' man Dune," the biggest of the three boys said. "Get outta here."

The three attackers scrambled to their feet and started running back the way they came. George stood over Jeff. For the first time he realized blood was running from his nose.

"What happened?" Graham sputtered as he ran up.

"They attacked us!" George shouted. "Came out of nowhere!"

"I know those boys," the principal growled. "Always been troublemakers around the school. I'll get 'em. Believe you me! I'll make 'em pay."

Jackie came running up and dropped to her knees to help Jeff. "Oh, son!" she said. "Are you hurt?"

"They had a knife," Jeff whimpered. "I thought they would cut us."

Graham looked at the principal. "Does this sort of thing happen around here often?"

The principal shook his head. "Too often, unfortunately."

CHAPTER 30

FEELING COMPLETELY DRAINED, the Pecks drove down the back roads, returning to their cabin in Tomahawk. Whatever their expectations had been, the experience at the Rhinelander school left them in shock and dismay. The institution remained far below their minimal level of standards, but the attack on the boys had turned dismay into horror.

"You guys doing okay?" Jackie asked over the seat for the third time.

George and Jeff both nodded without saying anything.

"We're just about home," Graham reassured them. "Look, you can see our house ahead." He pointed, but no one answered.

"Let's get them in the house as quickly as possible and see exactly how badly they are hurt," Jackie said.

"Of course." Graham pulled up and shut off the car. Matthew stuck his head up from the hiding place where he watched the house from a distance. Mary and Adah had to be inside.

"Go on in, boys," Jackie said. "We need to check your injuries." She ushered the boys into the house.

"I'm okay," George groused.

"I don't care what you say," Jackie said firmly. "George, take your shirt off and let us see where that boy's board hit you."

Painfully, George pulled his T-shirt over his head and

looked down. A dull red stripe ran across the middle of his chest.

"He really smacked you," Graham said. "It must hurt!"

"What in the world!" Mary walked in and stopped. Her mouth dropped in shock. "What happened to the boys?"

"They were jumped behind the public school," Graham said. "It appears assault and battery starts at an early age around that town."

"Good heavens!" Mary shrieked. "Look at the knot on the side of George's jaw!"

"That's where the big boy slugged me," George said.

"I'm not going to that school!" Mary protested. "They'd kill me on the first day."

"Nobody's going to that school," Graham assured her. "To say we were bitterly disappointed is an understatement."

Jackie came back with a bag of ice. "Put this on your jaw, George. It will help the swelling." She pressed the ice against the side of his face and wiped the dried blood from his nose.

"I still hurt where that boy kicked me," Jeff groaned.

"I know, I know, son." Graham drew him into his lap. "I can't tell you how sorry I am they attacked you."

Adah Honi walked in from the veranda. "Oh my goodness! What happened here?"

"Our boys were jumped," Graham said. "Looks like the public schools around here have bigger troubles than Chicago does."

Adah dropped to her knees in front of Jeff. "You poor,

dear boy." She patted him on the cheek. "What a terrible thing this is."

Mary compassionately hugged George. "Is there no end to what we have to suffer?"

No one said anything.

"Always your schools have been the best," Adah said, "but this is what the Tribulation we are living in has done to us. Matters will get worse."

"What do you mean?" Mary said.

"The book of Revelation calls this problem the 'wormwood phenomenon,' when the springs of the water of life are contaminated."

Graham blinked several times. "What in the world you are talking about?"

"Water is the New Testament way of talking about where we feed our spirits," Adah said. "Water is what keeps us alive mentally, spiritually, as well as physically. When I drink in philosophy and am educated, then I am feeding myself with waters of vitality. Yeshua, or Jesus, is the water of life."

"I'm not sure I understand," Jackie replied.

"The Bible says a star named 'Wormwood' will make the rivers bitter. It is the Scripture's way of warning that during the Tribulation, the educational and philosophical systems will spin out of control. Ideas will be infected and the children will suffer. This is what you saw today."

"I can't take any more of this!" Mary exploded. "Everywhere I see chaos, confusion, pain. Eldad was shot by some vagrant fool, and my brothers got stomped on by local delinquents." She pulled at her hair. "You sit here and spout that religious psychobabble! The world's gone completely stark-raving crazy!" Mary ran out and the front door slammed behind her.

"I didn't know she even cared about me," George said.

"Mary's hard to understand," Jackie finally said. "Let her be."

"Looks like we'll have to teach you boys at home," Graham said.

"Oh no!" George groaned. "I wanted to go to school with the other kids."

"Well, today wasn't much of a step in that direction," Graham answered.

CHAPTER 31

GRAHAM SAT on the veranda, watching George and Jeff playing down below the lofty walkway that ran around the front of the house. The playground incident in Rhinelander had seemingly slipped to the back of their minds, but Graham knew it was far from over for them.

Following his mother's death in Arlington Heights, Graham sank into despair over the shooting that killed her. Depression and grief had been pushed to one side as the discovery unfolded that the mayor's office had become the focal point for Borden Carson's schemes in the

United States. Graham had been totally shocked to discover Frank Bridges stood in the center of the entire mess. Eldad Rafaeli's death only added to the burden. When he thought of his Jewish friend, tears came to Graham's eyes. He blinked quickly and turned toward the boys.

Usually George and Jeff spent hours playing with a palm-sized transistorized magnifying system. The power of the batteries allowed the boys to enlarge microscopic particles to a size they could observe through the lens. But today they were engrossed in baseball.

George reached his baseball mitt high in the air, ready to catch the ball Jeff was trying to bat off the T-ball stand. You could never tell because Jeff might actually hit the ball. The boys seemed totally absorbed in their game and weren't even aware Graham was watching them.

And that was exactly the problem back in Chicago! Graham had been so lost in his job to reelect and politically position the mayor that he had failed to recognize the obvious. He couldn't afford to do so again. Maria, his mother, had warned him years earlier that he had a bad habit of being naive. She worried because Graham always assumed the best about people and that could get him in deep trouble.

It had.

During these past months, Adah and Eldad had taught him volumes about what the Bible said about life, values, hopes, morals, and what lay ahead. Hopefully he had absorbed their teachings because he needed every ounce of it. The death of Eldad, as well as the possibility of an attack on their home, had again plunged him into crisis. What happened in the Rhinelander schoolyard only brought the problem back into clearer focus. He needed to think clearly, accurately, and with no naïveté.

Ten feet away on the veranda's railing a blue jay landed. The bird hopped along the wooden pole, unaware a human was watching him, then suddenly twisted his head and saw Graham. For a moment the bird stared, as if trying to figure out what this strange creature was. Cocking his head, the bird pecked at the pole and then flew away to a tree. At the least, the blue jay didn't seem to be afraid of Graham. Maybe that was a good sign of better things to come.

Adah had shown Graham that the Bible taught he should be as harmless as a dove, *and* as wise as a serpent. Graham had to seem both harmless to a bird and deadly to an attacker, and he was certainly trying to fulfill that role. The Beatitudes instructed that he should be humble, self-contained, merciful, and peaceful. It was important to be honest so that no one could accuse him of falseness. But first and foremost, what should he remember as the chaos once more swirled around him? What was the paramount principle that must guide his life?

The wind picked up, blowing Jeff's ball off course and sending it bouncing into the trees. George went after it at a dead run. The current caught the blue jay and sent the bird sailing over the trees. Similar winds of change wouldn't stop blowing, and the family could be thrown off course as surely as the ball and the bird veered from theirs. Something more was needed.

And then he remembered that Adah had said the Bible taught that love should be his primary aim. Above all else, love should guide his every direction in life. Never before had that idea struck him with such force. He had learned what it was like to be clever and conniving, but not once had Graham taken seriously the idea that love should singularly guide him.

Sure, he loved his family. Jackie remained forever the light of his life, and Graham adored his children, but never before had he considered that love might guide what he did with and to other people. Time and time again in the last year, he had felt like vultures were diving at him with five-hundred-pound bombs strapped to their feet, but not once had he considered that love had the slightest place in what he did or how he responded.

Graham rubbed his chin and stared up into the clouds drifting by. "Okay, Lord," Graham prayed out loud. "You're the One who started this journey! I found love all through the Bible and certainly in the life of Jesus. I need to understand everything about what it fully means. I certainly can't be a passive idealist. We learned back in the last century that if we didn't fight for what's right, millions got killed, but how does that correlate with love? I don't know. You're going to have to show me!"

"Is somebody out here with you, Graham?" Jackie stuck her head out the doorway.

Graham jumped. "No! I mean, well, I was only talking to myself."

"You certainly were talking passionately," Jackie said and went back inside.

CHAPTER 32

HASSAN JAWHAR RASHID leaned back against the hospital pillow supporting his back and laid the thick file he was reading on the bed. His mind seemed to be operating correctly, but he continued to feel slightly woozy. Of course, the day of the shooting, as well as the three days following, had completely disappeared from his memory, yet today everything around him appeared far too vivid. The hospital room had become unbearably familiar, but the doctors warned he needed isolation to make sure no infection endangered the amazing progress he had made since the cranial operation. Obviously, the room had been professionally decorated to be the most luxurious in the hospital. An abundance of flowers nearly transformed the suite into a hothouse and truckloads of sprays had been sent elsewhere. Still, Hassan wanted out of this hospital as soon as possible.

"Sire?" Abu Shad closed the door behind him and walked over to the bed. "I trust you are feeling well today." He handed Rashid another file.

Rashid nodded. "As soon as the plastic surgery on my forehead and cheek is completed, I want out of here. Instantly!" The wound in his cheek made his words sound slurred.

"Of course. The doctors say that since the unusual

surgery with the material provided by the specialist from Illinois, your recovery has progressed splendidly. Thanks be to Allah that the bullet went down the middle of your brain, doing so little damage."

"Thanks be to modern science," Hassan snapped. "Human progress is what saved my life. Don't forget it!"

"Yes, sire." Abu bowed his head respectfully. "His Honor Mayor Bridges and his assistant are waiting outside to see you."

"Okay. Send them in."

Abu Shad opened the door and motioned for Bridges to enter.

"You may leave now," Rashid told his secretary.

"Ah!" Frank Bridges rushed through the door with his hands extended. "Al-sayyid Rashid, you're looking great!"

Rashid shook hands with both the mayor and his assistant, Al Meachem. "I'm sure with this clumsy bandage around my head and face, it appears they nearly cut off the top of my head. It makes me look like a fool."

"Oh no!" Bridges said with overwhelming enthusiasm. "No. Not at all!"

"Don't play the politician with me, Frank. I am lucky to be alive, but I still look like I was dumped out of a cement mixer."

"You have to expect to show a little wear and tear, Al-sayyid Rashid." Bridges shrugged. "But the truth is, you are looking amazingly well."

Rashid reached down and picked up a thick file that was bound at the seam. "I read the entire file you prepared on the investigation of your assistant Bill Marks. The security people have obviously done a considerable amount of investigation on this assassin."

"Absolutely." Bridges jutted his chin out confidently. "As I discussed earlier, no one, and I mean *no one*, had a clue that Marks had become involved with these right-wing lunatics. We knew a reactionary movement was creating the chaos and confusion that . . ."

"You mean crime and assaults everywhere were starting to upset them significantly," Rashid interjected.

"Yes. Of course." Bridges nodded. "We knew there were issues, but we couldn't have foreseen its affecting someone right in the midst of my administration."

"You blame a great deal of this man's behavior on his wife." Rashid started thumbing through the file. "I believe her name is Nancy Marks."

"That is correct, sir. Our investigators believe Nancy Marks initiated the problem with Bill Marks."

Rashid looked past Bridges. "You have caught this woman?"

Meachem nodded. "Yes sir! She fled the state to her parents' home in Little Rock, Arkansas. Our people captured her in the airport, preparing to fly out of the country. She's held in the Cook County Jail."

"Excellent." Rashid smiled at Meachem. "What have you learned from her?"

Bridges edged between Meachem and the bed. "The reactionary movement grew more rapidly than anyone in the United States government suspected. And it's better organized."

Rashid studied Frank Bridges' face. The mayor appeared nervous and probably was worrying that Rashid considered him guilty or incompetent for allowing Bill Marks such easy access. Having already studied the security tapes of the shooting, Rashid knew exactly what had occurred.

"As a matter of fact," Bridges continued, "we're concerned that an amalgamation of religious crazies and hostile militia groups could create a serious situation."

"You think I don't trust you, Frank?" Rashid said coolly.

Bridges stiffened and look frustrated. "No! I—I don't think any such thing, sir. Y-you know how profoundly I regret w-what's happened with this shooting."

"Relax," Rashid said forcefully. "Frank, if I didn't trust you, my security officers wouldn't have allowed you to enter this room."

Bridges' shoulders dropped and he swallowed hard. "Certainly. Thank you. Yes, thank you."

"I find your report to be thorough and complete." Rashid laid it on the bedside table. "I remain confident your analysis is correct and . . ." A surge of pain raced through his head, forcing the oil magnate to catch his breath.

"You all right?" Bridges extended his hand.

"Just a small bump in the road. Headache pains surface now and then." Rashid took another deep breath. "As I was saying, your assertion that the problem could quickly become serious is also correct. National attention is needed to stop this movement."

Bridges glanced frantically at Meachem. "We are doing everything possible to—"

"Fine." Rashid cut him off and smiled. "Your efforts are worthwhile, but we need something much, much larger."

"Larger?" Bridges frowned.

"Yes, and I have already identified the solution." Rashid picked up the file Abu Shad had brought in moments earlier. "You will find a prepared response in these pages." He handed the material to the mayor. "Abu Shad prepared this copy for you."

Bridges stared at the quarter-inch-thick file in his hand. "In order to coordinate the entire country for an attack on these insurgents, we are going to change the image of the Sunday Encounter Groups."

"Sunday Encounter Groups?" Bridges shrugged. "They're little more than time killers to keep people happy on weekends when they have nothing else to do. Those people provide tours, ski trips, nonsense like that."

"I understand they offer an opportunity for the people who once went to church to meet together," Rashid continued. "Rather impressive numbers of your population apparently are attending these groups every week."

"Well, yes. Sure. Lots of people attend."

"My sources also tell me that the Sunday Encounter Group members tend to vilify your extreme right-wing groups that attempted to assassinate me."

Bridges nodded his head up and down. "Y-yes. Encounter Group members certainly aren't part of the right-wing crowd."

"Excellent!" Rashid abruptly pounded the bed. "I am going to give them a new status, an unexpected position of power. They're going to reclaim the name 'church.' We will now call them 'The Restored Church,' the people of vision. They will change from being time killers to *people* killers."

Bridges rubbed his mouth. "I—I see."

"Nice people always have an amazing capacity to become meaner than junkyard dogs." Rashid raised an eyebrow condescendingly. "Sweet little old ladies can turn into ravenous wolves during a good old roaring church fight. Nice old men eat each other alive during such brawls. They remain perfect candidates to report deviates to the police. Am I right?"

"Certainly!" Bridges agreed. "Sure."

"You will find that I am recommending you do exactly what Constantine did in the third century when he took the Christians out of persecution and propelled them into one of the most powerful groups in the empire." Rashid smiled. "The Restored Church will become our national watchdogs to catch your extremists."

Bridges stared with his mouth partially open.

"Yes, my dear Frank, we are going to turn these encounter groups into national persecution societies. Every city, town, and burg, will have eyes watching up and down the streets to see what is going on. Don't worry. They'll help us wipe out all the opposition that you fear."

CHAPTER 33

I N A FEW DAYS, July 4 would slip around the corner, bringing with it the usual parades, picnics, fireworks, and celebrations of American independence. However, this year the merrymaking would be far more subdued. Citizens simply felt too much tension and apprehension to attend the festivities with their normal zeal. The Pecks certainly felt such hesitancy.

Watching out the back door of their cabin, Graham knew the children had gone on a walk through the woods, so no one was around to hear him. Matthew was with them to make sure nothing unexpected happened. "Jackie," he called into the kitchen. "How's Mary been lately?"

"Not good," Jackie said from the stove. "She seems despondent and depressed. The school episode seemed to almost finish her off. I know she hates being isolated out here in the woods."

"If Mary would only consider our faith and make an honest inquiry, I know she'd quickly find her way out of her confusion."

"Mary seems completely determined not to believe in anything but herself," Jackie said. "She's certainly not going to pay any attention to us because we're her parents."

"I guess you're right," Graham said sadly.

He punched the television remote, and the high resolution set hanging on the wall instantly came into focus. The clarity of the picture left the feeling that the announcer was literally sitting in the living room.

"And that completes our in-depth review of the recent war in India and Pakistan," Donald Ruther said. "Tragically many, many people were killed, but both countries are now back in compliance with the demands set by Royal Arab Petroleum for both services and political support of the company's position. Today we can expect the oil company to start looking at South America with greater interest." The announcer laid down his script page and looked directly into the camera. "Tonight we have just received notice of a special announcement from the mayor of Chicago. We are going live to the mayor's office."

"Hey!" Graham Peck yelled to Jackie. "Bridges is on national television. Take a look!"

Jackie turned around with a dishtowel in her hand. "Your ol' buddy's made it back on big-time television. My, my!" She sat down next to Graham. "What's the scoundrel up to now?"

The television camera panned across the conference room where Graham had sat so often on the other side of the table from Frank Bridges and discussed political strategy. Bridges sat at the end of the long mahogany table, hunched over with a serious look on his face.

"O-o-h! Frank's got on that 'I-mean-business' face," Graham said. "I imagine he's going to lay some heavy thoughts on us. Hunker down, Frankie boy."

Adah Honi walked in. "Oh! I know that man." She pointed at the screen. "The bad man."

"Only moments ago," Bridges began, "I completed a conversation with Creighton Lewis, leader of the Sunday Encounter Groups meeting weekly across the United States. Recognizing the need for spiritual renewal in the land, Borden Camber Carson encouraged me to suggest to Mr. Lewis that his movement ought to have greater visibility and recognition. Our citizens should be giving their serious attention to the ideas and procedures endorsed by the Encounter Groups. We believe in spiritual values."

Graham looked at his wife and frowned. "Don't tell me Bridges is going religious on us? That'd be bigger news than another terrorist attack."

"Creighton Lewis agreed with me that a new name is needed. Henceforth, we will use the title 'The Restored Church' for these groups. At Mr. Carson's urging, we are recommending that the country consider recognizing The Restored Church as a national religion. Americans can expect Creighton Lewis to be highly informed and make important pronouncements on issues of national concern. Dr. Creighton has just been given the title of 'Bishop in the Church of God.' The Restored Church will stand for national security, and you can expect their leadership to help our country maintain a high level of defense. Your involvement with The Restored Church will give you a renewed sense of personal protection."

"This has got to be a joke!" Jackie said. "What an absurdity."

"Good Lord!" Graham scooted forward in his chair. "They're creating a church they can control."

"I bet they've got Carson in the back room dictating their next copy of the Bible." Jackie rubbed her hands together nervously. "I'm getting to where I can read the signs of the times unfolding before us."

Adah narrowed her eyes. "How very interesting. Just this morning I get an insight. Suddenly, boom! The next shoe falls."

"What do you mean?" Graham asked.

Adah reached over to the coffee table and picked up her Bible. "I have been studying what the thirteenth chapter of Revelation tells us about this terrible shooting we have been watching on television. In the third verse, the beast, the Antichrist, is predicted to have a mortal head wound that healed. As unexpected as this passage seems, this prophecy we have seen in the Scripture has been fulfilled."

"The first time you showed me that passage," Graham said, "I was staggered." He glanced at the page. "But today the whole world has indeed *marveled* at Carson's recovery."

Jackie nodded. "Has it ever!"

"Farther down, we read in verse 11 about the lamb who speaks with the voice of the dragon."

Graham looked at the Bible.

"It doesn't take much thought to see the symbolism here," Adah said. "The voice of the dragon is how the Evil One speaks to us. Now, he is going to speak through the lamb, or the phony church. This 'church,' as Bridges calls it, is about to become the voice of the devil."

"Oh man!" Graham shuddered.

"A satanic trinity is slipping into place," the Jewish woman said. "In the seat of authority, the first person in this hierarchy is the Evil One. Behind the scenes of these diabolical ideas is always Satan." Adah pointed to the television. "This church we have just heard described is the next part of this trinity. The lamb with the dragon's voice is the second persona." She shook her finger. "Don't ever forget, there is a daily, practical aspect of this extension of evil that we must pay attention to. The beast with authority is runaway government doing the bidding of Lucifer. That's the third person. Government will take on a quality of anonymity about what it does. Evil will happen everywhere." Adah shook her finger at Graham and Jackie authoritatively. "Get ready! The satanic trinity is about to confront the world with more confusion."

CHAPTER 34

FRANK BRIDGES flashed another forceful smile and finished his television speech. "Your involvement with The Restored Church will give you a renewed sense of personal protection." He kept smiling, waiting for the light on the camera to switch off.

"Got it!" the cameraman said. "Donald Ruther in New York has already sent your message to millions of homes."

"Thank you." Bridges stood and briskly walked out of

the room. "Good job." He saw Al Meachem standing out in the hall waiting for him.

"We picked up Gillette," Meachem said. "He wasn't any happier this time than the last, but the good doctor's getting acquainted with the routine. This time he threw up his hands and marched out to our car immediately, without any screaming or yelling."

"Okay." Bridges nodded. "I want to observe this experiment. Let's hope it accomplishes our purposes."

"Where do you want to do it?"

Bridges thought a moment. "Gillette brought the top secret materials with him?"

"Sure. Got 'em hidden in the car."

"Where would he suggest they be released?"

"I asked him," Meachem said. "He thinks from some high place like the roof of this building."

"Sounds good enough to me, Al. Get him up on the roof."

"I'll be there in five minutes."

Bridges returned to his private office. He shut the door behind him. "Anyone else here?"

Connie Reeves smiled seductively. "Why? You looking for a new girlfriend?"

Bridges kissed her passionately. "How'd I look on television?"

"Good as always. The man of the hour."

"Think I snowed 'em?"

Connie kissed him again. "Like a blizzard."

"Any business I need to attend to before I go up to the roof?"

"No. None."

"Good! Good. Look, baby, this is top secret. Make sure my phone calls are covered."

"You bet." Connie waved him on. "Hurry along."

Bridges took the elevator on the other side of his inner office and in moments was on the roof of the thirty-story building. Al Meachem and Jack Stratton held Dr. Paul Gillette between them. At his feet sat a large metal trunk. On the top side had been stamped *Top Secret*.

"Dr. Gillette." Bridges rushed forward with his hands extended. "How good to see you again."

Gillette shook hands perfunctorily, but remained stone-faced.

"Looks like another of those freak storms is blowin' in," Jack Stratton mumbled as he glanced upward. "Clouds look bad."

"Yeah," Meachem agreed. "There've been tornadoes in Michigan and across Illinois. Strange for this late in the year for sure. I don't like it."

Gillette jutted out his chin. "We don't have much time," he said stiffly.

"I'm sure you're completely aware of what we need to do," Bridges began.

Gillette nodded his head, but he looked worried. "I'm not sure this project is at all ready to be released into the atmosphere," he said reluctantly. "We've had problems."

"Come now, come now," Frank cajoled. "Your staff at the nanotechnology lab has been working on this project for weeks. I trust your people."

Gillette glanced nervously at the mayor. "We've had significant problems."

Brushing the comment aside, Bridges pressed on. "How do these gizmos work?"

"Each camera is approximately one ten-billionth of an inch and shaped like a bullet. From the front end, the nanorobots send images to our computer system. They are propelled by the microtubules on the back side and float on the wind. The nanorobots are in the trunk, and I have only to release them and the project begins."

"Excellent!" Bridges beamed. "I understand that extraordinary possibilities are available to us."

"They have a miniature gallium arsenide photon detector in the front, which functions like the retina of the human eye," Gillette continued explaining. "In addition, a bioluminescent factor provides a unique source of light. These nanorobots operate something like a primitive camera."

"What ya mean?" Al Meachem asked.

"The idea of a camera obscura has been around for centuries. The Romans actually came up with the first one by making a small hole in the wall of a dark room and observing what light did. The image came through upside down on the opposite wall. Kids today do the same with their pinhole cameras. That's the way images will be sent to our computer system."

"Hmm." Bridges pondered. "Fascinating."

"That same idea is the principle behind these devices. When the nanorobots start performing, we've set up these particular robots to operate according to the algorithms our people developed," Gillette continued. "We believe they will merge together and form their own network."

"That's where each individual nanorobot will coordinate with the others and project a composite picture of what they see?" Bridges asked.

"Something like that," Gillette agreed. "We might think of it as a form of swarm intelligence. Because these camera nanorobots are so infinitesimal, we need every one of them to give us an orderly and structured picture of what they find."

"That's exactly what we're looking for." Bridges kept smiling. "We want your gadgets to locate a group of six people, then shoot an image of the group back to us. None have been tagged with security markings."

"As you instructed earlier, we think this group of nanorobots are so programmed."

"You keep saying *I think* or *I believe,* Dr. Gillette." Bridges frowned. "There's a problem here?"

"As I've tried to tell you many times," Gillette barked. "We're not sure what these gizmos will do. They could spin out of control."

Bridges chewed on his lip. "That would be most unfortunate."

"No!" Dr. Gillette said sharply. "That could be most *deadly.*"

CHAPTER 35

WITH THE FEROCITY of a sudden winter blizzard whirling down from Canada, the summer storm turned the clouds purple and sent hail flying across Wisconsin. Another outbreak of tornadoes smashed through Minnesota, hitting towns like Brainerd, Saint Cloud, and brushing over Minneapolis. The little town of Tomahawk braced itself as the unprecedented heavy rains washed through the forest and pounded roofs with golf-ball-sized hail.

"This storm looks like one of those dark passages from the book of Revelation," Graham told his wife. "The sun's blacked out, and it's almost as if the stars are crashing down on our roof."

"The weather's been strange for over a year," Jackie said. "For months the moon was red, but it's never looked any more frightening than this storm." She folded her hands. "Lord, keep us from a twister."

"I guess the children are okay," Graham said. "Aren't they?"

"I think they are downstairs." Jackie walked to the stairs leading to the second level. "George? Jeff? You down there?"

"Yes," Jeff's voice answered.

"And Mary?"

"No."

Jackie frowned. "What do you mean?"

"She's not here." George stuck his head around the door at the bottom of the stairs. "I haven't seen her all afternoon."

"That's strange." Jackie turned to Graham. "I'm going down there to see what's going on."

"How could Mary be out in this storm?" Graham scratched his head. "She's got to be down there hiding somewhere."

Jackie hurried down the stairs and found George and Jeff playing a game on the floor of their room. She smiled and went to the next room. Matt had pushed himself up against the head of his bed and was reading a book.

"Son, have you seen Mary this afternoon?"

Matt shook his head without looking up. "No," he said disinterestedly.

Jackie stepped across the hall and pushed open the door to Mary's room. The unmade bed was piled high with a tangle of sheets and a blanket heaped in the center of the mattress. Clothes were scattered everywhere.

"Mary?" Jackie got no reply. "You have to be here!" she said resolutely and jerked open the closet door. The only thing she noticed was that Mary's suitcase was not on the top self. Jackie felt her heart beat harder. She darted across the hall and pounded on Adah's door. "Is Mary in there with you? Have you seen her?"

Adah opened the door and stood with her Bible in hand. "Mary?" She shook her head. "I have not seen her all day."

Jackie's heart thumped like a bass drum. "Graham!" she screamed. "Mary's gone! Her suitcase is gone."

Graham bounded down the stairs, taking them two and three at a time. "She can't be!" he argued.

"No one's seen her all afternoon!" Jackie's voice trembled. "Her room's the usual mess. I think our daughter has run off!"

CHAPTER 36

FOR TWO DAYS the Peck family searched every possible trail, lane, and street in Tomahawk and the town of Rhinelander, believing Mary had hidden somewhere in one of those two places. Maybe she had made a friend in one of the towns and hadn't told anyone. When nothing turned up, they sought the help of Alice Masterson and a few of the believers in her study group. After looking for several hours without arousing suspicion, the searchers reassembled in the basement of the old church where Alice's group met.

"Has anyone found *anything*?" Graham begged. He had wanted to convey love to his daughter, the kind of affection that would crack the resistance and turn her back into a kind, thoughtful person who would embrace the faith. Instead, he had been swallowed by his own guilt. "Anything?" Graham repeated.

"I'm sorry," Alice answered. "I don't think so."

"Oh, please! Please tell us you've found at least a clue?" Jackie pleaded.

Alice looked around the basement. "I know these people well, and most of the town's people are also acquainted with them. They won't lie. Has anyone found out anything about the Pecks' daughter?"

The large man in overalls looked away, and an elderly lady stared at the floor. The other people didn't speak.

"I'm sorry, Graham, but these people would have discovered something if Mary was in Rhinelander."

"She's right, Dad," Matt added. "I walked a dozen blocks this afternoon. Nothing."

Graham's entire body sagged. "I simply can't make any sense out of where she's gone." He ran his hands nervously through his hair. "We're at least one hundred and seventy miles from the Illinois border and seventy-five from Michigan. She can't drive a car, and surely no one would pick up a child."

"She's not a child," Jackie insisted. "Mary's become a young woman and could pass for someone much older than she is. Dressed right, she might look close to twenty. No, Mary's capable of traveling a significant distance alone."

"Let's sit down," Alice suggested. "Everybody grab a chair. We've got to think together. Let's start by praying."

Without any more being said, they started to pray. After ten minutes, someone said, "Amen," and the praying was over.

"We've got to be even more careful these days," Alice

said. "You can't tell who's watching. Graham, think it over again," Alice instructed. "Where was she most likely to have gone?"

Graham looked at Jackie for a moment. "The only place that Mary knew anything about was Chicago, but that's simply too far away."

Alice grabbed his arm. "I hear something," she said in a low, quiet voice. "Listen!"

"Could be those people from that new Restored Church," the man in the overalls said. "I heard they was on the prowl."

Alice slipped next to the basement window and peered out for a moment. "Someone's out there circling the church building," she whispered. "We've got to get out of here. Graham, I'm sorry we couldn't do better. Time for us to run."

Graham nodded. "Sure. Thanks for the help." His heart felt heavy.

"Just get out and go to your cars or wherever," Alice Masterson said forcefully. "Try not to let anybody see you."

Graham took a deep breath. He could feel his anger building, but he didn't know what else to do. "Okay." He reached for Jackie's and Matthew's hands. "Let them get out and then we'll make a break for it. Matt, shut the door behind us."

Alice and her friends left in a single file, scampering up the back steps and disappearing down the alley. Everyone tried to make as little noise as possible.

"Follow me," Graham said to his family and dashed up the stairs with Jackie and Matt behind him. The basement door flew open and he trotted across the backyard. "Let's go." He started around the side of the church.

Two men suddenly stepped out from around the front of the church. "Where you people think yer goin'?" the larger of the two men said and crossed his arms defiantly over his chest.

"Just looking at your church building," Graham said. "Is it for sale?"

"He's interested in buyin' a church," the second man chided the first. "Now, ain't that somethin'. You goin' in the religion business?"

"No," Matthew said firmly. "Restaurant."

"In this old church? Now, ain't this young man got a smart mouth," the first man said. "I think you people is alyin' to us."

Graham studied their faces. Each man's eyes had a mean glint, and they were clearly looking for trouble. Maybe there were other people; maybe there weren't. The Pecks needed to get out of the area, and these men weren't to be toyed with.

"We're leaving," Graham said to the family and started walking.

"Now, I wouldn't be so fast," the smaller man said. "We didn't even get your name."

"Without your name, we can't sell you the building." The larger man reached for Graham's arm and gripped it firmly.

With everything he had, Graham swung for the man's stomach. He felt his fist sink into the man's fat belly. With a low groan, the large man went crashing into the weed-filled flower bed.

The second man stepped back. "Hey! Ya better not hit me!" he yelled and started scurrying toward the back of the church.

"Let's get out of here!" Graham said urgently under his breath. Grabbing Jackie's hand, he started running for the street.

"Man, you punched him out!" Matt said as he trotted alongside them. "Great hit!"

"We've got . . . to get . . . to the car and out of here," Graham said, gulping air. "We're not safe in this town."

Matthew grabbed the car door and jerked it open. Jackie tumbled in behind him. In seconds, Graham had the car started and pulled away from the curb. Without stopping, he headed for Highway 51 to get out of town.

"I'm not sure what's going on in that village, but the place has gotten scary." Graham kept watching the rearview mirror. "I think we got away, but it's still not clear where Mary is."

"You know," Jackie said thoughtfully, "that town still remains the best place for her to hide."

CHAPTER 37

THE PECKS WAITED a day after their hasty exit from Rhinelander before they made any further contacts. Graham finally drove down to the country store in Tomahawk and called.

"We don't have a telephone," Graham told Alice Masterson over a pay phone outside the store. "Keeps us more secluded. No one can trace where we are. Sorry. I guess I'll have to call you to make contact."

"I understand," Alice said. "However, we must be extremely cautious. My friends got away yesterday because those two men were in front of the church, but those clowns spread word all over Rhinelander that two militia vigilantes attacked them. Said you knocked one guy into the bushes."

"They're from this new Restored Church?"

"Exactly! These people are turning the town upside down looking for people they call 'the attackers.' They mean you! You're going to have to be doubly careful if you come back to this town."

"Hmm." Graham rubbed his chin. "Things are heating up in Rhinelander, huh?"

"That's right," Alice said. "Everyone in my group is concerned. We're afraid to become identified as a target for the nut fringe. We're not meeting at the church building for a while."

"I certainly understand," Graham said. "These Restored Church members sound like they've gone on a rampage."

"It's a witch hunt! They've turned all of their pent-up fears and anxieties loose on anyone who is different from them. It's like that ancient communist fighter Joe McCarthy has ridden into our town with an army of hellcats, spreading confusion everywhere."

"We'll pay close attention to them," Graham assured her. "I wanted you to know that Jackie still has a strong suspicion that our daughter might be hiding somewhere in Rhinelander. Please ask everyone to keep their eyes open."

"We certainly will. You remain in our prayers. Be careful. Like I told you earlier, I have that cabin over in Prentice. The key is always left hanging behind the welcome sign on the door. If things get tight, please, please, use that place."

"Thanks, Alice. You have certainly been more than a friend. You're a real sister in Christ."

"God bless you and your family, Graham. Goodbye." Alice hung up.

Graham slowly put the receiver back inside the telephone booth. Jackie sat in the car watching him. He walked back and told her what Alice had said.

"I can't believe Mary would do this to us," Jackie agonized. "We've given her nothing but the best. The first time I even got wind of her belligerence was when Matt came home from college with insights about the Christian faith. Mary turned into an overprivileged brat. If Mayor Bridges' men hadn't chased us out of town, she'd probably still be lined up with her atheistic friends, calling us fanatics behind our backs. Everything about her behavior scares me to death."

"She's had it too good," Graham said. "While millions of Americans struggle to survive every day, Mary lives like a princess with her friends as her court-in-waiting. Affluence breeds apathy, and in her case, it sparked hostility and defiance."

Jackie ran her hands nervously through her hair. "We can't give up looking for her."

Graham started the car and turned back in the direction of their cabin, driving slowly up the dirt road. "It's going to be tough to return to Rhinelander for a while. Sounds like my punching that country clod exploded into a lynching mob. We can't be seen on the streets."

"But we can't simply let her take off like this," Jackie objected.

"Really?" Graham raised an eyebrow. "And what control do we have over her right now?"

Jackie didn't say anything more. The car pulled up in front of the cabin and they went back inside. Matt, George, and Jeff were sitting around the breakfast table with Adah talking to them. They immediately stopped the conversation when their mother and father walked in.

"Things have heated up in Rhinelander," Graham told them. "The Restored Church leaders have turned into vigilantes, and we can't let ourselves be caught in town," he explained. "Your mother and I aren't sure what to do next."

The conversation around the table slipped into silence, with each person lost in their own thoughts. Even little Jeff looked worried.

"I still have trouble understanding my sister," Matt said. "Sure, she and I have had our fights through the years, but I've never seen Mary hold out so long about anything."

"Perhaps we should turn on the television and see what the news is this morning," Graham concluded. "I'll pick up that NBC news station from Chicago to see what's happening locally." He punched the remote and the screen instantly leaped to life. Graham started buttering a bagel.

"Looks like another summer day in Chicago," the weatherman concluded. "We hope none of those spontaneous strong storms that caused so much damage return. If the weather stays on an even keel, we will have a scorching July 4 and good picnic weather. Back to you at the anchor desk, Larry."

"Thank you for that update," Larry Daniels said. "We have one more item that has just come in to us. The Chicago police have picked up one of the members of the Graham Peck family attempting to enter the family home in Arlington Heights."

Graham dropped his knife on the floor. "*What!*" he shrieked.

"Apparently, teenager Mary Peck was trying to enter the back door when police posted in the trees saw her and apprehended the teenager today. She is being held incommunicado, since her father is now considered an armed and dangerous suspect."

"It can't be!" Jackie cried. "No! NO!"

"The police caught her at our house," Matthew moaned.

"Details are sketchy, but police have increased their search in the Chicago area for Graham Peck." Graham's face appeared on the screen. "If you've seen this man anywhere in the metroplex area, please call the police immediately, as he is armed and considered dangerous."

Graham dropped into the chair at the end of the table. His heart pounded like a drum. "God help us!" he cried out loud.

Adah grabbed Graham's arm. "Since they now have your daughter, will she talk?"

"Talk?" Graham looked at her, not comprehending.

"Will she tell them where we are?" Adah pressed.

Graham blinked several times. "I—I don't know."

"Mary can't handle pain," Jackie blurted out. "She's obstinate around us, but she will crumble in a hurry under police pressure."

"Absolutely," Graham muttered. "Yes. We've got to get out of here immediately." He suddenly stood up and blurted out, "Whether she intends to or not, Mary will probably reveal our location. Bridges' men could descend on us like hornets. Grab your things. We must run as fast as we can!"

CHAPTER 38

A T LINCOLN PARK, not far from Belmont
Harbor on Lake Michigan, a blue hydrogen-powered family van pulled up to one of the picnic sites where a wooden table and a rock fireplace promised a good setting for a family outing. The car doors quickly swung open, and the six members of the Rice family hopped out.

"Come on, Mom and Dad," Donna Rice chided her parents. "Let's see who's first to the picnic table."

"Oh," Donna's father groaned. "I'm an old man. Just get me out, Mother."

Donna's mother helped her husband slide out of the car as she always did, but the two children were gone in a second.

"Hey!" Robert Rice shouted at his sons. "You boys cool it. Get back here and help us carry the food to the picnic table."

"Rats," Ryan Rice growled. "We want to play softball."

"Yeah!" his brother Randy chimed in. "Carryin' stuff ain't our style."

"It is now," Donna insisted. "You boys come back here and help your grandparents."

Grumbling under their breaths, the boys slammed their large mitts to the grass, but returned to help.

"Put that six-pack of soda over there on the table," Robert told Ryan, "and make sure you don't drop it."

"I'm not a klutz," Ryan mumbled under his breath and picked up the drinks.

"Sure feels good to sit down out here in this nice breeze blowing off Lake Michigan," Donna's father said. "Certainly helps cool me off."

"Well, I'm hoping we don't have any more of those horrendous storms like the one that blew through the other day," Donna's mother added. "Scared me to death. Never seen anything come on so fast and furious. And the hail? Heaven help us, don't you know!"

"Yes." Donna set a cake on the table. "No one expected it when the sky started turning black. I wouldn't want one of those surprises *tonight*."

"Play ball with us," Ryan begged his father.

"I will after we eat," Robert assured him. "Why don't we cook some hot dogs first, and then we'll have a ball game with all six of us playing."

"Hey, wait a minute," Grandfather protested. "I'm not sure that I'm up to one of those rip-roarin' battles."

"Come on, Dad," Donna encouraged him. "You'll do fine."

"What is that?" Donna's mother pointed up to the sky. "It looks like sand, little gnats or something." She kept tracing the hazy air with her finger. "How peculiar."

"I don't see anything," Donna said.

"I do." Robert shielded his eyes. "One minute it's there, and the next it's gone, but it's like a slight discoloration sailing through the air."

"Come on," Donna chided her husband. "You been nipping on more than a soda?"

"Look!" Robert pointed at eye level. "It's changed course and isn't far from us . . . maybe twenty feet at most."

"Y-yes." Donna squinted. "How unusual. Like mosquitoes swarming, but lots smaller." She pointed. "Hey, it's gone!" She looked again. "No, it's back."

The boys pushed in around their grandparents, staring at the strange discoloration hovering in the air.

"What do you think it is?" Robert asked.

"Never seen anything like that," Donna's father said thoughtfully. "Bizarre. Looks more like . . . maybe . . . it's a gas of some kind."

Suddenly the cloud surged at the six people, swarming around their faces. The grandparents began coughing violently.

"My eyes!" Robert cried. "Something is burning in my eyes." He rubbed his face fiercely.

"I can't breathe!" Donna gasped. "M-my mouth feels like it's filling with s-sand." The normal healthy pink in her face faded, and Donna's lips began turning purple.

"A-a-ah!" Ryan screamed. "Help me!" He grabbed his throat. "I can't get any air!" Ryan fell backward.

Robert tried to reach out for his son, but he could hardly move his arms. At that moment he realized that Donna's mother and father had fallen facedown on the picnic table.

"R-Randy!" Robert gagged. "Wh-ere a-are you?" He felt himself losing breath and becoming uncontrollably light-headed. His vision blurred and he couldn't see. Only then did he realize that Randy was lying on the ground on the other side of the table.

"R-obert," Donna groaned and then slumped to the ground in silence.

"P-Please." Robert kept reaching, but he could no longer move. He forced his eyes open, and realized the entire family was sprawled unconscious around him. With his last ounce of energy, Robert fell to his knees, and then plopped facedown in the grass.

In less than five minutes they were all dead. Only after twenty minutes did anyone realize that the six people were lying motionless around the picnic table. A passerby finally noticed them and called the police, but of course it was far, far too late.

CHAPTER 39

AL MEACHEM WALKED BRISKLY into the mayor's inner office. "I've got something you should look at," Meachem said. "An incident happened at Lincoln Park yesterday." Wearing a faded black shirt and suit, Meachem looked more like a backroom operator than an officer of the city.

"I'm busy right now," Bridges said in a gruff voice. With his casual pullover T-shirt and khakis he wore when not making a television appearance, the mayor looked considerably laid-back.

"We're completing a letter to Washington, D.C.," Connie Reeves said with a hint of indignation in her voice. As always, Connie had a slightly seductive air to her appearance. "Is this really urgent?"

Meachem glanced back and forth between the two of them. He didn't think much work was actually going on here today. "Look," he said demandingly. "We've had six people killed in a park, and the circumstances are too suspicious to put this one on a back burner. It needs your immediate attention, boss."

"*Your Honor!*" Frank Bridges corrected him. "Can't you get that straight?" He held out his hand. "Okay. Give me the story."

"We're talking *six* people here," Meachem said. "Does that ring any bells?"

Bridges' eyes narrowed. "*Six?*"

"Yeah. They were found dead around a picnic table—like something strange swooped down on them from the sky. An initial examination indicated they suffocated in broad daylight with no apparent cause."

Bridges' eyes narrowed. "You're suggesting the camera nanorobots hit them, aren't you?"

Meachem nodded. "Word came up through the chain of command about this, so I ordered autopsies to be performed by our people."

"*And?*" Bridges beckoned for him to keep talking.

"The lab found their noses, windpipes, and throats filled with a black substance. Microscopic examination revealed thousands of nanorobots invaded their eyes, ears, throats, all over their bodies."

"Get Dr. Gillette on the videophone instantly," Bridges ordered his secretary. *"Do it at once."*

Connie Reeves rushed out of the room.

"Let's see what Gillette says," Bridges growled. "By the way, have you dragged anything out of Peck's daughter yet?"

Meachem shook his head. "She's turned out to be a tougher nut to crack than we thought. Won't tell us anything. I think we're going to have to use a little sodium Pentothol or something of that order on her if we're going to get any information out of the kid." Meachem rolled his deep-set eyes cynically. "Drugs usually pound the door down. Don't worry. We will break her."

"He's on the phone," Connie said from the door. "Turn on your wall receiver."

Bridges reached across the desk and hit a corner button. A large blank screen on the opposite wall sprang to life. Sitting in his office wearing a white lab coat, Dr. Paul Gillette had a worried look on his face.

"Ah, Dr. Gillette." Bridges instantly switched to a broad smile. "We need your assistance." Bridges kept the everything-is-okay countenance in place. "You see"—he cleared his throat—"we had a strange incident yesterday. A family of six were out in one of the parks when they suddenly died—"

"God help us!" Gillette cut him off. "I knew it!" He dropped his face into his hands. "I told you we weren't ready!"

Bridges' smile slid into a frown. "Please be more specific."

"I told you those nanorobots weren't entirely control-lable! Don't you remember the death of Dr. Allen Newton? The machines killed him!"

Bridges leaned forward. "I want to know how long they'll be out there flying around," he asked pointedly.

"Who knows?" Gillette fired back. "You stopped our experiments before we could compile data on such issues."

"But you can pull them back in," Bridges pursued the scientist. "Can't you electronically make them return to your lab, to our building, wherever?"

"You fool!" Gillette snarled uncharacteristically. "If these gizmos attacked someone rather than took their picture, do you think I have any control over them?" He smashed his fist on the desk. "My God, apparently they have developed a herd mentality, a sense of direction of their own! They are roaming across your city, doing whatever the swarm pleases." He suddenly stood up. "I don't care what you do to me. I want no more of this. Don't send those thugs back here again. Get out of my life!" He pointed a finger at the screen. "You come back here, and I'll talk to the press. You've released a plague that is running its own course. Like turning loose killer locusts and scorpions on the world, you've sent death out on the winds. Who knows what those malicious machines will do to *any group* of six people they find!"

The screen went blank.

CHAPTER 40

WHEN THE DAY of July 4 began, the sky looked normal, but only a few hours had passed when the summer sun started to fade. For a short period of time, a deadly stillness settled across the world, and a chill spread down the plains and over the Midwest. A volcano abruptly erupted in the middle of the Lewis and Clark National Forest, about sixty-five miles from Great Falls, Montana. The darkening sky silhouetted the exploding eruption of fire and lava. Ash caught the increasing wind and began to spread as a gray cloud down into Wyoming and into Idaho. By noon a threatening blackness had settled over the West. The volcano quickly grew into a large mountain.

Special celebrations were canceled, and some of the ash proved deadly. Not only in Montana, but in Wyoming and Idaho, as well as in North and South Dakota, people were dying from breathing the ash and poisonous gases now set loose across several states. The town of Cheyenne declared an emergency, insisting people tape their windows and doors to keep out the deadly dust. Deaths were reported in Ft. Collins and Greeley, Colorado. Terror spread through Minnesota and on toward Wisconsin.

"I think it's another one of those assaults from God," George told his father. "He's warning people to straighten up."

"I'd think they should have gotten the message by now," Jackie said. "If I didn't have a relationship with the Almighty, I'd be frightened to death."

"The world can see nothing but confusion," Adah added. "It is the Scripture that opens our eyes to the truth." She opened her Bible. "Chapter eight in Revelation tells us of what happens when the Holy One breaks open the seventh seal. Listen to what the book tells us." She started to read: " 'And hail and fire followed, mingled with blood, and they were thrown to the earth. And a third of the trees were burned up, and all green grass was burned up.' This I think is happening. Isn't a volcano like fire and blood mingled?"

"Yeah," Graham said glumly. "At least Alice Masterson saved us by allowing us to use this cabin," Graham said.

"And we have a phone now," Jackie added. "It helps to be able to call her."

"I am so sorry that Eldad was killed so early on," Adah added. "While this strange explosion leaves me in fear, he would have been fascinated."

"I wish Matthew would come back," Jackie added. "I don't like him hiding over there watching our cabin."

"Matt's clever," Graham said. "He has binoculars now; he can get the picture without getting too close."

"This house is really small," George said. "Half the size of our other one."

"But it's a roof over our heads," Jackie reminded him. "Never complain when we could be living out of the backseat of our car. I am sure many, many people are dying right now."

The wind picked up, sending an icy howl through the small cabin. Windows shook, and only the candles provided an eerie glow throughout the small house.

Graham looked out the window. "We can't simply let Mary sit in jail. We've got to contact her."

"They'd nail you on the spot," Jackie answered him. "Graham, you can't go anywhere without people recognizing you. The Chicago bosses have turned you into a wanted man."

"Maybe I could peroxide my hair," he said thoughtfully. "Grow a beard. Something of that order."

"It is an important idea," Adah said. "You must not be recognized easily."

"I keep thinking over and over about our daughter," Jackie said. "I pray a hundred times a day that God will keep His hand on her, no matter how rebellious she's been."

"Listen!" Adah said. "I think a car is coming."

Graham rushed to the window. "I can see the headlights. Yes! It's Matthew's car!"

The car pulled up near the front door, and Matt dashed into the house. Stamping his feet on the small rug near the door, he brushed small pieces of ash off his coat. "Everybody gather around the table," he said. "I've got plenty to tell you."

The family quickly settled around the wooden dining room table. No one spoke.

"This morning, shortly after the sky started to darken, a caravan of cars showed up at our cabin," Matt began. "They came fast and hit our house like commandos on a raid. In seconds, they'd gone through the entire house. I recognized the face of Al Meachem."

Graham's shoulders dropped, and he sighed. "Exactly what I was afraid of."

"Obviously, they knew exactly where they were going," Matt continued. "Of course, they didn't find anything."

"How long did they stay?" Jackie asked.

"Two hours at the most. One of the cars arrived with scientific equipment, and I think they must have gone over every inch of the place, but the sky kept getting darker. They turned on the lights, which allowed me to watch them through the windows easier without anybody seeing me."

"What happened next?" George asked.

"After about an hour and a half, the sky turned black, and the attackers looked worried. The men came back out and got in their cars, except for Meachem and some other man." Matthew stopped and took a deep breath. "You want me to go on?"

"Absolutely," Graham urged him. "We've got to know what they did."

Matt nodded his head slowly. "Well . . . they threw gasoline all over the house and tossed in a match. The cabin burned to the ground."

Jackie started crying, and Graham put his arm around her.

"Your beautiful house burned down?" Adah said with painful longing in her voice.

"Yeah, afraid so," Matthew said. "We no longer have a home in Tomahawk."

CHAPTER 41

"OUR ENEMIES HAVE TURNED us into wandering nomads," Jackie said thoughtfully as she listened to Matthew describe the burning of their Tomahawk cabin. "We have no place to live except where friends open a door to us."

"And Graham is now a criminal on the run," Adah added. "The Evil One has made him a wanted man everywhere."

"For doing nothing," Graham said. "Adah, are you sure you know what you are talking about from the book of Revelation? Sometimes I think it would have been much easier to have forgotten all of this Bible stuff and simply . . ."

"You *really* believe that?" Jackie asked.

Graham looked out the window thoughtfully. "No, of course I don't. I'm just feeling the pain of knowing thugs burned down our cabin, and we can't do anything about it."

"Not at this moment," Adah said. "But never forget, the future is on our side."

"Why do you say that so confidently?" Graham asked her.

"It is clear from the Bible. In the end, the believers win."

"That's a hard idea to hang on to right now," Graham said.

"Sure." Adah nodded her head. "But every prophecy in Revelation tells us this is true."

"I guess you're right," Graham said glumly. "It's simply hard to feel right now."

Adah picked up a piece of paper and quickly drew a wheel, with a hub in the center and spokes extending to the outer rim. "This is how the events in Revelation are arranged," she explained. "In the past, brilliant interpreters didn't understand the book correctly because they thought the events like broken seals, seven trumpets, and bowls of wrath were stepping-stones that had to follow one another chronologically. This I do not believe was correct."

Matthew looked at the wheel for a moment. "Then what is right?"

"Each of these unfolding visions is always the same pattern," Adah said. "Notice that fact. What occurs between people is different, but the pattern is identical for what follows." She pointed at the hub of the wheel. "Each prophecy begins with the proclamation of Christ as Lord. That's the hub. Once that word is preached, a battle with evil begins. That is the spoke of the wheel. After a period of warfare, it appears the Christians are in trouble, because chaos is so strong." A smile broke across her face. "Then a surprise occurs and God intervenes, just as He did for the Jews against Pharaoh, and the believers come out the victors. That is the outer rim. Each vision, whether it be trumpets or bowls of wrath, tells this story. Like spokes of a wheel, the pattern is repeated in each of these circumstances."

"That's amazing!" Matthew told Adah.

"You look and see." Adah pointed at Graham. "For yourself—find out. See if I am not correct."

"I'm not doubting you," Graham said. "I'm just deeply disturbed right now. We can't sit here and let Mary rot in the Cook County Jail! I must visit that jail and talk to her."

"You can't!" Jackie protested. "I'm sure they've got samples of your DNA, fingerprints, picture, and who knows what else. Bridges' people would grab you in an instant."

"She's absolutely right," Matthew agreed. "Dad, if there's anybody who needs to stay hidden, it's you."

Graham rubbed his hands over his face and shook his head.

"In fact," Matthew continued, "there's only one person who hasn't received publicity during this period, and that's who must go."

"Who?" Graham frowned.

"Me!" Matthew said. "Haven't you noticed that I'm never on the news or in any of these reports? They haven't thought of looking for a likeness of me yet."

"You can't go into that jail," Graham protested. "Why, they'd grab you in—"

"Wait!" Adah interrupted him. "I think your son has a point. Look at him." Adah pointed at Matt's face. "He's grown a beard and a mustache in these weeks. Dye his hair dark black, and Matt would look like an entirely different man from months ago."

Jackie eyed her son's face. "I hate to admit it, but Adah is right. Matt has matured during this last year."

"It's out of the question," Graham insisted.

"Dad, I'm not a child anymore," Matthew said. "I've grown up. Don't be afraid. I can go to Chicago, and if there's a way to see Mary, I'll get in."

"And I will go with him," Adah insisted. "Two people will be needed for this task, and no one knows me."

Graham rubbed his hands together nervously. "Neither of you knows that jail," he said. "I do. Remember? I was on the committee that helped design the new building. I know every detail of that prison. That's why—"

"That's why you need to teach me," Matthew said. "Draw a map. Go over it with me. I can learn what you know."

"I'm not convinced," Graham said.

"You, too, must change your appearance," Adah told Graham. "Obviously, Bridges' people will be looking for you in Wisconsin. Make your hair blond. Grow a mustache, but keep out of sight."

Graham still shook his head. "The entire idea worries me."

"I understand," Matthew said. "But we're your only hope. Adah and I will get ready to return to Chicago. Dad, start telling me everything you know about that jail. We'll be ready."

Graham took a deep breath. "I guess I don't have much alternative." He picked up a pencil. "Okay. Let's go over a diagram of how the jail is laid out."

CHAPTER 42

MAYOR FRANK BRIDGES, Al Meachem, and Jack Stratton stepped off a private jet and into a limousine waiting for them at the La Guardia airport. The driver whisked them away in the direction of Hassan Rashid's New York offices on Fifty-ninth Street across from Central Park on Manhattan Island.

"How's Rashid doing?" Meachem asked. "Still recovering?"

"Actually the plastic surgery went well, and Carson—I mean Rashid—is back in his offices," Frank Bridges said. "Looks like he's recovering very well."

"Has that United Nations speech he was going to make come back to his mind?" Stratton asked.

"Fortunately, it hasn't," Bridges said. "I think Rashid would be in big trouble if he'd blasted the General Assembly in a grab for power. He hasn't brought it up again, and we're sure not going to mention it." He looked at both men with one eyebrow slightly raised. "Got me?"

"Sure, boss." Meachem grabbed his mouth. "I mean, *Your Honor.*"

"What's the latest report on the effects of the volcano and the subsequent storms?" Bridges asked.

"The volcano hasn't subsided a bit," Meachem said. "They've got big trouble in Great Falls, Bozeman, and Billings, as well as Helena. In Wyoming, they've closed

Yellowstone Park and are concerned about the number of animals that may die."

Bridges nodded his head. "We've certainly got our problems in Chicago. I hate these strange environmental problems that keep coming up." He cursed violently. "I thought the sky was falling on us when that crater erupted."

"Yeah," Meachem said. "I guess you know one of our cars crashed coming back from the attack on Peck's cabin."

"I heard," Bridges said. "Can't you find people who know how to drive?"

"Listen, Frank. It got black so quickly, we had a hard time even finding the highway."

"Humph!" Bridges snorted. "Any of those people drinking?"

"Oh, no, sir!"

"They better not have been!" Bridges looked menacing. "We can't afford any scandals." He cleared his throat. Contamination from the atmosphere had infected his sinuses. "The only good thing to come out of this volcano eruption is that it gives us a logical reason for those six deaths in Lincoln Park. We've taken the position that they died from poison volcanic gas."

"But they died before the volcano erupted," Stratton objected.

"Never mind," Bridges snapped. "Our position is the same."

"I'm worried about Gillette," Meachem said.

"Me too," Stratton added. "I'd have to track him

down since he's flown the coop, but do you want me to kill him? I could assassinate him through a window, something of that order."

"No," Bridges said. "If you find him, we might need him again before this nanorobot mess is over."

The limousine pulled up in front of a skyscraper with a large sign proclaiming "Royal Arab Petroleum Company" across the first floor. The driver hopped out and hurried around to open the car doors. The three men quickly entered the building and walked down a long hall.

"Remember," Bridges told Jack Stratton, "you stay outside Rashid's door and guard the entrance. I don't want another one of those United Nations experiences!"

"Yes sir. I'll pay careful attention."

"Look sharp," Bridges whispered out the side of his mouth to Meachem. "These meetings are extremely important."

"Certainly."

A guard immediately whipped open the massive door as the three men approached. Bridges and Meachem walked into a large board room. Stratton stood outside. Across the ceiling were scrolls painted gold. The room looked elegant.

"Wow!" Meachem gasped. "This is some kind of palace."

Abu Shad marched in from a side entrance. "Please be seated," he snapped. "Al-sayyid Rashid will be with you momentarily. In the meantime, please read this statement he will be releasing to the press later in the day." The secretary handed each man a copy of a formal statement and then left the room.

Bridges quickly scanned the copy. His mouth dropped slightly. He said nothing.

Five minutes later, Hassan Jawhar Rashid walked into the room from the same door Abu Shad had entered. "Good day to you, gentlemen."

Bridges immediately leaped to his feet. "Al-sayyid Rashid! You are looking well!" He tried not to cringe, but Rashid's cheek was still sunken and the side of his face drooped, radically altering his appearance.

Rashid felt the small bandage on his forehead. "I certainly look better than the last time you saw me. We now have hair covering the back of my head to conceal the surgery." He motioned for them to be seated. He didn't mention the bandage on the side of his face. "People still seem amazed by my rapid recovery."

"Of course! Your healing has been a miracle." Bridges pointed at the paper in his hand. "This is an amazing statement we have just read."

Rashid sat down, a slight smile crossing his face. "You like it?"

"If this agreement with Israel can be consummated, you will be bringing peace to the entire world," Bridges said.

"The Israelis and the Palestinians have fought back and forth for decades, as we all know," Rashid said. "In the past, a peace agreement would almost be completed and then the wars would explode again. I think I can end that problem."

"You will do so with the use of your petroleum resources?" Bridges asked.

"If the Israelis agree to join the oil distribution system I now have in place in many other countries, it will allow me to turn to my Arab friends and insist they comply with the terms of peace. Because of my relationship with Turkey, I am part of a country with a history of dealing with this region. I have a natural platform to demand compliance."

"You have intelligence needs?" Bridges asked. "Of course, we are ready to respond. What can we do?"

"Thank you, Frank." Rashid's voice remained smooth and calm. "However, I have another system in place for this part of the world." A slight grin edged up the side of his mouth. "I already know everything necessary to complete this deal."

"What if the leadership of Israel refuses to comply?" Bridges ventured gingerly.

"I'll have their throats slit!" Rashid exploded. "They'll die like street dogs!"

"I—I see," Bridges mumbled.

Rashid took a deep breath. "Let us not quibble over insignificant issues." The cool voice returned. "Do you have any insight into the horrendous storm and volcanic activity that has been occurring? I understand several million have died."

Bridges had avoided numbering the dead, but since Rashid seldom was inaccurate when he used numbers, he knew to not attempt to manipulate the man. He had to be straightforward. "We have no insight into the cause of these strange experiences."

"And I understand you captured Mary Peck, the daughter of Graham Peck?" Rashid's voice abruptly conveyed the all-knowing quality that was always so unsettling. "You are making progress in catching this man?"

Bridges nodded perfunctorily. "Yes sir."

"What have you learned?"

"After we used sodium Pentothol, the girl revealed where the family was hiding." Bridges kept speaking in a factual voice, avoiding saying more than he could support. "It turns out they were living in Wisconsin, and had retreated to another location before we arrived. We burned their house down."

"Excellent!" Rashid pounded the table. "I like a violent response. I trust you will soon have this man who could create so much trouble for us."

"We have made him into a criminal in the media," Bridges continued. "With the services of the police, the public, and The Restored Church groups in particular, today we have a much larger dragnet in place to catch Peck."

"Good. Good." Rashid drummed on the table with his fingertips. "I am concerned that this volcano could create serious problems across your country. Do you think your president is on top of this situation?"

"I am sure he is responding quickly to the crisis. Of course, what could anyone do?"

"Exactly!" Rashid's eyes sparkled as he leaned forward. "I want you to use the complexity of this problem as an opportunity for more attacks on the president. Get on your television and call the president a traitor, a fool, an incompetent. Hang the impossibility of his doing anything around his neck like a ball and chain!"

"Yes sir!" Bridges agreed, but he felt uneasy. The public would quickly recognize there was little anyone could do to combat the effects of a volcano, but he must attempt to do what Rashid expected.

CHAPTER 43

THE MOUNTING DEATH TOLL from the Montana volcano sent shock waves across the country. Depending on the drift of the wind, the sky remained dark or sometimes became opaque. Effects of the poisonous gases subsided to a degree, but thousands and thousands of people were found dead in their cars, in out-of-the-way motels, on back roads, as well as among the populations of large cities. The elderly died quickly. Television stations continuously flashed scenes of these ghastly scenarios.

Graham knew these deaths had to be affecting public opinion. He had followed such events carefully when it was his job on the political beat to keep the mayor informed about any changing mentality. People's ideas about political officials' performance were always shaped by gigantic catastrophes politicians had no control over. When Bridges blasted the president for not doing more, Graham sensed something strange was going on behind the mayor's blistering attacks. Borden Camber Carson had to be hiding in the shadows.

Matthew came out of his bedroom. "I think I have all of my equipment." He looked at his watch. "Time's flying. Adah and I ought to leave for Chicago in a few minutes."

"I don't want you to go," Graham exclaimed.

"Dad, we've been over this twenty times," Matt answered. "You're the one who's got to stay in hiding."

Graham took a deep breath and shook his head. "I don't know," he mumbled. "The whole idea terrifies me."

"Driving that car we borrowed from Alice Masterson will help," Jackie added. "No one in Chicago has a clue who she is."

"And I look different." Matt glanced in the mirror. "Dying my hair black makes me look like Adah's brother. We'll do okay."

"You've got that diagram I made for you of the inside of the Cook County Jail?" Graham asked.

"Yes," Matt said. "I bet I know more about that prison than the cops do."

"Remember to check and find out if any of Mary's friends have been visiting her," Graham added. "That's your clue as to whether it's safe to attempt a drop-in at the jail."

"Dad, we have to trust God to protect us," Matt said. "It's the only hope we've got, and it's the biggest shield on the planet."

Graham nodded. "Sure, but it's easier to affirm than practice."

Carrying a backpack, Adah came out of the workroom where she slept. "I think I have everything I need," she said and set the bag on the table. "Looks like we are ready to go." She hugged Jackie and shook Graham's hand. "Don't stop praying for us."

"You can bet we won't," Jackie said.

"And get Graham's hair turned yellow," Adah said. "He must look different." She opened the back door and started toward the car. "We're on our way."

"Remember the electronic cameras and sensors," Graham said, giving Matt a final warning. "They'll be watching you everywhere you go."

"You bet." Matt waved and shut the car door. "Bye!" he waved out the window and started the car down the road.

"What do you think will happen?" Jackie asked as the auto disappeared in a cloud of dust.

Graham bit his lip. "Anything!" he said thoughtfully. "Absolutely anything is possible."

CHAPTER 44

A DETAILED PLAN of what the Israelis had been doing militarily for the last several months lay on Rashid's desk. He picked up the report and read it carefully. Continuing tension with Arab terrorists and the surrounding Islamic nations had caused the prime minister, Dov Landau, to arbitrarily remove the

Muslim Wakf, Jordan's select temple guards and land trust, from the control of *Haram es-Sharif*, the Temple Mount in Jerusalem. Rashid's report also contained a speech Landau made in the Knesset, calling for the rebuilding of the ancient Jewish temple so the Jewish nation would forever have a place to worship. Work had begun immediately, and the Arab world had predictably reacted violently, but Israel's military strength remained too great to be toyed with. Some national leaders of Islamic states had even cited Adolf Hitler's actions as an example of the response needed at this exact moment, but none came.

Borden Camber Carson, or Hassan Jahwar Rashid, as he now preferred to be called, had studied the history of Adolf Hitler from every possible angle. He was impressed that he and the German dictator shared many unexpected characteristics. Rashid was convinced that Hitler had been betrayed by arrogant generals who despised his ability, and that brought the defeat of Germany. Learning from Hitler's journey to and through World War II, Hassan would never make the mistake of letting presumptuous subordinates gain the upper hand. He kept his thumb on everything.

"Sire, the paperwork is done." Abu Shad walked into Rashid's Istanbul office overlooking the Black Sea. "I have made the adjustments to the proclamation that indicates you will also be called *Supreme Commander in Chief*." He placed the documents on Rashid's desk. "It also indicates you will be known in working relationships as only *Chief*."

Rashid studied Abu Shad's face. The man always had a look of complicity and kept his eyes looking down like an obedient pup. There was no reason to worry about Abu. He met all the specifications for a compliant servant.

"You have notified the television networks that I will make a statement later in the day?" Rashid asked.

"Yes, sire." Abu Shad continued to look down as he nodded his head. "They are preparing for a global hookup."

"At that time, I will also make a report on my progress in establishing peace between the Jews and Arabs," Rashid continued. "I know that statement will create worldwide interest."

"Of course."

Rashid glanced at the dark clouds outside. "Are we still struggling with the effects of that volcano in the United States?"

"To some extent the weather has been affected."

"Yes, I expected this, but I hope it doesn't detract from the television appearance tonight."

"I'm sure nothing will affect that event negatively," the secretary said.

"Excellent." Rashid pushed him away. "I will read these documents alone." He watched Abu Shad walk out like a chambermaid. "I'll call you when I need something more."

The truth was, he didn't actually trust even Abu Shad. He didn't trust anyone. Like Bismarck and his Prussian predecessor Frederick the Great, he didn't trust democracy or any rule of the people. Only a supreme monarch could guide the world out of the morass of its troubles. And Rashid was that man.

In studying the rise of the Third Reich, Hassan had carefully scrutinized German history. When Kaiser Wilhelm was crowned in 1871, the foundation had been laid for the rise of the great German state that would eventually be formed in Berlin. In turn, Bismarck had created the *Reichstag*, the German Parliament, but he didn't trust the corporate voice. He defiantly said, "The great questions of the day will not be settled by resolution and majority votes . . . but by blood and iron."

And if Rashid believed in anything, it was the rule of blood and iron. Only if he created an army greater than the combined military forces of the world would he be able to put in place a system of world government and unity to create a unified globe.

When World War I began long, long ago at the start of the twentieth century, the German General von Moltke had said war would unleash "the noblest virtues of courage, self-renunciation, loyalty, and willingness to sacrifice with one's life." Hitler had deeply embraced those ideas and immediately volunteered for the army. Rashid was always moved by these same goals.

The prime minister of Turkey got up from his desk and walked across and out to the veranda. He always enjoyed the cool breeze blowing in from the Black Sea. The gentle wind restored tranquillity.

He considered the title *Chief* much like Hitler's laying claim to *Fuhrer*. The designation was singular, obvious, and clarifying, as well as demanding. Using this word, the multitudes would salute him and instantly give their supreme allegiance to what he dictated.

Rashid's thoughts returned to his study of history. Unfortunately, the United States had entered the First World War, tipping the balance of power and forcing Kaiser Wilhelm II to surrender and go into exile in the Netherlands. Rashid remained fascinated that the old monarch had spent the rest of his life studying occult writers and seeking explanations from soothsayers about why Germany had lost the war. Even Houston Chamberlain, the famous student of the secret and the superhuman, had whispered in Wilhelm's ear that Germany would rise again in glorious power. Never mind that many of these prognosticators at the war's outset also taught that Germany would win World War I before Christmas. The fact that a German kaiser studied the occult fascinated Rashid.

The occult had a central place in Rashid's thinking. After that extraordinary experience, which he shared with *no one*, Rashid began his rise to power, even as Hitler had taken on extraordinary speaking capacities after studying occult ideas. No matter what anyone said, evil offered its own gifts, capacities, and powers to those who saluted its colors.

Rashid closed the door to the veranda and returned to his desk. Hopefully in a matter of days, he would make his treaty with the Israelis, propelling himself to a new level of extraordinary global power. Nothing must impede this step.

The face of Graham Peck flashed across his mind. He remembered the first time he saw this man in Frank Bridges' office. Something undefinable was hidden in the American's eyes. The man seemed to have a quality of character, of strength, of honesty and determination that particularly bothered Rashid. Peck might be a threat to everything Rashid had planned. No, he wasn't a statesman or a politician of a stature that could thwart Rashid's carefully laid plans, but he could derail the train by talking to the right people in the government and press. Rashid pounded his desk. Peck had to be killed!

Hitler's example had taught Rashid that death was a tool, a basic political tool, to be used judiciously. These times demanded executions, just as Hitler had attempted to execute the Jews. Of course, that was the one part of Adolf Hitler's strategy that bothered Rashid the most. No, it wasn't the killing that disturbed Rashid, it was killing the *Jews*. Recognizing that mass extermination had been aimed at this one simple, quiet population lurking in the back streams of Europe still troubled Rashid. The extermination of the six million caused him to keep one aspect of his life totally and completely confidential.

Although no one in the world knew, *Rashid's mother was Jewish.*

TERROR ON THE HORIZON | III

Behold, a white horse,
and its rider had a bow;
and a crown was given to him,
and he went out conquering
and to conquer.

REVELATION 6:2

THE TRIP FROM TOMAHAWK to Illinois was filled with fear. Matthew Peck kept remembering the earlier terrifying chase out of Arlington Heights that had ended in the car wreck that killed one of Bridges' men, Jake Pemrose. Matt didn't want any more violent scenes. The possibility of electronic surveillance and detection stayed upmost in his mind.

Driving a ten-year-old hydrogen-propelled four-seater they had obtained from Alice Masterson, Matthew and Adah arrived in Chicago early enough to check out visitation at the Cook County Jail. Matthew quickly confirmed that Mary had been moved to regular confinement, and some of her friends had visited her. Apparently, all Matt and Adah needed to do was show up within the normal visiting hours, and they could talk to her through a thick glass shield in a special unit, but both Matt and Adah knew they were walking far out on the end of a thin branch. One step inside the county jail was a dangerous journey for anyone named Peck.

After circling the block several times, Matt said, "Fierce-looking place. I'm not sure I want to go in."

"Yes," Adah said. "Escaping from inside that brick building appears to be impossible."

"That's what we're counting on, Adah. We're going to take a very different route out of this place than the police would ever expect. Dad had special insight into how the jail fits together."

"Okay, but we must pray for God to protect us or we will be in a cell with Mary."

A large car pulled out and a parking slot opened in front of them. Matt immediately pulled in and stopped. "So far so good," he said. "It's time to get into our in-style teenager looks." He reached in the backseat. "This blond wig will certainly give you a different appearance."

Matt opened the glove compartment and took out a small box. "Alice Masterson also obtained these for you." He put the container in her hands. "As soon as you put in these contact lenses, your brown eyes will be blue. I'd say that ought to give your face a completely different look."

Adah stared at the little box. "You are changing me into a completely different person!"

"I certainly hope so!"

Adah pulled the wig over her head, and Matt slipped on a T-shirt like those worn by most of the kids. Black pull-on boots purchased in Rhinelander fit the hip image. He quickly split his hair down the middle and combed it back on one side like all the young boys did. With his hair dyed black and a stubbly beard, he no longer looked like the regular Matthew Peck.

After ten minutes of working in front of mirrors, Matt and Adah emerged looking like a pair of rockers. Getting out of the car, they looked at each other in disdain.

"Pretty weird, huh?" Matt said.

"No worse than me." Adah took a deep breath. "Have

you considered they could have set a trap for your family, and are ready to arrest us as we walk into that jail?"

"It's possible. Wouldn't take much to grab us. That jail is a massive holding tank."

Adah nodded. "Makes me shiver."

"Put these dark glasses on." Matt handed her sunglasses. "I've got a pair for me." He took her arm. "Just walk slow and casual."

"I'll try." Adah started walking with a swing. She bowed her head, but kept her eyes open. *"Please, please, help us, Lord."*

Easing along at a nonchalant pace, Matt walked up the steps and through a door marked "Visitors." Holding Adah's hand, they ambled down a long corridor toward a metal detector. After ten feet, the hallway felt like a chute that would eventually dump visitors into a pit waiting at the other end. Obviously, once they started down the path, there was no way out. The green light on the detector clicked "on," and a voice echoed from somewhere: "Put purses and shoes on the conveyer belt. Go on through."

Matt sauntered through with Adah following behind him. No bells went off.

"Leave your purse and personal belongings out there for the check," the heavyset police inspector instructed. "Who'd you want to see?" He got up out of a metal chair and picked up a clipboard filled with lists. "Give me the deadbeat's name," he said with supreme indifference and disinterest.

"Mary Peck," Matt said with no show of emotion. "She's no crook."

The cop jerked slightly and looked at him more closely. "How'd you know her?"

"I'm one of her old buddies," Matt said. "We're long-time friends."

The policeman studied his face for a moment. "Hmm," he mumbled. "She's an *unusual* person," he said suspiciously.

Matt shrugged. "Ain't we all!"

Quickly flipping through his list again, the cop checked Mary Peck's name twice. "Okay. The sheet says she can have visitors. Put your shoes on and go up to the fifth floor. Unit six."

"Sure, man," Matt said with disinterest. "Thanks." He grabbed his boots and slipped them on.

"Take the elevator straight ahead of you." The officer studied him intently.

"Come on." Matt beckoned for Adah to follow him. "We're going up." He forced himself to keep his slow ambling pace toward the elevator.

"Hey!" the cop yelled. "Stop!"

Matt froze. He was already on the other side of the metal detector, and they couldn't run even if they wanted to. Matt turned around slowly, dreading the worst.

"The woman left her purse." The policeman held out Adah's small handbag. "I imagine she wants it."

"Thanks, man." Matt walked back and took the purse. "Appreciate it."

The policeman kept glowering at them, but the elevator door opened and closed. Matt and Adah started up to the fifth floor.

CHAPTER 46

THE ELEVATOR DOOR opened on the fifth floor. A sign with the words "Unit Six" pointed to the left, indicating the visitation area. Matt and Adah started down the hall.

"I guess the police inspector called the guards in the detention area and told them we were coming," Matthew said. "Remember, you sit down first. Break the ice with Mary before we allow her to know who I am. We've got to make sure she's not going to scream and alert them to us. I'll keep my back to the window."

"Okay," Adah said. "I will."

"And *quietly*. If possible, we don't want anyone to notice your accent."

Matt opened a heavy metal door, and they walked into a room with dirty, smeared walls. Fortunately, no one else was sitting in front of any of the three thick glass windows and visitation cubicles. On the other side of the glass, he could see a narrow shelf and a simple straight-backed chair. Matt turned and faced the entry door to make sure no one slipped in behind them.

After ten minutes, Matt and Adah heard a door open and knew someone was entering on the back side of the glass divide. A policeman came in leading a girl in handcuffs and wearing a bright orange jumpsuit. Mary looked bent, frightened, and like she might have been treated badly by the authorities. She kept her eyes fixed on the floor.

Adah adjusted her sunglasses and studied Mary's shuffling steps across the room. She had radically changed from a rebellious teenager to a broken child.

"Sit down!" the cop demanded, and Mary Peck slipped silently into the chair. "You got fifteen minutes, and that's it!" He walked away and disappeared through the far door.

Mary Peck slowly looked up with red eyes ringed by dark circles. Her dark hair hung over her eyes in un-combed strands that looked dirty and matted. "Do—do I know you?"

"Not well," the Jewish woman answered, "but you've met me before."

Mary frowned. "Forgive me, but your face doesn't ring a bell."

"Are you okay?" Adah pushed on.

"That accent!" Mary leaned forward and blinked several times. "I know that accent!"

"You okay?" Adah repeated.

Mary's hand came up to her mouth. "Are you . . . that Jewish woman . . . Adah Honi?"

Adah took off her glasses. "I've changed my appearance," she said. "We must come here disguised."

"We?" Mary looked over Adah's shoulder for the first time. "Who's we?" Excitement filled her voice.

Matt turned around slowly and took off his sunglasses. "Remember me?"

Mary's mouth dropped. She stared in shock and then

suddenly broke into tears. "Matthew! Oh, God help us! It's you! Matt! I wouldn't have recognized you." Mary sobbed. "God bless you for coming."

Matt quickly got as close to the glass screen as he could. "Mary, we came to get you out. Do you want our help?"

"Want it?" Mary sobbed. "Oh, Matt! I've been such a pigheaded fool. I can't believe you've put yourself at such a huge risk to see me. How can I ever thank you!"

"Tell us what happened," Matt pushed.

"Oh, I got my head all twisted on backward." Mary kept crying as she talked. "I wanted to get away, so I caught a ride with a truck driver and rode all the way to Arlington Heights. I called a friend and she took me to the house. That's where I got caught."

"A truck driver?" Matt shook his head. "We never guessed it."

"Listen!" Mary put her hand up to the glass. "I want Mom and Dad to know I didn't talk voluntarily. They drugged me, and I'm still not sure what I told the police."

"It's all right, Mary," Adah said. "Your folks are fine, and they pray for you every day. They sent us."

"I can't believe it." Mary shook her head. "After all the trouble I've caused everybody. I know I've been very hard to live with. I'm so sorry."

"We're here to get you out of this place," Matt repeated.

"You can't," Mary wailed. "They watch me like a hawk. Cameras are concealed everywhere. The only time I'm alone is in this visitation booth. I've had a few friends visit, but then the police scared their parents and they won't come back." She shook her head in lament. "I'm so lonely in this torture chamber."

"You don't see anyone else?" Adah asked.

"Well, actually there's another person in the cell next to me that knew our family. Her name is Nancy Marks."

"Nancy Marks!" Matt nearly shouted. "Do you know what her husband, Bill Marks, did?"

Mary shook her head. "No. What?"

Matt rubbed his chin thoughtfully. "She's important. Try to get better acquainted with her, but don't tell her about our coming to see you."

"Okay," Mary said.

"We understand the emptiness in here," Matt said. "We're going to do our best to get you out."

"No! No!" Mary wailed. "I made my big mistake by not listening to Adah, and everything you tried to tell me. Now I have to pay the price for being a fool." She rubbed her brow. "Bridges' men rubbed my forehead with a cotton swab. They've marked me with the sign of the beast."

"Oh!" Matt exclaimed.

"This isn't good," Adah whispered.

"Listen, Mary." Matt put his mouth as close to the microphone as he could and spoke softly. "We are living through a terrible time. The tension is out of sight, and all we can do is try our best even when it's hard. You simply made a mistake."

Mary wiped her eyes. "I listened to the wrong people. Sitting in this dirty, empty jail, I realized that the only people who weren't struggling with confusion were Adah and my family. That's when I began to understand. It's taken a while, but I've finally seen the light."

"The light? What do you mean?" Adah asked.

"The reason my family knew where they were going was because everyone but me believed in Jesus Christ and read the Bible," Mary said. "My mistake was I didn't know how important it is to have your priorities right." She bowed her head and then looked up, a fresh resoluteness in her eyes. "I'm through listening to my friends, and I'm not confused anymore about what counts." Mary smiled. "I've given my life to Jesus Christ."

CHAPTER 47

THE HELICOPTER carrying Hassan Jawhar Rashid circled the cement pad behind St. Peter's Basilica on Vatican Hill and slowly settled to the ground. A cluster of dignitaries, waiting for the prime minister of Turkey and now international leader to arrive, waved and saluted as the craft came down. Dr. Creighton Lewis, the bishop of The Restored Church, stood next to the intelligence chief and still mayor of Chicago, Frank Bridges, and his assistant Al Meachem.

"Do you know what is *really* happening today?" Lewis shouted to Bridges above the roar of the helicopter's motor.

"Supposed to be an important public statement,"

Frank Bridges said. "Nothing more's been released, but we erected a glass shield in front of the speaker's stand for protection. It's virtually impossible to see the deflector."

Creighton Lewis nodded. "You never know, but when Hassan Rashid calls, everyone pays attention."

The helicopter's engines shut down. Hassan Jawhar Rashid hustled off the vehicle and walked through the line of officials, greeting each person as if they were Rahsid's most intimate friend.

"Creighton—" Rashid exclaimed. "I understand The Restored Church is making tremendous progress these days."

"Thank you, sir. Since you made it possible for us to obtain these ancient facilities that once belonged to the Vatican, we have gained new heights of international respect."

"Good! Good!" Rashid turned to Bridges. "Frank, you're always looking well. I trust life in Chicago is under control."

"Indeed!" Bridges shook his hand firmly. "We have the podium prepared as you directed."

Rashid smiled broadly. "I think you'll like my speech today."

"I always do."

Rashid turned away, and the group quickly followed him through the garden area then hurried toward the front of St. Peter's where a platform had been erected. The enormous crowd milling around in front of the podium broke into raucous cheers when the entourage appeared.

"You've really produced a multitude," Frank Bridges told Creighton Lewis.

A slight grin crossed the bishop's face. "We have our methods."

"Wasn't easy to find that many people," Bridges quipped.

Creighton sobered. "Times are hard," he said quietly. "People are bewildered, confused. No, it wasn't easy."

Rashid immediately launched into his speech, predicting that The Restored Church would bring hope and renewed vitality to a broken world. Heaping praise on the church's new role in society, Rashid proclaimed they would be part of restoring global peace.

The crowd roared back their applause, and television cameras swept across the mob, recording an affirmation of everything Rashid said.

"Our plans for a Middle Eastern peace settlement are moving on schedule," Rashid continued. "I am hopeful I will be able to return to Jerusalem in the immediate future and pave the way for a permanent settlement of all Arab and Jewish differences. I will be coming as the prince of peace."

Once again the crowd applauded wildly. The roar echoed across the massive square.

"Today I am relinquishing my role as the prime minister of Turkey as my global responsibilities are increasing," Hassan Rashid continued. "I will be uniting the armies of Europe and the Middle East into the most powerful allegiance the world has ever known. As soon as this process is complete, I will become the supreme commander of the global army."

People looked shocked and surprised. Silence settled

over the crowd. Even Creighton Lewis's rabble weren't sure of the meaning of what they were hearing. Frank Bridges sensed uncertainty as the announcement caught him off guard as well.

"In the future, I will be known simply as *Chief*." Rashid paused, then a frown crawled across his face.

"The crowd isn't excited by what they are hearing," Creighton Lewis whispered in Bridges' ear. "I'm not sure what's going on, but I sense serious unrest."

Bridges said nothing but gritted his teeth. He didn't like the sudden change in the mood of the assembly.

"In the future, you will salute me as your chief," Rashid continued, "and, in turn, I will protect you from all the negative forces permeating the world today." He raised his hand forcefully. "Along with the leadership of The Restored Church, we will immediately—"

A brigade of men rushed out from the front of the crowd and dropped to their knees. Leveling rifles and MP5 machine guns at Rashid and the dignitaries, they started firing.

Bridges instantly pressed the button on an alert device in his pocket. Sirens blasted, but nothing could stop the burst of bullets. Rashid's soldiers, placed in reserve for such an event, ran out from behind the speaker's platform and started returning gunfire. The crowd screamed and dispersed, stumbling in every direction.

"Get down!" Bridges screamed at the dignitaries around him. "Hit the floor!"

One of the attackers leaped up and hurled a grenade at the mayor's side of the platform. Instantly, Bridges dived behind the bleachers. The ground shook and chairs shattered in every direction. Holding his ears, Bridges rolled up in a ball next to a piece of twisted metal torn from the stands.

Gunfire continued for several more seconds then abruptly stopped. Bridges could hear Rashid's men yelling and running away from the platform area. Apparently they had won the battle. He slowly peered over the shattered bleachers.

Everywhere Frank Bridges looked, people were lying on the ground. Dignitaries had been hit and many were dead. Creighton Lewis lay sprawled over a pile of chairs, but he was still breathing. Bridges leaped over the wreckage and ran to find Rashid.

The protective glass plate had been shattered in a hundred places by bullets and metal fragments, but there was no sign of Rashid. For the first time, Frank felt pain, and he realized that his pants were torn. His leg was bleeding, but he didn't stop looking. Bridges saw a figure crouching inside the broad podium. Hassan Rashid slowly crawled out from inside the steel-encased wooden stand.

"You're all right?" Bridges blurted out.

Rashid dusted off his silk suit and glared over the bodies lying everywhere. "Of course!" His eyes flashed with anger and fury. "They can't kill me."

"We had security!" Bridges tried to reassure Rashid. "Our men were everywhere. I don't know where these terrorists came from!"

Rashid ran his hand over his hair and suddenly the

look of intense hostility turned into a smile. "Don't worry, Frank." He patted Bridges on the arm. "We will find these people and kill every last one of them."

CHAPTER 48

THE DEADLY ASSAULT in front of St. Peter's gripped people's imaginations so fiercely that Hassan Rashid's message was swept into the backwaters of worldwide attention. The impact of declaring that nations recognize him as "Chief" shrank against the story of death and reactionary resistance to his authority that had instantly spread around the world. The assassination attempt only added to the confusion in the streets.

Initial television reports speculated that the attackers had come from the Ukraine. When Rashid put together his initial allegiance in Europe, the Ukraine had been passed over because he suspected the country lacked the military resources to make a significant difference. With time, Ukrainian anger turned into deep resentment and hostility.

Because Creighton Lewis had been injured, some questioned the role of The Restored Church, but the church's membership reacted with vehement anger. In many small American towns, vigilante groups attacked anyone suspected of what they considered questionable relationships or possible allegiance to any fringe group not considered completely loyal to Rashid's regime. The volcano in Montana had created fear, but the reaction of The Restored Church brought panic. Adah and Matt realized that in addition to the electronic surveillance, they also had an army of spies walking the streets looking for people like them. They had to pay even closer attention to avoid detection.

Adah and Matt talked over breakfast in a small café in a Chicago suburb at the corner of Cicero and Ninety-fifth Street. "What do you think about the attack on Rasshid that happened overnight?" Adah said. "How does it look this morning to you?"

Matt sipped his coffee and thought out loud. "Of course, I was astounded to hear what happened in Europe, but I kept thinking about Nancy Marks being imprisoned at such close proximity to Mary. She adds a completely new dimension to the situation."

"How?"

"Because her husband tried to kill the Antichrist, Nancy becomes a much more important person. We must think about getting her out, too."

Adah looked out the window. "I don't know, Matt. Events everywhere are headed on a worldwide collision course. Some people have made politics into their religion." She shrugged. "Maybe Nancy Marks is to us more of an obstacle. The newspapers didn't push the story this morning, but Rashid is hell-bent on forcing Israel to sign an agreement. That's simply another big piece of the prophecy puzzle in place."

"If Nancy Marks were in your shoes, would you want her help in trying to get out of jail?"

"Of course!"

"Does that answer your question?"

Adah's sly grin communicated her thoughts. "I think you are playing Christian on me now. Yes, of course, I would help. My question is answered."

"What I'm most worried about is the fact that Mary's forehead has been marked with the sign. We've got to get around that problem."

"Matt!" Adah grabbed his hand. "There are people across the street looking into this window!"

Trying not to react, Matt looked out the corner of his eye. "Looks like ordinary citizens."

"No. Watch them. One of them has a cell phone and is making a call right now. They are watching us through the window."

Matt peered straight out the window. "Adah, why would they be watching us?"

"I don't know, but it scares me."

Matt thought for a moment. "Look at your shoes." He brought his foot up over his knees and glanced at the sole. "Nothing here." He glanced at the other foot.

"Oh no!" Adah pulled off her sandal. "Look." She pointed to a small brown dot attached to the heel of her shoe.

"The jailer must have tagged you at the Cook County Jail." Matt glanced out the window again. "I'm sure they figured out by now that we don't have security markings on our foreheads, and that's what tipped them off. They've probably been watching us since early this morning."

"What'll I do?" Adah's eyes widened.

Matt pulled a pocketknife from his pocket and carefully scratched off the dot. He took a napkin and wiped the blade, leaving the marking on the napkin.

"Did you get it all?"

"I don't know, but we'll find out soon enough." He nodded toward the restroom. "Go back there and then duck out the back door. I'll try the front door and see if I can shake them. We need to give each other at least thirty minutes to see if this ploy has worked. State Street cuts through this section of town at an angle. Meet me on the corner of State and Eighty-seventh in around thirty minutes."

"What if this isn't the only tag they put on us?"

Matt could see Adah looked more than concerned, but he had to be honest. "Then they may well catch us when we show up on Eighty-seventh."

Adah swallowed hard. "God help us." She slid out and walked quickly down the hall.

CHAPTER 49

MATT RUSHED OUT the front door of the restaurant and ran east on Ninety-fifth Street. At the street corner, he glanced over his shoulder and saw a man and a woman still following him. Without waiting for the light to change, he dashed across the street. The couple broke into a trot.

They're too obvious, Matt thought as he ran. *Trained police wouldn't stay out in the open. They have to be vigilantes, Restored Church members, plain old citizens. I've got a real chance to lose them!*

A narrow space between two apartment buildings opened in front of him, and he darted between the buildings. Matt came to the alley, and he ran even harder. When he reached the end of the next block, he stopped and peered over the top of a large trash bin. He could see the man and woman standing in the alley a couple of blocks back. They kept walking around and looking behind barrels. Turning in the opposite direction from him, they continued searching at the opposite end of the alley.

"Wh-e-e!" Matt wiped his forehead and had just started south when a police cruiser turned the street corner ahead of him. He froze but realized he mustn't look suspicious and started walking again. The car didn't slow down when it passed him. He kept moving.

In ten minutes he reached the corner of State and Eighty-seventh Street. Adah wasn't in sight! Fighting panic, Matt started slowly walking east on Eighty-seventh. At the end of the block, he turned around and came back.

"They caught her!" he mumbled under his breath. "Must have!" Matt tightened his fists in desperation.

"P-s-s-t!" a voice whispered from behind him.

Matt whirled around and saw a small form standing behind a telephone booth. "Adah!" he gasped.

"Quick," the Jewish woman said. "Over here."

Hurrying to the back of the obscure battered booth,

Matt hugged his friend fiercely. "For a minute I thought they'd grabbed you."

"No," Adah said. "They didn't even realize I went out the back kitchen door. No one followed me."

"Praise God!" Matt hugged her again. "At least we're next to a phone booth. I think we should check in with my parents. Let's call the house in Wisconsin."

"Sure." Adah pushed the phone booth door open for him.

Matt dialed the number, and his father answered the phone.

"We didn't call you earlier," Matt explained, "because I wanted to make sure no one had zeroed in on us and might trace the call. I'm certain that we're okay."

"Good, son. What did you find out?"

Matt quickly detailed the experience at the jail. "And we found Nancy Marks," he concluded. "She's in a cell close to Mary."

"That's a surprise," Graham said. "Be careful. I'm sure both Mary and Nancy are prime candidates for close surveilance." Graham thought a moment. "On the other hand, the police may not associate Nancy as having any relationship with us, since Mary is so much younger and only my daughter. I always maintained a distance from Bill Marks."

"Interesting thought," Matt said. "We're staying with the original plan you worked out for me before we left. We'll see if we can work Nancy in."

"Good."

"There is one problem. Mary's forehead has been

marked with the nanorobots. She's no longer free of the curse."

"Oh," Graham groaned. "We will have to think carefully about that . . . because it is a problem."

"What do you think, Dad?"

"I simply don't know. Let me think about it overnight. Son, never in your life has it been so important to be extremely careful. Bridges never was a fool, and now he's increased his capabilities with everything from electronic surveillance to an army of civilian spies. You're in an extremely dangerous place. Pay attention to everything!"

CHAPTER 50

HASSAN JAWHAR RASHID had stewed day and night since the attack at St. Peter's. He had anticipated some opposition, but nothing of these proportions. Seldom caught off guard, the suddenness and scope of the attack profoundly angered him. Bill Marks' attempted assassination at the United Nations Building proved to be the first clue that security issues were far more serious than he had suspected, but the audacity and ferocity of the second assassination attempt in Rome had astounded him. Fortunately, he had made security arrangements broad enough to protect himself, but others whose advice he valued had been killed. Sitting in his spacious and luxurious offices in New York City, one conclusion was clear. Rashid was determined to stop these capricious assaults. He needed to find a new and more powerful means to control the masses.

When Peck's face abruptly floated through his mind, it bothered Hassan. Somewhat to his surprise, he still worried about what had become of Graham Peck. Rashid thought Bridges should have captured the man long before now. Locking up Peck's daughter was a step in the right direction, but only a very small step. He couldn't quite put his finger on what it was, but this man remained a threat in Rashid's thinking, and he was determined to wipe Peck out. Sooner or later, they'd catch and kill this irritant.

The large ornate clock on the wall struck the hour. It was time for the next important meeting to begin. Abu Shad should have everything in place, and the delegates would be present by now. Hassan reached up and felt his brow. While a touch of makeup here and there concealed the scar adequately, he could feel the effects of the gunshot wound. His cheek remained shrunken and distorted his face. He hated the mutilation. A sobering reminder, indeed! Nothing of such magnitude must ever again escape his personal attention.

Pushing back from the mammoth mahogany desk and adjusting the collar on his Nehru jacket, Rashid walked resolutely toward the conference room down the hall. Assistants immediately opened the tall doors as he approached.

In addition to ten generals from across Europe and Frank Bridges, Dr. Creighton Lewis sat at the table with his arm in a sling. Five key administrators from his international oil consortium had been stationed at the far end of the table. Everyone stood when Rashid walked in.

"Thank you, gentlemen." Rashid motioned for them to be seated. "Our meeting today is of primary importance. Since the unfortunate incident in Rome, it has become clear that we must stop these arbitrary attacks, which serve only to deter us from our resolute course." He pointed to Frank Bridges. "What have the most recent intelligence efforts revealed?"

Bridges pulled a file out of his briefcase. "We scoured all possible details obtained from the bodies of the assailants, and made a thorough investigation of each attacker's personal history. To our surprise we found that they were from France, Germany, Poland, the Netherlands, and even a few from Turkey. They *were not* from countries outside your alliances."

Rashid stiffened but said nothing.

"We were concerned by their Western European orientation," Bridges continued. "Apparently tensions created by economics, confusion, weather disasters, and political unrest have proved more significant than we would have concluded."

Hassan Rashid nodded. "People have to eat to live. Economic problems twist their minds. We can expect the recent shortages to have created problems. Am I wrong?"

All heads around the table nodded agreement.

"As you know, Dr. Creighton Lewis is bishop of The Restored Church," Rashid continued. "How do you ac-

cess the outreach and growth of your religious movement? Please be perfectly candid."

Lewis squirmed nervously in his chair. "We have
picked up many people who once had relationships of
some variety with Christian churches. In addition, our
members have reacted in the ways we desired and have
searched out many subversives, particularly in the United
States." He paused and took a deep breath. "However, we
have also been surprised by the recent negative reactions
of citizens in many countries. A sense of confusion appears to be turning into hostility toward the establishment." He coughed. "Al-sayyid Rashid, *you* are becoming
the establishment."

Rashid nodded. "I am aware that prominence can
create misunderstanding. No surprise there. Globalism
is already recognized as a powerful political force across
the world. What we must do is reduce individualism
and help dissidents become a part of the common
cause. They need to be caught up in the vision and
dreams of the larger national body. Their personal fears
must be sublimated by a new allegiance to the collective good of all the people. They should recognize The
Restored Church as their hope, their salvation." He
smiled. "Nothing is more powerful than religious moti-
vation."

Creighton Lewis raised his hand. "I would add another thought to the concept you are developing. Not in-
tending to be technical or theological, I must point out
what the meaning of the word 'god' actually is. Anything
that gives our lives meaning and ultimate direction is our

god, whether it be business, politics, or money. We give our ultimate allegiance to whatever is truly our god." He pointed at Rashid. "While we recognize and support your leadership in the church, Al-sayyid Rashid, I believe we must make the ideas you stand for more final, more enduring, more conclusive."

Rashid blinked several times. Lewis's line of thought caught him off guard and wasn't what he expected. "I'm not sure I am following you."

"If you become ultimate to these people," Lewis said. "You actually become their god. Whether they use the word or not, you will be their divinity."

"Extremely interesting," Rashid said slowly as the idea grabbed his imagination. "Very good. I want you to work on this approach, Creighton. Yes, I want you to refine what you suggested. Perhaps this concept is *exactly* what we need right now. How can I be made into their god!"

CHAPTER 51

WITH A RESOLUTE but dramatic flourish, Hassan Jawhar Rashid walked from the conference room. The generals and petroleum executives immediately broke into a discussion of how to proceed with the chief's directives. Bishop Creighton Lewis turned to Frank Bridges and smiled.

"I think he liked my suggestions about upping the

ante on how people see his status," he joked. "Everybody wants to be god."

Bridges nodded. "Good idea, Bishop. I sensed our chief was a bit edgy today."

Lewis nodded. "Yeah, I noticed he seemed slightly more nervous than usual." Creighton leaned back in his chair. "We're both on the top level of how this operation is playing out. We can be candid. What's your evaluation on how matters are unfolding in America?"

Frank Bridges pursed his lips and studied Lewis for a moment. The bishop had always been a straightforward and candid type of man. While exercising caution, Frank sensed he could be fairly honest with Lewis. "I think the status of the president of the United States has been minimized by such recent events as the volcano eruption in Montana," Bridges began. "Citizens aren't sure if anyone's actually running the ship. That particular problem is good for the chief's interest."

"I sense the same thing. We're finding our church members to be increasingly uneasy about the capacity of the president to actually keep the country on course. As a matter of fact, that's part of what's creating this new dangerous political polarity."

"Ever hear of groups of six people dying at one time?" Bridges asked.

The bishop frowned and shook his head. "No, I don't think so. Sounds rather gruesome."

"Hmm. Interesting. Seems to be happening around Chicago. Well, we both have to be concerned with stopping the radicals from recruiting people who could turn into enemy troops. Your boys have done quite a job hitting the troublemakers across America."

"Which reminds me," Lewis said. "We haven't even picked up a hint of a lead on this Graham Peck guy you're looking for. Of course, Chicago is a big city."

"We're still looking for him," Bridges said. "If your people get a drop on him, kill the man on the spot. That little action would make Rashid very, very happy."

Creighton Lewis jerked and blinked a couple of times. "I see," he said, all levity disappearing from his voice. "Well, got to run." He stood and hurried out the door. "Stay in touch," he said over his shoulder.

Frank Bridges watched the bishop walk away, realizing the man lacked any sort of killer instinct. He was bright, but no more than a functionary, a paper shuffler. And what Bridges needed was a plain and simple killer. He and his people had to keep looking for Graham Peck themselves.

CHAPTER 52

VOLCANIC ASH, small pumice bombs, and pyroclastic fragments floated through the air even though the Montana volcano eruption had subsided. The moon stayed behind the thick clouds of dust, turning the evening pitch-black. By midnight, it was virtually impossible to see anything more than a couple of feet ahead. The eerie cast of the sky kept people indoors, but it provided the ideal setting for sneaking through the night unobserved.

Parking their car five miles away, Matt and Adah walked cautiously down the avenues toward the Peck home in Arlington Heights. Streetlights provided an obscure glow, which made the boulevards appear more like fog-covered old alleys in London. Wearing totally black clothing, Matt and Adah faded into the dismal night scene.

Matt maintained a fast clip down familiar streets. Adah said nothing but kept up with his pace. Two blocks from the Pecks' former residence, he stopped.

"From here on we must assume they've got cameras or police stationed close by," Matt said. "We can't possibly spot the electronic surveillance, so we'll have to trust the dark night to shield us."

Adah momentarily closed her eyes and prayed. "Lord, please protect us." She abruptly smiled. "Okay, I'm ready."

"I'm not," Matt said. "We're going to have to carefully cut through backyards. I did such rooting around when I was a child, but nobody would have shot me then. Today, they'd fire first and ask questions later."

"I understand."

"All right. Stay close to me, and keep low and out of sight." Matt pointed to the fashionable and expensive homes in front of them. "We can't say a word. If we get caught here, it's all over not only for us, but Mary as well."

"I will be careful," Adah said.

"Let's go."

Without anything more being said, Matt bent low and slipped into the bushes leading into the next backyard. Carefully moving in and out of the shrubs, he worked his way into the grassy area behind the house. Matt climbed the fence at the side of the house, Adah staying right behind him. Once on the other side, they worked their way carefully through the next yard.

"There's no fence here," Matt whispered. "We can walk faster."

Suddenly a light came on in a kitchen. Matt grabbed Adah's arm, nearly sending her sprawling in the grass. He could feel his heart beating faster and feared they had been spotted.

For a moment nothing happened, then a man walked into the kitchen wearing only an undershirt and boxer shorts. He opened the refrigerator and took out a quart of milk. After slowly pouring himself a glass, he drank it and put the milk back in the refrigerator. The light went off, and he disappeared.

"Whoa," Matt wheezed, and motioned for Adah to follow him.

The next houses went by quickly and they soon came to the end of the block. "I'm going to cross the street first," Matt whispered. "Wait a solid five minutes and then come across. If I get caught, retreat, get out of here."

Adah nodded.

On tiptoes, Matt darted across the street and dived behind a big oak tree. He lay in the grass, expecting someone to grab him, but he heard and felt nothing. Five minutes later, Adah hurried across the street.

"Do exactly as I do," Matthew whispered into her ear. "Remember, if people attack, we split, and you simply run. Here we go."

Twisting through the thick shrubs, Matt wiggled his way into the backyard adjacent to their home. Crawling with his face nearly on the ground, he wormed his way through the back hedge and passed through a hole at the bottom of the wooden fence. Inching his way forward on his stomach, he avoided the back door to the home and kept creeping around the side of the house without making a sound.

Only when he reached the garage door did he check to see if Adah was still behind him. He pointed to a doggy door and made a waving motion with his hand. Like a snake, he pushed the dog's entry open and slithered into the garage. Adah crawled in behind him.

Walking on his knees, Matt crept across the empty garage and up to the back door. He waited a moment, but heard nothing. Very slowly, he opened the door that led into the kitchen. On his hands and knees, he inched forward but didn't hear a sound.

"Mary came walking across the backyard like an elephant marching into a circus," Matt whispered in Adah's ear. "She also tried to enter the back door, where a camera was undoubtedly aimed. We missed those traps. So far so good."

Without saying more, he quickly crawled down the hall and up the stairs that led to his father's office. At the top of the steps, Matt stopped and looked around. Everything was just as they left it. Last year's Christmas decorations were still up, and brightly colored baubbles still hung on the dried pine tree downstairs. Only a few months ago, this was their home, the center of their lives, and now . . . Well, *now* they were crawling around in the dark like rats on the prowl.

Silently, with Adah behind him, Matt slipped into his father's office. As his father had warned him, Bridges' men had already rifled through his files and slung papers everywhere. The office had been thoroughly ransacked, and looked like a train had torn through the walls.

"Is it in here?" Adah whispered.

Matt shook his head. "I certainly hope so! Bridges' boys obviously tore the files apart. Let's see what I can find."

He carefully pulled the top drawer out of his father's desk. Someone had already gone through the contents, but Matt dumped the few remaining items on the floor. Taking a small flashlight from his pocket, Matt held it in his teeth while he examined the bottom of the drawer. As his father had instructed him, he could feel small pins along the edge of the sides. Quickly removing them, he lifted out the false bottom.

"Ah!" he gasped. "Here it is! The file marked 'Identi-fication.'"

"We've got it!" Adah said.

"Let's get out of here—just like we came in and with just as much care."

"I'm right behind you."

Matt started crawling out of the room but stopped. He noticed something. On the bottom shelf of a book-case was an object he'd missed seeing when coming in. It looked like a camera lens. He darted across the room and yanked it away from the shelf.

"Oh! It's only a small video camera our family used a long time ago. Actually it can also be used as a projector. I thought it was a security device."

"Let's go," Adah urged.

"Okay." Matt started to put the camera down. "No, wait a minute. We might use the camera. We'll take it with us."

"Whatever. Let's move."

Without making a sound, Matt and Adah crawled out of the office and started down the stairs.

CHAPTER 53

ONCE MATT AND ADAH returned to their motel, they slept until nearly noon the next day. When Matt finally awoke, he felt groggy and exhausted. Midnight romps through his old neighborhood were not his style. It took him several minutes to become fully alert. Adah slept soundly on the other bed.

Matt sat down at the small table in the corner and carefully examined his father's file. Inside he found the basic documents used to create his father's identification tag that Graham used inside the Cook County Jail. Underneath lay a similar tag for his former secretary Sarah Cates to wear when she'd had to enter the prison. Every detail was as his father had told him it would be.

"What are you studying?" Adah sat up and rubbed her eyes.

"We've found the forms we're going to alter," Matt explained. "These ID certificates are our ticket back inside the jail."

"How so?" Adah crawled off the bed and straightened her black clothing. "I don't understand."

"The names on these ID tags are for my father and his secretary. We're going to change them. They will be for Al Meachem and Bridges' secretary, Connie Reeves. Virtually no one's seen either one of them around Chicago in public."

Adah frowned. "I'm still not sure that I quite understand."

"You are going to become Connie Reeves, and I'll be good ol' Al Meachem."

"Oh!"

"We've got to change the names and get the IDs in plastic covers," Matt explained. "Once we've got this job done well, we're about 90 percent there."

"We have something else to do?"

"Yeah. I'm going to shave off the beard, but leave a mustache. We need some new clothes. The teenage rocker look has to go. We've got to have an adult semiprofessional appearance. We'll also need to pick up some simple chemicals. Once we've got the supplies, we're ready to return."

"How will we get back in?" Adah sat down at the table opposite Matt.

"We're going to take a service personnel entrance

where employees enter the jail. Once inside, we'll request to see Mary and Nancy Marks in the room where attorneys talk to their clients. My father's ID gives us great latitude."

Adah nodded. "And what chemicals do we have to pick up?"

"Several different kinds. Ever hear of thermite?"

"No."

Matt grinned. "It will eat the socks right off your feet, and finish off your toes next. You're going to be extremely surprised to watch my little friend Mr. Thermite go to work."

CHAPTER 54

WHILE MATTHEW PECK and Adah Honi finished picking up clothing and the chemicals they needed, unexpected events were rapidly occurring in the international scene. With no previous warning, Hassan Jawhar Rashid announced he intended to speak to the United Nations General Assembly. Because his earlier speech had been canceled due to the assassination attempt, he demanded immediate access to the podium.

Rashid pushed hard, catching everyone off guard, including Frank Bridges and his Chicago staff. Because of the chaos sweeping across every continent, Secretary General Anjem Choudray cleared the calendar and gave

Rashid access to speak that afternoon. Television cameramen raced to the scene.

Frank Bridges remained in his office with Al Meachem and Connie Reeves to watch television's "big show." Bridges kept chewing at his fingernails nervously.

"What's he going to say, boss . . . I mean, Your Honor?" Meachem asked.

"I don't know. Anything is possible."

"Let me fix you a drink," Connie said. "It makes you less nervous."

"Okay," Frank said, "and make sure we don't get any phone calls. I don't want any interruptions during this speech."

"Sure thing, honey." Connie picked up the phone and notified the switchboard to hold all calls until further notification.

Bridges plopped down in his large leather chair. "I'm concerned he's going to blast the world and start another backlash. The entire planet is teetering on the edge as it is. We don't need an attack that will destroy all remaining stability."

"Drink this." Connie handed Frank a stiff whiskey and water.

"Are your people poised to handle any problems that might erupt in the streets?" Bridges asked Meachem.

"I have to tell you that most people are simply trying to survive. Food's been scarce since that volcano cut loose. I don't think the rank and file care what Rashid says as long as he promises them more bread."

Bridges took a drink of whiskey and water. "You're right."

For thirty minutes, the threesome watched, waiting for Rashid to appear. Political commentators droned on in endless speculation about what he would say. Eventually Rashid entered the United Nations chamber. The delegations rose and gave him enthusiastic applause.

Rashid proved to be in excellent form. Beginning with a casualness contrived to indicate a close personal relationship with Secretary General Choudray, as well as the other delegates seated around the vast chamber, he described in detail his hopes of an immediate agreement with Israel that would bring peace to the Middle East. Delegates applauded, and a sense of well-being emanated from the General Assembly.

"I have a specific request for you, my friends," Rashid continued. "As my armed forces have increased around the world, our new military presence has changed the world posture. This new status has imparted to me the new title of Supreme Commander in Chief. In order to achieve a world order of peace and harmony, I request that the United Nations change its charter." His voice shifted and took on a hard, demanding sound. "I ask that you eliminate the current Security Council and replace it with my European Union."

Silence fell over the room. Delegates looked at each other in stunned silence as if they didn't hear correctly. The idea sounded crazy, bizarre, and sure to create harsh confrontations.

"As you are aware, the United Nations Peacekeeping

Forces are completely unequal to my army. In order to make the world a genuinely peaceful place for all peoples, you must recognize the priority of my troops. I will expect immediate response."

From some corner of the chambers, a delegate shouted a resounding "No!" Other voices joined in.

Commotion broke out across the hall. Rashid stopped and stared at the uproar as if he didn't seem to care, but was surprised. The noise increased.

"Good Lord!" Bridges gasped. "He's set off a bomb at the United Nations. This response is worse than I expected."

Meachem pinched his bottom lip. "They ain't going to buy that idea," he said slowly.

"But he's exposed the weakness of the UN," Connie said. "He's thrown the whole assembly off."

"I'm not sure what his purpose is, but he's gutted the authority of the international body," Bridges said.

Rashid continued talking, and the uproar slowly died out. While he maintained the gentle tone of which he was a master, it was clear there was nothing subtle about his intentions. Like Adolf Hitler taking Poland and moving on to absorb the rest of Europe, Hassan Jawhar Rashid had made it clear that he had elevated himself into a world dictator.

"Keep the phones turned off," Bridges snapped. "We've got to reflect on what we've just heard. Connie, set up a conference call with Creighton Lewis and Rashid's top generals. I want to know what's happening out there."

CHAPTER 55

IN THE LATE AFTERNOON, Matthew Peck
and Adah Honi walked through the service
entrance of the Cook County Jail without any problems.
The hustle and bustle of the day's business had passed,
and everyone was preoccupied with what had occurred
earlier in the day at the United Nations.

Wearing a dark brown pullover shirt and lightweight
brown pants, Matt flashed his plastic ID card, and the
guard passed it under the security light with no problem.
Adah had pulled her hair back in a ponytail and changed
into a casual but attractive blue blouse. The guard
seemed so taken with her that he hardly paid attention to
the scan. The officer said nothing about the large brief-
cases Matt and Adah were carrying.

"Please send two prisoners down to the attorneys' interview room on the second floor," Matt said in a highly
professional manner. "As soon as possible, I want to talk
with a Mary Peck, and . . . let's see . . ." He flipped
through a notebook as if reminding himself of the name.
"Oh yes, her name is Nancy Marks."

The officer nodded. "Sure thing. I'll have 'em sent
down immediately."

"Thank you, Officer." Matt smiled and kept walking
with the briefcase dangling at his side. "I'll remember
your name."

Taking the fire exit staircase, Matt and Adah climbed to the second floor. Matt stopped and made sure no security cameras were aimed at them. The staircase was nothing but unadorned cement.

"Let's review our plan," Matt said. "Once I get inside the interview room, I will immediately pour the thermite on the floor. It will take a few minutes for it to eat through, but I guarantee you it will devour tile, cement, brick—everything! There's a space between the first and second floors where all the wiring and heat ducts run. That's our way out of this joint."

"I understand." Adah looked up the narrow stairway. "You want me on the fourth floor just outside the entry door."

"Exactly. I put a couple of cigarettes in there. To kill time, act like you're standing out in this stairway smoking. In your briefcase are materials used in race car fuel and amateur rocket experiments. It's an assortment of stuff like nitromethane, nitrophane, hydrazine percholorate, and methyl nitrate, ready to be laced together with a large amount of sodium nitrate you will pour in at the last minute. Remember, once that stuff is ignited, it may well blow the door off the wall, but it will certainly fill this staircase with billowing smoke. The explosion will go in every direction."

Adah nodded her head soberly. "I realize this is dangerous."

"You bet. You've got to get out of there quickly, but give me ten minutes to burn through the floor before you set off the electronic detonating device. Timing is everything."

Adah bit her lip. "I will do my best."

"Don't worry. You'll do fine." Matt watched her continue on up the stairs. "Remember. If we get separated, don't try to look for me. Run!"

Matt opened the exit door and walked down the hall. He entered the interview room door only to find a cop with Nancy Marks and his sister.

"Oh, hello, Mr. Meachem," the policeman said. "We got these people down here as quickly as we could."

"Thank you for your speed, Officer. I'll take it from here."

"You bet." The cop saluted informally and walked out the back door.

Mary stared at her brother, almost unable to speak. Nancy Marks obviously couldn't figure out what was going on. Matt placed the briefcase on the table and opened it quickly. He pulled out a large can of thermite.

"Ladies, don't move," he said. "It'll take about ten minutes, but I'm going to cut a hole in this floor and then we're all flying the coop."

CHAPTER 56

IN THE COOK COUNTY JAIL'S central security offices, a guard making a secondary check of anyone entering with special identification credentials noticed a red light blinking on the computer. He pushed a button and waited for the sheet to print out.

"How strange." The policeman read the numbers a second time. "It doesn't match." Several moments passed and a second printout came out of the machine. "This one doesn't fit either." He reached for the phone. "Give me John Peters on the entry desk for service personnel," he told the operator.

"Peters here."

"This is Smith up in central security. Did you take an ID for a man named Graham Peck about five minutes ago?"

"No," Peters said. "Haven't had anybody by that name come through all day."

Smith looked at the printout a third time. "Something's not adding up here. The ID numbers match a man in the mayor's office named Graham Peck, and there's a second one for a woman named Sarah Cates."

"Graham Peck!" John Peters said. "Wait a minute. Now, that name rings a bell. That's the guy we've been trying to catch. Remember? His daughter is in here. She's a . . . Mary Peck . . . I believe."

"Yeah. That's right."

"Hey, wait a minute. Five minutes ago I had a young attorney come in with a woman named Connie Reeves asking for Mary Peck."

"What was his name?"

"I believe . . . it was . . . Al Meachem."

"Meachem?" Smith thought for a minute. "There's an Al Meachem that's a big dog with the mayor. Must be some kind of mix-up with these name tags. Meachem is an important man. I'll check with the mayor's office."

"Sure," Peters said. "Let me know if there's a problem." He hung up.

Smith quickly dialed the number on his confidential security sheet.

"City of Chicago," the operator said. "Mayor's offices."

"This is Officer Smith in the Cook County Jail. I have an important call for the mayor."

"I'm sorry," the operator said. "All calls are being suspended for the moment. Leave your number, and I'll put it through when the line opens."

"Look, lady! This is a top-level security matter. Put me through."

"Sorry." The operator hung up.

CHAPTER 57

MATTHEW PECK poured thermite on the prison floor in a two-foot-wide circle. Instantly steam bubbled up from the tile, and an acrid smell drifted across the room intertwined with the smoke. He walked around the circle a second time, pouring more of the chemical into the channels forming in the tiles.

"You don't know who I am," he told Nancy Marks, "and for the moment it's better that you don't. I've come to get you and Mary out of this jail."

"I—I'd be extremely grateful," the young woman

said. Nancy's brunette hair surrounded her youthful-appearing face with a touch of class. Her large brown eyes stayed fixed on Matt, mesmerized by what he was doing. "I truly, truly want out of this dump."

Matt set down the thermite and pulled the video camera from his briefcase. "Both of you, look at me like I'm an attorney talking to you. I've got to get you down on tape, so act normal." He set the video camera on a small table and aimed it at the women.

While Mary and Nancy talked into the lens, Matt inspected the floor again. The chemical was cutting as quickly as he expected, but the scent of the chemical burned his eyes. He picked up the can and poured more solution into the ruts burning through the cement.

"In a few moments, I'm going to give you some clothing. I want you to get out of those orange jail suits and into these duds as quickly as you can. When this section falls out of the floor, you're going to jump into the hole. It's about a five-foot drop. When you hit the bottom, follow me, and I'll get us out of here."

After a couple of minutes, Matt switched off the camera and tossed the clothing at the women. "Change quickly," he said, "while I get this VCR unit in place. Fortunately, it's one of those new cameras that projects a digitally refined picture. You'll look natural." He pulled the small table in front of the window mirror.

Matt quickly positioned the VCR so it projected on the back wall opposite the large two-way mirror behind him. A picture flashed on the white wall that looked exactly like Mary and Nancy sitting there talking to someone. He flipped the repeat switch and the endless loop began.

"We're ready," Mary said. "You tell us when and we'll jump."

Matt watched the circle burning through the floor. "Let's see what's left." He stomped in the center. A cracking sound echoed across the room. "Here we go." Matt grabbed one of the chairs and pushed it against the ring.

With a crumbling noise the two-foot circle of floor broke loose and crashed down below them. Matt grabbed the women's orange jumpsuits and threw them in the hole. "Cushions your jump and keeps them out of sight," Matt said.

Mary stared into the black hole. "Absolutely awesome!"

"Follow me," Matt instructed the women. "Stay close."

"I'm ready," Nancy said.

Matt dropped into the hole and Nancy followed him. Mary brought up the rear. The three huddled beneath the low ceiling with pipes and wires running everywhere. The area smelled musty, like no one had been in there for years.

"I locked the door when I came in," Matt said. "They'll have to break it down to get in. Through the two-way mirror they can only see images being projected on the wall. Those little adjustments should slow the cops down for a while."

Suddenly a dull boom echoed down the walkway. In

a moment a strange smell drifted across the pipes and wire cables.

"Run," Matt said. "Adah's set off an explosion on the fourth floor. Stay with me, and I'll lead you out of here!"

CHAPTER 58

BECAUSE SHE HAD COMPLETELY under-estimated the force of the explosion, it knocked Adah backward, rolling her down the next section of stairs. Hovering on the landing of the third floor under a cloud of smoke, Adah lay stunned on the cement floor. Slowly her awareness returned, but she couldn't hear a sound.

"Got to get out of here," Adah mumbled to herself. "Must get up."

Her knees ached, and her back throbbed. Adah felt along the side of her face and discovered her nose was bleeding. Blood ran down the side of her face from a cut on the side of her forehead.

I don't think I can move, Adah thought. *Maybe I broke a bone, a rib . . . but . . . I've got to get up . . . get out of here.*

Adah remembered the plugs in her ears and carefully removed them. Somewhere above her she heard people coughing and a few voices shouting.

"Smoke! Get out of here!"

"Run!"

Adah knew she had to get up off the floor and force herself down the stairs. The smoke was beginning to make her dizzy, and she feared passing out again. The acrid smell lingering in the air carried an awful stench. She reached for the handrail to pull herself up but fell back on the landing.

———————

A cop burst into the central security office. "There's been an explosion on the fourth floor!" he shouted. "Can you pick it up on your cameras?"

Smith rushed to the monitors. All he could see on the fourth floor were clouds of smoke obscuring everything. "Lord help us! We've got a big problem up there."

"I don't know what's happening," the policeman said. "I can't find any evidence that prisoners have escaped yet."

Smith picked up the telephone again and dialed the mayor's office.

"City of Chicago," the operator said. "Office of . . ."

"Listen," Smith barked. "Don't you shut me off again. This is Smith over in Central Security in the Cook County Jail. We've just had an explosion over here. Now, you get the mayor on the line right now!"

The operator hesitated a moment. "Okay," she finally answered.

After thirty seconds, Connie Reeves answered. "This is the mayor's office. Is there a problem?"

"You bet there is!" Smith pushed. "We've had an explosion at the jail, and someone is running around using an ID tag with Al Meachem's name while the card is marked with numbers for Graham Peck."

"*What?*" Reeves's voice elevated.

"And we have another ID for Connie Reeves."

"I'm Connie Reeves! And I'm not there in the jail!"

"Well, the numbers fit a secretary we have listed as Sarah Cates."

"On my God!" Reeves gasped. "Here's the mayor."

Smith quickly explained the situation to Bridges. "We don't know who's loose over here," he concluded. "Al Meachem, Graham Peck, Sarah Cates, who?"

"Listen to me carefully," the mayor said. "Al Meachem is standing here next to me. You have *Graham Peck* loose in your building. Call in maximum security for the entire jail. I'm on my way over there!"

CHAPTER 59

A STRONG HAND REACHED under Adah Honi's body and lifted her up. The policeman glanced at the ID tag identifying her as Connie Reeves, and then pulled Adah to her feet.

"Connie, we've got to get you out of here." The policeman started walking her down the stairs.

"Thank you," Adah barely mumbled. "I fell down."

"Yeah," the cop said, "and you need to get out of this smoke. I'll get you down to the bottom exit."

They struggled down the three flights of stairs. When

they reached the bottom, an officer was standing at the door with his gun drawn.

"Got to get her out into the fresh air," the policeman said. "She's one of us."

The officer at the door nodded. "Move it," he said.

By this time, Adah's legs felt stronger, and she was walking. "Thanks," she barely gasped.

"Sit down here on this metal bench," the policeman said. "I'm going back in to help other people."

Adah nodded silently. "Thanks." The man disappeared back inside the open door.

Sirens were blasting away with an unbearable sound, and people were running everywhere.

"Got to get away," Adah said to herself. She stood up and covered her ears. With her ID tag swinging around her neck, Adah stumbled down the street. She glanced over her shoulder and saw smoke pouring out the fourth-floor windows of the jail. Adah kept walking down the street.

At the corner, she stopped to get her bearings. At first nothing made any sense, but finally the lay of the land came into focus. Matt's car had to be two streets over. With all the strength she could muster, Adah crossed the street and walked down the alley. The sirens continued to blare across the boulevards with nonstop insistency.

At the end of the alley, she looked across the street, hoping to see the ten-year-old hydrogen-propelled vehicle they had obtained from Alice Masterson. The space was empty.

Adah blinked several times but slowly realized the

truth. It had taken her much longer to get out of the building than she realized. The fall and the bump on her head had left her on the floor for who knew how long. Matt had done exactly as he should have by leaving. He concluded she might have been captured and took off with the other two women.

Adah sagged against the building. She had to get out of there before the police caught her. Limping, Adah hurried down the street in an unknown direction with no idea where she was going.

CHAPTER 60

WHEN THE MAYOR'S LIMOUSINE pulled up in front of the Cook County Jail, Frank Bridges could see policemen standing everywhere with guns drawn. Several fire engines were already on the scene, but the smoke had disappeared from the windows. Bridges and Meachem rushed from the car and broke through the police lines.

"Where's an officer in the internal security unit named Smith?" Bridges barked. "Central Security?"

"I'm not sure," the policeman said. "The jail's turned into a madhouse. You'll have to keep asking."

Bridges and Meachem started running from policeman to policeman, looking for the one man. After five minutes, they found Officer Smith standing with a group of five policemen.

"I'm the mayor," Bridges began, "and *this* is Al Meachem. What's going on inside the jail?"

"That's my question," Officer Smith said. "We got an ID number for Graham Peck with Meachem's name on it. Connie Reeves's ID came through for a woman named Cates. About that time we had an explosion on the fourth floor. This place went crazy."

"Okay, okay," Bridges said. "Where did this man calling himself Meachem go?"

"We're not sure. He had two prisoners brought down to the attorneys' interview room on the second floor. From there, we lost track of 'em."

Bridges beckoned for Meachem to follow him and hurried into the building. Quickly clearing all the security checkpoints, they took the elevator to the second floor. Several policemen were guarding the hall.

"Get me into the interview room right now," Bridges ordered one of the cops.

"Certainly." The officer tried the door. "It's locked," he said. "Strange. Hmm. There's a two-way mirror on the other side. We can look in and see who's there before we break it down."

"Do it!" the mayor ordered.

The officer opened the next door down the hall and the three men entered. "The glass makes people look a little distant," the cop explained.

"Look!" Meachem said. "It's them! The two women! Peck's daughter and Nancy Marks."

Bridges stared. "How come they didn't get away? And Graham Peck's not in there!"

"They're just sitting there talking," the officer said.

"Turn on the mike," the mayor ordered, "I want to hear what they're saying."

The policeman threw the switch. No sound came out. He wiggled the switch back and forth. "I don't understand. It's never done this before. We always hear what they're saying."

Meachem pressed closer to the glass. "Hey!" he said. "I don't think there's people in that room. Those are video images."

"Break that door down!" Bridges shouted. "Get in there."

The men rushed toward the interview room door. Meachem and the cop hit the door with the full force of their combined weight. Instantly the lock broke and the door banged open.

Bridges stared at the pictures flashing against the back wall and the hole in the floor under a small table that concealed it from anyone looking through the mirror. He walked slowly across the room and stared into the black hole. Down at the bottom he could see two orange jail suits.

"Graham Peck's been here!" Bridges declared in disgust. "This is his work. He's floating around here somewhere. I'll give him one thing, Peck is one smart man."

Meachem stared in amazement.

"Sir!" Another policeman broke into the room. "Something's happening outside you need to know about." He kept gasping for air.

"What?" Bridges snapped. He didn't like being interrupted at such moments.

"Those six policemen you were talking to," the man said, huffing and puffing, "they all fell on the ground. Something's hit 'em! No one knows whether it's the smoke, gas, what. We think they're dying!"

"*Six* men?" Meachem's question held a strange air of knowing suspicion.

"Yeah, six of 'em!"

Bridges looked at Meachem in disgust. "We don't need this problem on top of everything else that's happened!"

CHAPTER 61

EVENING HAD BEGUN to fall when the mayor started winding up his investigation. The darkness of the sky returned and it was becoming difficult to see much.

"As best we can understand," Al Meachem said, "a crude bomb was set off on the fourth-floor fire escape. While it knocked the door off the hinges, it didn't really do that much damage except for spreading smoke everywhere. The hole in the floor in the interview room is another matter."

"And those six policemen that died out front?" Bridges pushed.

"Has to be the nanorobots," Meachem concluded. "The smoke in the building smelled bad, but it wouldn't kill anybody outside. We couldn't find any other effects in the building." Meachem scratched his head and raised his eyebrows. "I'm afraid that horde of invisible killers struck again."

"Have you found Dr. Gillette?"

Meachem shook his head. "No. The man's hiding somewhere, but no one will give us any clues."

"When you find him, get mean!" Bridges sneered. "Rough him up! I need him to give us some idea of how long those killer robots can float through the sky."

"Believe me, we're lookin'."

Bridges thought for a moment. "Warn the jail personnel not to discuss what happened with anyone. And I mean *anyone*. I don't want Rashid getting wind of the two women's escape until I tell him." The mayor ran his hands through his hair nervously. "That'll send him into orbit. Maybe we can catch them with Graham Peck before I have to discuss the matter with him."

"Rashid's got his own set of issues after that speech today," Meachem added. "He probably won't be thinking about these people."

Bridges raised one eyebrow. "That's the problem. He'll resurrect the issue of Peck out of nowhere one of these days. I hope to be ready for him when he does."

"We've got every highway going north out of town covered with roadblocks, and our men have fresh pictures of Graham Peck. They'll nail him if he tries to get away."

The mayor shook his head. "Your men *better catch him*, or you'll all be looking for work."

Adah jumped on a bus and slipped into a seat in the back. Unsure of where she was going, Adah needed to get out of the downtown area no matter had bad she felt. Somewhere along the way she could change buses and keep moving. It was the only hope she had.

She thought about where Matt would go. He would avoid the Arlington Heights area for sure. The only logical place seemed to be the motel where they stayed last night. If she could get there . . .

The bus pulled up to a stop and people got on. Before long, the rear end would fill up. Passengers started sitting around her. Adah noticed a few of them staring, and they seemed to be looking at her face.

She glanced into the window to catch the reflection. The cut on her forehead had swollen and was turning into an ugly bruise. In addition, the side of her cheek was scratched. Adah's hair hung down in disarray. In general, she looked like a thug had rolled her. She quickly pulled the identification tag from her neck and shoved it into her pocket. Best to keep all names out of sight.

The bus rumbled on into the night while Adah silently prayed.

CHAPTER 62

MATTHEW PECK pulled up in front of one of the city's forehead marking stations and turned off the car. "I'm not sure what happened to

Adah," he said. "She knew to get out of the area around the jail as fast as possible. Fortunately, she wasn't marked, so computers and satellites can't track her. I just pray the cops didn't catch Adah. Our problem now is that both of you still have the marks on your foreheads."

Nancy Marks reached over and squeezed Matt's hand. "How can I ever thank you for getting me away from those terrible men?"

"We wanted to help you escape and certainly hoped to stop any torture," Matt said.

"I—I can't tell you what they did to me." Tears welled up in Nancy's eyes. "Fortunately, Bill and I didn't have any children yet . . . but I—I miss him so much." She started crying.

Mary Peck put her arm around Nancy. "You're with us now. Don't worry. We're going to take care of you."

Nancy again squeezed Matt's hand. "Thank you so much."

"Dad had an idea that might help us," Matt said. "He reasoned there has to be some difference in how applications of identification nanorobots operate or everyone would be sending the same signal. He thinks there's a strong possibility that a second application might short out the first application. If the computer signals were nullified, that's all we'd need."

"I'll try anything," Mary said.

"Okay." Matt pointed toward the entrance. "Both of you go into that office, and tell them you've been out of the country. Ask for the swab treatment. We can only pray that it works."

Nancy and Mary hurried inside. In five minutes they returned.

"You got the mark?" Matt asked.

Both women nodded their heads.

"Dad had one more idea," Matt continued. "In the Scripture, Christians often prayed for healing and were cured of their diseases. The mark on your heads is mechanical, but it's still a disease." Matt took out a small Bible. "He said I should read to you this passage from the end of Revelation when the city of evil is destroyed."

"Do it," Mary said. "You won't find any resistance from me."

Matt smiled. "Good." He started reading. "'After these things I saw another angel coming down from heaven, having great authority, and the earth was illuminated with his glory.' Dad thought we should ask this angel with authority to come and touch your foreheads. If the placing of a second sign on the forehead didn't help, surely the touch of an angel wouldn't hurt."

"I never went to church," Nancy said, "and I don't know anything about the Bible. But Bill and I realized we were wrong about many issues. I don't understand anything about angels, but I want God's assistance. I'm glad to ask Him to be with us."

Matt rolled up the windows. "The summer heat may make the car get hot fast, but I don't want anyone on the street to hear us. We've still got to protect ourselves. Let's join hands and ask God to help us with this forehead problem."

The three friends clasped hands and closed their

eyes. Matthew fervently prayed that a "touch of authority" would cancel the effects of evil. He called on the angels of God to walk among them.

"And please forgive me of my sin," Nancy added. "I don't know what's the right thing to say, but I want to believe and be one of Your people, God. I want Jesus Christ in my life. Please, please help me."

"Me too," Mary added.

Matthew suddenly sensed light filling the car. The intensity of the glow was so strong, he squinted and feared to open his eyes. After a few moments, Matt felt the light subsiding.

"Did you see that?" he asked in awe.

"See what?" Nancy asked.

"A powerful light flooded our car," Matt explained. "I'm sure I didn't hallucinate."

"God *really was here!*" Mary said fervently.

"Oh, I pray so!" Nancy said. "With all my heart, I pray so."

CHAPTER 63

MATT PULLED UP in front of the motel around ten o'clock. The residue of volcanic smoke had once again turned the night into blackness. Only the haze around the streetlights gave him any sense of direction.

"This is the motel where Adah and I have been staying," he said. "We have no reason to think it's not safe, unless computers are still following the mark on your foreheads. We have no alternative but to trust that God has done something to break the spell."

"I'm playing with a new deck of cards," Mary Peck said. "I'll trust His hand to deliver us anywhere."

"Me too," Nancy added.

Matt turned off the engine and pulled out the key to the room. With the two women following him, he cautiously put the key in the lock and slowly opened the door. Without making a sound, he pushed the door open wider. His heart nearly stopped. Someone was stretched across the bed.

Pushing Nancy and Mary back, Matt pulled the small penlight out of his pocket and flashed the beam on the shape.

"It's Adah!" he gasped. "Oh, man! I nearly had a heart attack!"

"*Shalom?*" the sleepy-eyed woman said and blinked several times. "Matt?"

Mary rushed in and grabbed the Jewish woman. "Adah, we are so grateful to you! Thank you, thank you."

Adah sat up and rubbed her eyes. "Sure. It's okay. I had a hard journey getting across town."

"You look tired and beat up," Matt said. "The blast got you?"

"Afraid so." Adah pushed her disheveled hair out of her face. "I stayed too close."

"I hate to wake you up, but I think we should leave tonight. We don't know if Mary's and Nancy's forehead markings have been neutralized. The sooner we get out of Chicago the better."

"Won't they be watching the roads to the north?" Mary said.

"Did you know Al Meachem and a group of his henchmen attacked our cabin in Tomahawk and burned it down?" Matt asked his sister.

Mary started crying. "No." She sobbed. "D—did I tell them where the cabin was? I don't remember."

"It doesn't matter," Mark said. "We all escaped, but you're correct. Bridges' people will assume we'll take a northern route. Dad told me to drop south on Interstate 55 to Joliet and then drive west to Davenport, Iowa. We're going to take a long back way up through Dubuque, but it should be more secure."

Adah nodded. "I am ready to go when everyone else is." She pushed her hair back. "Thank God we are all safe."

The sound of a helicopter circling the area drifted across the motel.

"Think they're looking for us?" Mary asked.

"Could be a routine security vehicle," Matt said. "I sure pray it is, but let's get out of here."

CHAPTER 64

EVERY MORNING before he got out of bed, Hassan Jawhar Rashid talked to his god. These quiet meditations gave him a sense of purpose, direction, stability. Often, before he had to make an important decision, Rashid would lapse into an inner dialogue with the divinity, and from these moments of communication, he found the precise path he needed to follow.

During one of these periods of quiet reflection many years earlier, he had "heard" the directive to develop two names. One for the Eastern world; one for the Western world. From this insight, Rashid had suddenly thought of the name Borden Camber Carson and experienced the urge to use this name as his public persona until otherwise notified. He much preferred his original name of Rashid, but immediately saw the value in creating a camouflage, a subterfuge to work behind.

His ability "to hear" was key in his religious life because the divine intervention was actually identical with his thought life. Insights, intuitions, ideas came out of nowhere, and this *voice* was similar to his normal way of thinking. Sometimes *the voice* would simply bubble up while he was reflecting on another matter, and he knew god wanted to speak to him.

Early on, Hassan Rashid had worried that he might turn into a schizophrenic and could start becoming disoriented. He worried that he might go crazy. Then Rashid realized that only one voice ever spoke to him, and it was always the same voice. Well, sometimes it was hard to differentiate between his thoughts and this voice, but the voice left him energized and gifted. Could that be crazy? Certainly not.

Rashid had grown up in a poor family on the edge of

the desert with an overwhelming amount of religious confusion swirling around him. At age two, he started recognizing words, and before anyone instructed him, Hassan taught himself to read, devouring every book in sight. Rashid quickly realized his father's modicum of Muslim faith made him distrust his Jewish mother's religion, and both had disdain for Christianity. As time went by, he discovered that the villagers hated Jews, and he must completely obscure this part of his identity. Quite perplexing!

Rashid's neighborhood swirled in such contradictions. Heredity was confusing. His father's lineage ran back literally to the Caesars. He had plenty of good, strong genes, but Rashid also realized the Islamic world churned with hatred for the West, and many Muslims proved to be extremely narrow-minded. Because he had inherited a fear of what Christians would do if they got the opportunity, Rashid had never seriously looked at the Christian religion. As he grew into adolescence, he seemed to only step from one puddle of pitch to the other.

One afternoon as he walked across the burning sand of the desert with the sun blaring down on him, Hassan Rashid abruptly decided he would create his own religion. With the hot sand oozing up between Rashid's toes, the idea seemed exciting and promising. Pulling together something from each of the three faiths, he would mold a new lump of dough and break his own bread! Standing on a height of his own creation, Hassan would throw himself down to the world in a burst of his own glory.

Casting the ancient ways aside, Hassan Jawhar Rashid would walk on a path of his own making.

At that moment, Rashid suddenly experienced an impartation of power. He felt as if the blinding sun had swooped down on him and burned hot energy into his brain. When he walked out of the desert that evening, he knew exactly what needed to happen with his mundane job at the oil company. Rashid recognized a path out of his humble origins straight to the top of the ladder, the world of wealth.

The first sign of change came when he discovered that he could now read people and perceive their intentions. Again, the ability wasn't a mystery as much as an insight that simply arose in his mind, enabling him to perceive the other person's core values. He could quickly decide where their thoughts would take the individual. In effect, it was almost like reading minds. He seldom missed. His capacity to "read them" was the key to constantly evolving success.

Rashid often thought about that afternoon in the desert. Sometimes the day seemed so revolutionary he wondered if it had even really happened, *but it had*. His life had changed. Progress escalated and wealth poured in. Of course, he kept this mountaintop moment in the depths of the desert to himself. No one knew, but those hours would forever remain the guiding fire in his soul.

CHAPTER 65

FOR SEVERAL MOMENTS Hassan Jawhar Rashid listened without comment. The prime minister of Israel, Dov Landau, kept pushing to make his point. Their conversation had been long and arduous. Landau argued that they both knew Iran was behind the current military tension, and that the Iranians had sponsored terrorism. Since that long-ago invasion of Afghanistan by the United States, Iran had supported the Taliban–al-Qaeda axis. Landau wanted to know if such manipulations were going to stop.

"Yes, my friend," Rashid said. "If you sign an agreement with me, I will guarantee Iran will retreat from attacks on Israel."

"And Syria? Saudi Arabia? The Emirates?"

"Of course. I control the military in these countries," Rashid said with such cavalier indifference it had to chill Landau. "They have not always acted in ways that I approved, but I am telling you they will respect a treaty . . . if you sign it."

For several moments silence filled the telephone line. Finally, Prime Minister Dov Landau answered. "In that case, and on the basis of your personal guarantee, my cabinet has instructed me to tell you we will sign."

"Excellent! I can assure you that your actions will

open the door to a new day of peace and tranquillity for the entire Middle East."

"I trust so. We will hold you to your word guaranteeing that it shall be so."

"And I have one more detail," Rashid continued. "I understand that since you took control of *Haram es-Sharif* from the Wakf, your people are constructing a third temple between the Dome of the Rock and the El-Aqsa Mosque. Am I correct?"

"Since the first and second temples were on this mount, we have every right to do so," Landau argued.

"How is the construction coming?" Rashid asked casually.

"Acceptably," the prime minister said without elaboration.

"Good, good. I would like for us to sign this treaty on the steps of your new temple. I think your people would accept such an event as a divine blessing. It would be a sign to the Arab world."

"Really!" Dov Landau sounded completely caught off guard. "I see no problem in signing there. It would be a highly significant political step. Of course, the Arab's won't like it."

"Excellent! I am going to release a statement indicating that we will sign an accord on the Temple Mount. Are you prepared to do so . . . in, let's say, oh . . . three days?"

"Three days!" The prime minister coughed. "That's rather soon!"

"Isn't the sooner the better for your citizens?"

"Well . . . I suppose so. Yes. We will sign."

"Ah, Dov. You are a good man. I trust this event will be the most important deed of your life."

"I hope so," the prime minister said with lingering hesitancy in his voice.

"Good-bye, Mr. Prime Minister. I will see you on the Temple Mount in three days. Our people can mutually work out the details." Rashid hung up the phone and turned to the four men gathered in front of him. Each was removing earphones from his head through which they had been listening to both sides of the conversation. "Well, gentlemen?"

"He took the bait?" Ali al-Hakim, the defense minister of Iran, asked.

"And they will sign?" Muhammad Baqer Hussein of Syria pushed.

"Gentlemen, gentlemen!" Rashid held up his hand to stop the onslaught of questions. "You heard the entire conversation with your earphones. You already know the answers. The point is that Landau does not realize he will be militarizing their temple. We have tricked him into taking a blasphemous step."

"Dov Landau is no fool," said Abdel Sharif, the prime minister of Egypt. "I am surprised he doesn't suspect something ominous behind your offer."

"The Israelis need this step out of political tension," Rashid said. "He may smell a rat, but that is now his problem, not ours. I will sign this agreement, which should bring relaxation of Israel's military defenses as well as their nuclear capacities. That result is the only one we are concerned about."

"Indeed!" Anat Berko said. "But our people in Jordan will not be happy with this turn of events. In fact, you can expect rioting in the streets and revolt by the people."

"Please!" Rashid kept smiling as he talked. "I brought you here today for exactly this reason. You must assure your people that more is working behind the scenes than they can see at this moment. In the near future the entire scheme will become visible, and matters will not be good for the state of Israel."

"Do not ever forget," Ali al-Hakim said, "the Prophet Muhammad said that the resurrection of the dead will not come until we do battle with the Jews and kill them. We will be on the east side of the river, and they on the west side."

"I know," Rashid said uncomfortably. "*I know.*"

THE DRAGON ATTACKS | IV

The dragon was angry with the woman,
and went off to make war on the rest of her offspring,
on those who keep the commandments of God
and bear testimony to Jesus.
And he stood on the sand of the sea.

REVELATION 12:17

THE LONG NIGHT'S JOURNEY proved more arduous than Matthew expected. A roadside park turned up outside Dubuque, and they pulled over so everyone could sleep. The next morning they wound their way up to La Crosse and finally got on Interstate 94, which took them through Eau Claire and up to the crossroad at Highway 8 where they turned east toward the town of Prentice. When they crossed the Big Jump South Fork River, Matt knew they were home. While they had been gone only days, it felt like months.

"Son!" Graham Peck ran out of the house when Matt drove into the driveway. "Thank God, you made it!"

Mary Peck slowly opened the back door of the car and got out without saying a word. Graham stopped, stared, and rushed toward his daughter, grabbing and hugging her neck.

"Praise God!" Graham sobbed. "Mary, you are alive!"

"I'm sorry, Daddy." Mary began weeping. "I have so much to apologize for."

Graham whirled her around him. "We're so thankful you're home. We love you, love you, love you!"

Jackie Peck rushed out of the house. "My daughter's back!" she yelled, swinging her arms in the air. "Oh, my daughter is home!" Jackie ran down the steps and threw her arms around Graham and Mary, hugging them both. George and Jeff came out the door behind her.

"I've never seen Dad so demonstrative," Matthew said. Adah and Nancy got out of the car behind him, shutting the doors slowly. "It's been a hard time for Mom and Dad since Mary ran off," he said.

"And Nancy Marks!" Graham turned toward their new guest. "You're here! Welcome to our house."

"Thank you." Nancy extended her hand. "I can't tell you how much I—"

Graham went past the extended hand and hugged Nancy. "We're so glad you're alive and with us."

"Not as much as I am to be with you," Nancy said. "It's been a long, gruesome road."

The family broke into conversation with everybody talking at the same time, hugging each other, and sounding like a gigantic party. George and little Jeff kept jumping up and down and hugging Mary.

"Let's go in the house," Jackie finally said. "We need to sit down. This family reunion's overwhelming me."

Everyone followed her into the small living room of Alice Masterson's cabin. Jackie quickly prepared a cold drink, and the little boys passed the glasses around while conversation broke out again.

Finally Graham turned to Nancy Marks. "I usually kept some distance from your husband, Bill," he began. "Of course, Jackie and I saw you at political events, but Nancy, we don't really know you."

Nancy nodded her head soberly. "I always stayed in the background because I wasn't comfortable with much

of the political nonsense that went along with Bill's job."
She leaned back in the chair and stared up at the ceiling
for a few moments. "We've never been church people in
any way, shape, or form, but I did know the difference between good and bad. I simply couldn't stand it when the
mayor pushed my husband to do things that were wrong."

"Wrong?" Jackie frowned.

"Like the night he, Pemrose, and Meachem raided
your home in Arlington Heights," Nancy said. "Yeah, intrusions like that!"

"Bill was there with those men?" Graham gasped.

Nancy nodded her head. "In the beginning, the
mayor said it was a routine security check, but Bill was
gone virtually all night because they were trying to catch
you. When he came back, Bill was deeply disturbed. Not
only was what they were doing illegal, he knew it violated
everything you stood for, Graham."

"He chased us?" Matthew asked.

"Not out of town," Nancy said. "Bill ended up trying
to run down those college students that were meeting in
your home. Remember Jennifer Andrews?"

"Remember her?" Matthew exploded. "Listen. She
was nearly my girlfriend until we discovered her father
worked for Bridges and she was a spy!"

"Bill kept her with him so she could identify the kids
escaping and running for the train station," Nancy continued. "They chased them all over Arlington Heights."

"Did they catch anyone?" Matthew asked soberly.

"Not in Arlington Heights. The college kids proved
to be quite elusive." Nancy stopped and bit her lip.

"The next day Jennifer guided Bill and the other thugs around Northwestern University, and . . . they picked them up."

"*And?*" Matthew motioned with his hand. "What happened to them?"

"Jennifer Andrews knew, but no one told Bill," Nancy said. "They simply disappeared."

CHAPTER 67

EXPLOSIONS from the Montana volcano had perpetuated a blackness across the sky, but it had also distorted the weather, causing violent swings from unusual cold to hot temperatures. Hot summer weather bore down on Alice Masterson's little cabin hidden in the woods near Prentice as the Peck family sat around the small living room and listened carefully. Nancy Marks described her journey—from being angry about the treatment Bill Marks received at the hands of Frank Bridges to the discovery that they could no longer passively stand by and allow the outrages to continue. The strain in her face added painful nuances to her story.

"You didn't know Bill very well," Mary told Graham, "but behind his silence was a man with conviction. When an idea gripped him, Bill wasn't afraid to follow his heart."

"You're right," Graham said. "I didn't hear Bill say

much, and he seemed more like a silent sentinel. I simply assumed Bridges had him in his pocket."

"The mayor thought so, too," Nancy said. "He figured a few yanks on the puppet strings would start Bill dancing like a marionette. Obviously, the mayor missed the truth by a million miles."

"I don't want to push," Jackie said. "I know this experience will always be filled with extreme pain, but we were totally blown away when Bill shot Carson in the United Nations Building. Can you tell us anything more?" Jackie stopped and smiled compassionately. "If you're comfortable doing so."

"After those college students he picked up at Northwestern University disappeared, Bill became distraught," Nancy said. "No one would tell him anything about what had happened, but several bodies surfaced in Lake Michigan. When the stories were suppressed, that gave him an important clue. Bill realized the issues had become life-and-death. He couldn't remain passive. One afternoon he sat in on one of the mayor's holographic conversations with Borden Camber Carson, or Hassan Rashid as nearly everyone calls him today. That conversation pushed Bill over the edge."

"I understand," Graham said.

"For the first time, Bill realized Frank Bridges wasn't simply seeking some high national office like the presidency. He realized Carson had complete control of the mayor, and murder was no problem. Bridges would do anything this megalomaniac from the Middle East told him. That night Bill came home completely distraught.

He realized someone had to stop these homicidal maniacs. Bill knew he had to break Carson's grip on the international avalanche the man was starting, or the world would face disaster."

"Amazing," Graham said. "We had no idea Bill had such insights." He looked around the room at his children. Even little Jeff sat like a statue, absorbing every word. "That's when he decided to shoot Carson?"

"No," Nancy said. "We secretly joined an underground group of people who were angry over the deterioration of the country and the violence in the streets. Everyone was confused, and we banded together to seek clarity. I believe it was the encouragement of the men in that group that caused Bill to realize he might have to sacrifice his life to stop Carson."

"A religious group?" Matt asked.

"No." Nancy shook her head. "Just everyday upset citizens. But Bill's respect for you, Graham, kept growing all the time behind the scenes."

"*Me?*"

"Bill recognized that you couldn't be manipulated by Bridges. He could see that you escaped to avoid falling under the control of this oil tyrant who had slipped in under the mayor's door, and he figured that you knew Carson's plans to make himself into an international dictator. When Carson set up his speech at the United Nations, Bill fully understood why both Carson and Bridges kept chasing you."

"Wait." Graham held up his hand. "What you've just said is extremely important to me. Look, Nancy, I'm a nobody, a cog in the machine. Why in the world would these men of power and money keep chasing me and our family for months?"

"You really don't get it, Graham?" Nancy asked.

"No. We've been hiding out more than a year. I expected by now that Bridges would have called off the dogs and given up on catching me."

"Bill realized they can't stop! Whether they fully recognize it or not, you scare them," Nancy said.

Graham laughed. "Come on!"

"Listen to me." Nancy's voice intensified. "Everyone Carson deals with ends up bowing to him and falling under his control . . . except you. While he can't completely define it, you're the man he can't dominate or master. Carson knows you stand outside the net in which he's captured everyone else. Bill realized that once Carson discovered your independence, you were forever a threat to his plans."

Graham stared at Nancy, unable to find the words to express his consternation.

"Look," Nancy said, "you're a modest man with independent ideas. Carson wants a world of slaves who bow every time they hear the word 'Chief.' As long as there is one person out there he can't control, Mr. Supreme Commander is threatened. Looking into your eyes, Carson saw an independent set of values and that you had a mind of your own. These thugs have to catch you, Graham, because you will forever be a threat to Carson's capacity to rule the world!"

Silence fell over the room. Mary walked over and put

her arms around her father. "And you didn't mention that my dad also had the ability to find his way to God and take his family with him. He also knows what is eternally true."

"For Carson," Nancy said, "that's the worst!"

CHAPTER 68

GRAHAM THOUGHT about Nancy Marks's observations for several days. Walking slowly in front of Alice's cabin, Graham pondered Nancy's assertions. Apparently, her husband, Bill, realized many things that Graham had totally missed. She was right; Bridges had buckled under to Rashid, but Graham hadn't. As a result, this so-called *chief* wanted him dead. What a fool this man was! He might be pulling half the world around on a string like a yo-yo, but Rashid actually teetered on a tightrope stretched across an expanse the size of the Grand Canyon. If he was afraid of someone like Graham Peck, one of these days, the man would fall, headfirst.

"Graham!" Jackie called from the back porch. "Hurry in here. Alice Masterson is on the phone."

"Sure." Graham walked back to the house.

"She sounds terrified." Jackie handed him the telephone. "Find out what's happening."

"Alice, you okay?"

"No!" Alice said. "Hell's broken loose. The town of Rhinelander is being twisted inside out."

"What's happened?"

"Apparently an electronic surveillance device in Chicago took a picture of Matt in my car with two women that must have been your daughter and another woman from the jail. It took them a while to run the data down, but once they identified the license was from Wisconsin, they were on to me."

"Where are you?"

"I'm hiding at a friend's house. Remember the man in the overalls that came to our meetings?"

"Sure."

"I'm at his place, but I can't stay here long. Apparently, some head honcho in Chicago activated the Restored Church people in Rhinelander and they are in a townwide hunt to find me."

"Alice, come out here."

"That's why I'm calling. Many people around here know about my place in Prentice. You need to get out of there immediately. These Restored Church people have gone berserk. Remember those two men you confronted by the side of the church some weeks ago?"

"Sure."

"Well, they beat to death one of the men in my study group an hour ago. I'm not sure if I will get out of this scrape alive."

"Alice, we're coming in for you."

"No," Alice said firmly. "You must take your things and run before they figure out I could be hiding at my cabin, or that you might be there. They will eventually drive out there to check it out. Leave my car hidden somewhere in the trees. I'll find it later . . . if I'm alive. Get out now!"

"You're our friend," Graham agonized. "We can't simply . . ."

"Yes, you can, and you must. God has a special plan for your life. I realized that the first day I met you. You can't jeopardize that plan for me or anyone else. God's got His eye on you; now, you and your family go! God bless you, Graham. Good-bye, my friend. The Lord is with you." Alice hung up.

Graham stared at the silent telephone in astonishment, holding it in front of him as if he expected Alice's voice to continue rolling out.

"If you wish to make another call," the distant voice of some operator said. "Please hang up the phone and try again."

Graham slowly placed the telephone back in the cradle.

"What's happened?" Jackie said.

"Apparently we're going to have to run again."

"Where?"

"I don't know." Graham looked like a man with the weight of the world on his shoulders.

"I do!" Adah Honi said from the doorway. "I've been expecting something of this order to happen ever since we came from Chicago."

Matt walked in from his bedroom. "I overheard the conversation," he said. "Sounds like we're in trouble again."

Mary bounced out of the small room where she and

Nancy were staying. "You can hear everything said in this house. Nancy and I couldn't avoid overhearing what's going on out here. We want in on the decisions."

"Sure," Graham said and plopped down in an old chair at the table. "It's simple. We have a limited amount of time before Bridges' boys show up at our front gate."

"It is the hour for us to return to Israel," Adah said firmly. "The only safe place for the Peck family is with us where Frank Bridges' long arms can't reach."

"You're kidding," Jackie said.

"Not at all." Adah smiled. "If there is anybody in the world who knows how important it is to have the right hiding place when evil men are chasing you, it is the children of Holocaust survivors. We must get on an airplane and fly to Israel."

Graham scrutinized Adah's face. Not only was she not joking, she was probably right.

"I was looking at a map," Matthew said. "And it's only a hundred miles to Michigan and a short dash across the Upper Peninsula to Sault Sainte Marie, and we're in Canada."

"*Canada?*" Graham blinked.

"Sure, Dad. All we would need to do is drive to the Toronto airport, and that's less than a day's drive. No one would expect us to take such an international route. We could immediately catch a plane to Tel Aviv."

Adah smiled. "Your son is a very capable young man. I think he is right."

"There is only one problem," Graham said slowly. "Since Bridges' people identified Alice's car, we can guess they are on Mary's trail. We don't know for sure that the mark on her and Nancy's foreheads was neutralized. It's an assumption we've made, but we can't be certain."

Mary and Nancy looked at each other with speculation in their eyes. "Could they trace us across Canada?" Mary asked.

"I don't know," Graham said. "But it's a better risk than waiting here in Wisconsin where they already attacked and burned our last house to the ground." Graham thought for a minute. "They haven't located those checking accounts I set up before we first left Arlington Heights. Would there be ATMs in Israel?"

Adah nodded. "Sure. What's good here will work there."

Graham rubbed his temples. "Alice wouldn't mislead us. I think we need to get out of here in thirty minutes. Can we do it?"

"Sure, Dad," little Jeff said. "We can run like rabbits."

Graham looked around the room at each family member. "When I first heard of the biblical notion of the Tribulation, I had no idea we would be faced with these constant and difficult problems!" He shrugged. "Are we all in? Does everybody agree that we should go?" Graham looked around the circle. Each of the six persons firmly nodded their approval.

"Okay, bunnies! It's time to hop. Let's be on the road in thirty minutes!"

CHAPTER 69

IN ORDER TO AVOID the growing chaos in Rhinelander, the Peck family caravan went north to Fifield before turning through Chequamegon National Forest and on to Eagle River. While crossing over into Michigan, they noticed that the sky remained dark and overcast with the smell of stale smoke lingering in the air. On the other side of the state line, Graham flipped on the car radio to pick up a weather report.

"At this time," the announcer said, "police units from as far away as Merrill and Wausau have been dispatched to Rhinelander, Wisconsin. Fierce rioting has broken out across the entire town, and a number of people have already been killed."

Jackie grabbed Graham's arm. "Listen! It's even worse than Alice told us."

"Apparently a hotbed of reactionary militants have been identified as hiding in Rhinelander. Local citizens are protecting themselves and their homes," the announcer continued. "Shootings are occurring across the town. National Guard units have also been sent in to restore order. Please stay tuned. We will be reporting conditions as we receive them."

"I pray our friends have survived," Jackie said. "God help them!"

Graham glanced in the rearview mirror. Driving with Mary and Nancy Marks, Adah was staying a safe distance behind him while Matt brought up the rear. "I certainly pray for Alice," he said.

Jackie looked over the seat at George and Jeff in the rear. They appeared engrossed in the books they were reading. She leaned next to Graham's ear. "What do you really think about the marks on Mary's and Nancy's foreheads? Are they safe?"

Graham ran his hand nervously through his hair. "I think it's possible that the second swab application affected the computers while they were escaping from Chicago, but with time it's possible some computer expert has sorted out the varying signals," he said in a quiet, low voice. "It's highly conceivable that Bridges' agents may still be after them."

Jackie bit her lip. "I pray we can get into Canada before the Highway Patrol or some National Guard unit heads us off."

"I'm guessing we've got between seventy and a hundred miles before we get to Sault Sainte Marie. Let's hope and pray."

Jackie took his hand resting on the seat. "Let's silently ask God to protect us while we drive." She settled back against the seat and closed her eyes. Jackie's lips moved noiselessly while they sped down the highway.

For both Graham and Jackie, the miles dragged by, but their caravan didn't slow down or hesitate. Graham kept his eyes on the road and stayed exactly at the speed limit to avoid giving anyone an excuse to stop them. Just as they had fled from Illinois into Wisconsin months ago, now their family was fleeing the United States. Of course, Eldad Rafaeli had been with them then, and now he was buried in an obscure grave near their burned-down summer home in Tomahawk. The memory remained painful. So much had occurred with the violent incident and chases in Rhinelander, as well as Mary's attempt to run away turning into capture that it almost made Graham's head spin.

"Look!" George leaned over the seat and pointed. "That sign says we're about to leave the United States."

"Good job," Graham told his son. "You spotted the warning sign that we're almost to Sault Sainte Marie."

Suddenly Graham heard the unmistakable *thump-thump* of helicopter rotor. He glanced up and discovered a military helicopter flying directly above them. Jerking his hand free from Jackie's grip, he grabbed the steering wheel tightly.

"What is it?" Jackie asked.

"A helicopter is flying over us," Graham said. "We don't have time to waste." Quickly rolling down the window, he stuck his arm out and motioned for Adah and Matt to follow him in the bizarre turn he was about to make. "Hang on!" He jerked their car to the right.

Graham hit the gas and bumped onto the shoulder, illegally passing everyone in front of him. A quick glance in the rearview mirror revealed Adah and Matt were following close behind.

Drivers to his left stared in disbelief as Graham passed, but he only drove faster.

"Watch out, Graham!" Jackie warned. "If someone pulled over . . ."

"We'd be in a disastrous wreck," Graham finished the sentence for her. "I'm not going to let one of Bridges' helicopters stop us this close to the border." He blared the car's horn as they came to the end of the stretch pouring cars into the entrance to Canada. The car directly in front of him screeched to a halt, and Graham shot past and back onto the highway ahead of the vehicle. Without slowing down, he aimed for the Canadian gateway while he waved his arm up and down out the window. Graham could hear the helicopter getting louder, and he knew it was landing. At the last possible moment, he came to a screeching halt in front of an officer.

"What's going on here?" the Canadian border agent held up his hand and asked harshly while unfastening the gun on his hip.

"We're American political refugees!" Graham shouted out the window. "That chopper setting down is following us, and they mean business. We're being chased."

The Canadian agent looked up at the helicopter roaring louder as it came nearer the grass. Men with MP5 submachine guns and AK-47 rifles were poised to leap out. "Over there!" He pointed to a side road. "You people pull into that chute! You're now on Canadian soil. Those people can't touch you unless they want a full-scale war with us!"

CHAPTER 70

THE ENTIRE TOP FLOOR of Jerusalem's King David Hotel had been set aside for Hassan Rashid's party. The large entourage included people from around the world as well as major figures in the movement Rashid was creating. Leaders from Turkey were given special preference. Rashid's friends strolled around the elegant hotel, chatting, drinking, promenading, while he remained upstairs.

Because of the turmoil Rashid left behind in New York City, no official delegates from the United Nations were part of the chief's party. Fierce arguments continued over substituting the European Union for the Security Council, and the debate subsequently stopped all significant forward progress. Rashid had short-circuited the entire international organization.

Hassan Rashid also remained visibly in control of every aspect of the extraordinary treaty event. Having set up the signing in the new Jewish temple, he was carefully studying the treaty one more time to make sure his demands and intentions had been encoded in the document. As Rashid read, he liked what he saw.

Abu Shad burst into the room, waving a piece of paper in the air. "Sire!" he addressed Rashid. "A new discovery has just been sent to us from the European Space Agency. You must be aware of its contents."

Rashid looked up slowly from his final reading of the treaty. "This is *not* a good time for an interruption," he said coldly.

"Of course," Abu Shad agreed. "But a killer asteroid has been discovered coming directly toward the earth."

Rashid stopped and frowned. "What do you mean?"

"A large chunk of rock and ice abruptly went off course and is projected to strike around the area of New Zealand," Shad explained. "A researcher at the University of Pisa in Italy believes millions of people in that country and Australia could be killed. Darkness may well return over the entire world, and the economy of those two countries would be destroyed."

Rashid stiffened. "When is this supposed to occur?"

"Researchers are projecting it will happen in this time zone late this afternoon."

"I see." Rashid slowly rubbed his chin. "Interesting. At least we will have completed the signing by then, and it will have been carried on television all over the globe so no fool could have missed it. Even if the transmission is interrupted, we will still have accomplished our major goal today."

"But sire," Abu Shad protested, "millions could be killed!"

"I can't stop that from happening!" Rashid snapped. "We must concentrate on what is under our control. Do you understand?"

The secretary again bowed his head and nodded.

"This runaway asteroid event will be our rival for television coverage," Rashid thought out loud. "We must do

everything possible to make sure every nation under-
stands what I have accomplished." He pointed his finger
at the secretary. "Get out there and drum up media coverage. Make sure our television distribution across the
globe is total, and nothing about our signing is to be cut
off the air."

"As you say." Abu Shad bowed and started backing
out.

"One more thing. Is Frank Bridges out there?"

"Indeed."

"Send Bridges in at once."

Hassan Rashid returned to his reading of the treaty.
He didn't even look up when Bridges walked in, leaving
the mayor standing nervously in front of him. Finally,
Rashid turned over the last page. "Frank! Please sit
down."

"Thank you." Bridges slowly sat down.

"How is business going in Chicago?" Rashid asked
with almost idle indifference.

"Fine, sir." Bridges smiled. "Making excellent
progress. I left Meachem to handle unfinished business."

"Good. Good." Rashid smiled broadly. "Everything's
under control?"

Bridges squirmed. "I believe so."

"Believe so?" Rashid stood up and walked around to
the front of his desk. "*Believe* is such an, shall we say, *in-
definite* word. I prefer people who *know*, not believe."

Frank Bridges looked uncomfortable but said nothing.

"For example, months ago I asked you to find Graham

Peck." The sound of Rashid's voice kept getting louder. He leaned over until he was only inches from Bridges' nose. "Not only did you not obey that order, I understand Peck returned *to your jail* and stole his daughter out from under *your nose*, along with this Nancy Marks character whose husband tried to kill me!"

Bridges jumped. "How'd you find out?"

"I make it my business to know *everything*." Rashid pounded the corner of his desk.

"W-we're about to catch them," Bridges mumbled apologetically.

"And I've heard you use that phrase a hundred times before!" Rashid ranted. "You're always 'about' to do something. Well, I no longer have time for you to *about* do anything! You have failed me miserably, Frank."

Bridges cringed. "I am sure we will have this man back in custody by this evening."

"By this evening half of the world may be gone!" Rashid screamed. "I am getting ready to establish peace in Israel, which no one has been able to do, and you can't even catch one little man who once worked for you!" he mocked Bridges.

"But . . . ," Frank Bridges began.

"You are through!" Rashid drowned him out. "Finished! You are no longer on my staff. Get out of here!" His voice rose even higher. "I don't want ever to see you again!" Rashid pushed a button on his desk and two burly men hurried in.

"Please," Bridges begged. "I assure you we will find Peck quickly."

"*Out!*" Rashid shrieked. "Throw this guttersnipe into the street! Shoot him! Anything!"

The bodyguards grabbed Bridges' arms and hauled him from the room.

"Don't ever let me see your ungrateful, incompetent face again!" the chief yelled like a madman.

CHAPTER 71

FOR AN HOUR the Canadian border guards confronted and argued with the Illinois National Guard troopers who had leaped from the helicopter. In their own official uniforms, Canadian police squatted in position with their rifles aimed at the American military during the entire confrontation. Hundreds of people trying to cross the border had jumped out of their cars and were hiding behind trees or lying along the ditches. An atmosphere of fear and apprehension hung over the standoff, but the Canadian officers wouldn't back down. Eventually, the American National Guard soldiers got back in the helicopter. With the heavy *thump-thump* of the craft's motor rising into the sky, the Americans finally lifted off.

"You're safe now," the border agent in charge told Graham. "You can breathe easy. Those boys won't be back."

"You saved our lives. We will always remain grateful."

"Well, I know *you*," the Canadian said in a good ol'

boy tone. "The Americans sent us your picture several months ago. I always scrutinize those flyers when they come in, and I particularly noticed your face. Your hair's a different color, but when you came driving up today I knew at once who you were." He grinned. "*Real bad criminals!*"

Graham forced a smile.

The border agent chuckled. "I immediately saw the implications of their goings-on when I read that description of why they were chasing you, Mr. Peck. Sounds like the Americans thought you were quite a wild man. Typical political nonsense."

"It hasn't been easy," Graham said. "They gave us a good run for our money."

"And the rest of your trip won't be easy either. Just before this attack occurred, we received a warning that an asteroid may hit the other side of the world. No one knows what it will do, but we're going to have problems. Looks like the world's going to get a real shakin'. I'd suggest you get on your way quickly."

"Thank you, sir." Graham shook hands with the man. "We'll pay careful attention." He quickly returned to the family cars where all six people were huddled together.

"What'd the man say?" Matthew asked.

"He thinks we're safe now, but we need to get on our way because a meteor of some sort is going to hit the other side of the earth later in the day. Big problems are projected to follow."

"Remember what the book of Revelation warned?" Adah Honi exclaimed. "The angel will blow his trumpet and a mountain of fire will fall into the sea killing millions of people and destroying many ships. Is that not what is coming?" She glanced around at each person. "We must prepare for a difficult experience. No one can know what this will do to Canada."

"That's a cheery thought!" Graham said sardonically. "I think it means we better drive like maniacs toward the Toronto airport."

Adah glanced at her watch. "In Jerusalem, on the other side of the world, the Antichrist is about to sign his infamous treaty with Israel. I—I think this asteroid is the Lord's warning to the world about what this political action means."

"But will anyone understand?" Mary asked.

"If Alice Masterson is still alive," Graham answered, "she certainly will!"

CHAPTER 72

AN ISRAELI ORCHESTRA assembled especially for the treaty signing huddled together at the back of the sloping courtyard in front of the ancient Western Wall. The large orchestra played triumphant entry marches continuously while the delegates filed in for the historic moment proclaimed around the world. A recently installed speaker system blared the music across the top of the entire Temple Mount.

Days earlier Israeli troops had cordoned off the entire Jewish section of the Old City and scoured every inch of the area to guarantee complete security for such a momentous occasion. Limousines pulled up in front of the rock walls of the Dung Gate entrance into the ancient city, and dignitaries from nations all over the world confidently crossed the entryway and ascended the steps to the Holy Mount.

Between the Dome of the Rock and the Al-Aqsa Mosques, an incomplete but imposing temple had been erected. Lacking the marble-and-gold exterior that would eventually complete the outside of the lofty structure, the building still towered above the Dome of the Rock, or, as it was often called, the Mosque of Omar. Obviously every Muslim in the world had been offended by the construction as well as the height. Many of the outer courts had not been completed, but the entire edifice stood as a lasting offense to the Islamic world.

Nothing like a Solomon's Porch or Beautiful Gate had yet been constructed around the building, but the plans for the present temple had followed along the original lines of the first structure built by Solomon in 960 BC, and later destroyed by the Babylonians. Standing on a platform ten feet higher than the surrounding ground area, the temple had ten steps up to the platform that ran inside to a bronze altar used for burnt offerings, and behind it was the sacred room known as the Holy of Holies. The area for the treaty signing had been planned on this ten-foot-high outer platform just in front of the final entry into the temple proper. Rashid obviously believed it provided the perfect setting not only for today's event, but for his future plans as well.

The hot sun burned with blistering heat while numerous television cameras captured every aspect of the celebration. Continuing their musical backdrop, the Israeli orchestra played passionately as the delegates took their seats in chairs in front of the temple proper. At five minutes to the hour, Israeli Prime Minister Dov Landau walked in with his cabinet, and they sat in their seats on the platform immediately in front of the temple entrance. The orchestra picked up the pace and the force of the music conveyed a majestic aura of hallowedness over the entire Mount.

Exactly on the hour a helicopter descended on the large empty area behind the Mosque of Omar, and only Hassan Jawhar Rashid got out of the chopper. In an unusual gesture, he wore a black cape over his shoulders with a golden lining that shimmered in the bright sunlight. Walking with determination, Rashid marched in front of the assembly with a sense of absolute authority and took his place opposite Prime Minister Landau and his cabinet. The throng of dignitaries broke into raucous cheering and applause.

Landau's minister of defense walked to the recently constructed speaker's podium and welcomed the delegates by announcing the purpose of the occasion. He was followed by Dov Landau, who made a statement about Israeli hopes for future peace and the desire to live in harmony with their neighbors. The prime minister then turned to the small table and signed the treaty. The crowd roared its applause.

Finally, all eyes turned to Rashid. Slowly and with great dignity, the chief stood like the king of beasts and walked to the table holding the treaty. With a single, quick swipe of the pen, he signed the document and then turned to the podium.

"This day marks a turning point in world history," Rashid began. "I thank the prime minister of Israel and his cabinet for their farsightedness in signing this document, which will end hostility between the Arab world and the nation of Israel. We can now turn our expectations to years of peace and prosperity." The assembly of significant and pompous functionaries broke into enthusiastic applause. Rashid smiled and nodded his appreciation.

"It is important that we recognize how this moment has come to pass," Rashid continued. "Using all the resources I have with *my* oil industry, *my* military capacities, and *my* diplomatic contacts around the globe, *I* have stopped the military opposition Israel faced. *I* did not accomplish this with threats of destruction or oppression, but by appealing to the best intentions of all parties involved."

Rashid stopped and let total silence fall over the entire crowd. "I have given new meaning to your struggles, new purpose to your labors. *I am* the source of ultimate meaning for citizens around this globe. You can call on me to protect you, provide for you, and sustain you. *I am* your hope and the completion of your dreams. You can trust in me forever. Lean on me and you will find fulfillment. *I am* your peace."

Many of the delegates squinted in the hot sunlight, not sure they had heard Rashid correctly.

"*I am* now your chief and the supreme commander of the mightiest army the world has ever known. It is I who will guarantee your security. You can rest in the knowledge that *I am* your hope."

At that moment the ground started to shake slightly. Clouds churned, and blotches of deep purple mingled with streaks of angry red shot across the sky. Murmurs of fear arose from the audience, and Rashid gripped the podium tightly, knowing the asteroid had already struck. The platform beneath his feet trembled slightly, and he noticed the sky was turning dark across the far horizon.

"Fear not!" Rashid shouted. "*I am* here that you may have life! *I am* your stability."

The ground continued to quiver, and the delegates turned to one another in concern. Rashid watched their consternation carefully. At this moment, only he completely appreciated the pinnacle on which he was poised. Not only did he command an invincible military force, he had declared himself to be divine. These slow onlookers hadn't gotten it yet, but their chief was positioned to be the religious authority of the entire world. Hassan Jawhar Rashid was mighty, and he would never again need anyone! After he worked his way inside Israel's nuclear power plant at Dimona where they stored enough radioactive material to fashion three to four hundred nuclear bombs, *then he would crush Israel.*

CHAPTER 73

THE PECKS' CARAVAN wound across Canada and above Lake Huron while summer kept the sun up longer. After passing Sudbury, Ontario, Graham headed south toward Toronto. The sun was starting to set when he realized that the highway had started shaking. Immediately slowing the car, he noticed the sky. Clouds appeared to be racing away from them.

"What in the world is going on?" Jackie asked.

"I don't know." Graham thought for a moment. "Yes, I do! It's the *asteroid*! There must have been an impact somewhere on the other side of the globe."

"Could it make the world shake?" Dismay filled Jackie's voice.

"Probably not," Graham said, "but it could cause the plates underneath the land masses to move, and that would create earthquakes, volcanos, tremors, anything. We better check on our other cars."

Pulling over to the shoulder of the highway, Graham stopped the car. Adah and Matthew drove up behind him.

Adah stuck her head out the car window. "There's a problem. My car shakes."

"Yeah," Graham said. "It's the highway."

Matthew got out of his vehicle. "Did I feel the ground rolling?"

"Afraid so," Graham said. "I think an asteroid hit somewhere, and we're now feeling the repercussion." He looked up at the sky. "Clouds are getting strange."

Matt studied the huge white pillow-like forms racing to the north. "The collision must have happened to the south."

"Quite possibly," Graham said. "I'm sure conditions will worsen. We need to move on as quickly as we can."

"We have no alternative but to drive faster?" Adah asked.

"No," Graham said, "we must drive more carefully. I have no idea what will follow, but the sky could well turn black." He hurried back to his car. "Let's get out of here."

The sky soon darkened, and the winds picked up with treacherous force. Slowing down to fifty miles per hour, Graham's vehicle swayed back and forth as the powerful winds shook them. Eventually he could see only the yellow line dividing the highway and had to slow down to thirty miles per hour.

"Maybe we ought to pull over and stop," Jackie said to Graham. "I'm afraid it's getting too dangerous to continue."

"Yeah, I think you're right. Let's see what we can pick up." He pulled to the side of the road and turned on the radio.

Breaking up with static and poor reception, little seemed to be coming in but garbled sounds. Finally Graham tuned in a continuous news station broadcast from Toronto.

"As was anticipated, Chief Hassan Jawhar Rashid

signed a treaty with Israel today, and promised to end all hostilities with that country. The chief made it clear these efforts were singularly the result of his doings, and Rashid insisted he had personally become the guarantor of world stability."

"Adah's search of the Scripture certainly proved to be exactly on target," Jackie said. "The Antichrist has made an agreement with Israel that will prove to be a source of great pain for that nation as well as the world."

"Now to the major story gripping the entire world tonight," the announcer continued. "An asteroid has smashed into the Coral Sea off the tip of Papua New Guinea and the east coast of Australia. Estimating the size of the meteor to be somewhere around one kilometer, the collision has shaken the world's core and has sent tidal waves across New Guinea and down Australia's coastline beyond Brisbane and down toward Sydney. Coastal towns like Cooktown, Townsville, and Mackay have been completely destroyed. Early estimates indicate at least five million people have been killed, but no one is certain. Conditions in New Guinea prevent estimates of a death toll there yet, but southern coastal towns around the South Cape are completely gone. Probably several million citizens have died. At this time, no one is able to identify how many ships and boats have been lost, but the number remains perilously high."

"Conditions sound as bad as we feared," Jackie said. "Bless all those people who died." She tapped the radio tune bar. "Our reception certainly is badly distorted. I've never heard the static so intense."

"Many countries in Southeast Asia and the Middle East experienced severe earthquakes. In Canada, we have . . ." Suddenly the static completely drowned out all reception.

Graham turned off the radio. "That's unfortunate! We can't find out what's ahead of us, and we need to know."

"Do you think air travel will be affected?" Jackie asked.

"I don't know," Graham said. "Quite possibly. That's our next big hurdle."

CHAPTER 74

THE PECKS' CARAVAN pulled into the parking garage of the Toronto airport at ten o'clock in the morning. The sky remained overcast with black clouds, and the radio reception continued to be somewhat distorted, but it appeared airplanes were flying. Gathering only what they could carry, the family hurried into the terminal to search for the El Al Airlines desk. Graham brought up the rear, carrying his briefcase containing their passports, papers, and documents.

"I know we are leaving many important items behind," Jackie told the children, "but we must travel light, and we'll find new toys in Israel."

"Yeah," Jeff said. "New stuff!"

"It's okay," George said. "I've still got my palm-sized transistorized magnifier. We're just glad to be here."

"You've got fine kids," Nancy Marks said.

"Absolutely." Jackie hugged both the boys. "You're good guys."

"There it is!" Adah pointed to her left. "There's El Al!"

The family quickly joined the passenger line. In five minutes Graham stood in front of the agent, presenting passports, payments, the political asylum order, anything needed to purchase a one-way ticket to Israel.

"One way?" Jackie mused. "Sounds *so* painful."

Graham hugged her. "Don't worry. We're going to be okay. We've made it through the dark night. Our problems are over."

Jackie forced a smile, but her eyes teared. "I—I just find it *so hard* to leave our home, our country." She buried her face in Graham's shirt.

The ticket agent quickly tagged their luggage and slung the pieces onto the slow-moving line of bags. In a matter of minutes their few remaining possessions had been tagged and were drifting down the conveyor belt to disappear into the black hole at the end of the counter.

"I believe everyone is ready," the agent finally said. "We do not expect any problems after this asteroid collision. Our planes are flying acceptably this morning. You are seated together, and you should board in forty-five minutes at Gate 33." The woman smiled. "Have a nice trip."

The family turned away from the desk and started walking, much more slowly than they had come in, toward the escalator that would take them up to the passenger lounges. With a final feeling of nostalgia, Graham turned for one last look at the terminal, the ticket counter, the world they were leaving behind. At that instant, he felt like lightning hit him!

Moving up through the line to the El Al ticket agent was a man he knew all too well. With his sinister eyes locked on the woman ticket agent, the thug would forever and always be terrifying to Graham. They were being followed *by Al Meachem*!

"Quick!" Graham said, pulling the family close to him. "Don't look back! Get on this escalator and walk through the security check as fast as you can. We're being followed!"

"God help us!" Adah exploded. A man going down the escalator turned and looked at her in surprise. "We are so close to escaping!"

"Listen to me carefully," Graham told the family. "When we get to the top, I'm going back, but you go on. If I'm not there when they load the airplane, you get on that jet and get out of here. Do you understand?"

"We can't leave without you!" Jackie protested.

"Yes! You must!" Graham insisted. "Matthew, make sure everyone is on that airplane. You got me?"

"Yes sir," Matt said slowly.

Graham kissed his wife. "I'll be fine and probably nothing will happen, but keep walking." He pressed the briefcase into Jackie's hand, turned, and started back down the escalator.

"Graham . . . ," Jackie called after him, but he didn't look back.

CHAPTER 75

G RAHAM PECK didn't look back at his family as he descended the escalator. He couldn't let them see in his eyes the apprehension he felt building, but Graham knew that a severe response might be required from him in the next few minutes. He had to resolutely set his face toward the hard task ahead.

The chances were good that he would be forced to confront Meachem, and that would be dangerous. The only way Al could have found them was to trace the nanorobot markings on his daughter's and Nancy Marks's foreheads. No question about it! Meachem must have been behind them somewhere when they entered Canada. Unless Graham could stop Meachem, the man would follow them around the world until he killed them. It would be far better to confront Meachem now and let the family escape than to have everyone taken captive by this vicious deputy of the mayor. If nothing else, he would fight Meachem to the death in front of the ticket counter rather than allow him to cause his family harm.

At the bottom of the escalator, Graham ducked his head and quickly walked up behind the ticket line Meachem was standing in. Instantly, Graham realized that a large support pole in front of him ran up to the ceiling. He darted behind the white metal shaft, which would partially conceal him if Meachem looked around. He was still close enough to both see and hear what went on at the ticket counter.

The lady in front of Al Meachem collected her tickets and walked away. Meachem stepped forward and slipped something out of his pocket that he flashed in the agent's face. The woman looked at what he held and frowned.

"I'm an emissary of the American government," Meachem said. "I need your help in finding a fugitive fleeing from justice with his family. Graham Peck is the man's name."

"I'm sorry," the agent said. "We just sell tickets."

Graham saw Meachem lean forward and mumble something Graham couldn't understand. The agent looked taken aback and didn't respond.

"I don't have any time to wait," Meachem said forcefully. "Don't fool with me!"

Graham could see that the woman looked angry. She reached out her arm as if fumbling for a signal on the counter. "Please leave," the ticket agent said forcefully.

"I'm not going anywhere." Meachem's voice became more pointed. "You'll give me assistance, or I'll have the police all over you."

Suddenly two plainclothesmen rushed past Graham and grabbed each side of Meachem, pushing him forward across the top of the ticket counter. The agents started frisking Al before Meachem even realized what was happening.

One of the agents pulled an electronic device out of

Meachem's coat pocket that must have been what he was using to follow Mary. The other man slapped a small handgun taken out of Meachem's shoulder holster up on the counter. Without saying a word, they pulled Al's arms behind his back and handcuffed him.

The ticket agent shook her finger in Meachem's face. "This clown was trying to force me to give out information on passengers," she charged. "What a jerk!"

"I'm with the United States government!" Meachem shouted back.

"Yeah? Well, we're plainclothes officers with the RCMP," one of the men said. "You'd better be able to fully substantiate your claims, or you're going to be with us for a good long visit."

The Mounties jerked Meachem around, marched him across the ticket line, and down the hall. Peck slowly slid around the other side of the metal pole and walked up to the woman at the desk.

"Thank you," Graham said. "I appreciate your help."

"I read your political asylum form when you picked up the tickets," the agent said. "And this nut was flashing a card that identified him as working for the mayor of Chicago. That meaningless badge won't buy him a bag of peanuts up here in Canada."

Graham shook her hand. "But it may get him a free stay in your slammer for a while."

"We don't get one of these thrills every day," the woman said with a grin. "But it certainly keeps business from getting dull."

CHAPTER 76

G RAHAM HURRIEDLY CLIMBED the escalator again and rushed down the hall. He struggled to keep a casual demeanor through the security check, but once past the metal detector, Graham ran down the hallway toward Gate 33 as fast as his feet would carry him. He slowed when he saw the family huddled together near the far wall in front of the door leading to the airplane. Obviously they were silently praying.

"Your prayers were answered," Graham puffed as he walked up. "We're fine now."

"What happened?" Matthew frantically asked.

"Al Meachem was taken into custody by the Royal Canadian Mounted Police. He pushed his luck with the wrong ticket agent."

Nancy Marks started crying softly. "I was so afraid! That evil man terrorized me in the prison." She wiped her eyes. "I feared he'd catch me again."

Adah patted Nancy on her shoulder. "We're going to board this airplane in a few moments. Once it's off the ground, we won't be worrying anymore about those gangsters from Chicago ever again."

"Dad?" Mary beckoned to Graham to follow her. "Come over here a second."

Graham followed his daughter to an isolated portion of the passenger lounge. "Yes, Mary?"

"That man followed us because he picked up on the forehead markings that Nancy and I have, didn't he?"

Graham shook his head. "It doesn't make any difference now," he said.

"Yes, it does!" Mary held her ground. "I want to know the truth. That's how they caught up with us, right?"

Graham nodded slowly. "I'm afraid so."

"I've worried about the marking every since Bridges' people put it on me." Mary folded her arms over her chest. "I don't want to leave this country and take the problem with me to Israel. It has to stop right here."

"But there isn't anything we can do."

"Yes, there is," Mary insisted. "Remember that device with the red and green buttons that your secretary, Sarah Cates, sneaked out of the mayor's offices?"

"Yes," Graham said carefully.

"You used that gadget the night Jake Pemrose was chasing us out of Chicago. When you pressed the red button, it caused the nanorobots to bore into his head, and that's what caused the car wreck."

"And?"

"For weeks I've been thinking about the green button. Why wouldn't that disarm the nanorobot markings?"

"Mary, we have no earthly way to know what the green button would do."

"The gizmo was made by some scientist at the Microfabrication Research Lab. Remember? The green color has to be positive. I want you to try it on me right now."

"I can't do that!" Graham protested. "If the red button killed Jake Pemrose, what might the green one do? The results could be devastating."

"Green is a good color," Mary argued back. "That button has to stand for something positive, and I want to try it right now."

"Look," Graham said dogmatically, "we can't experiment with something so potentially dangerous in the middle of this airport."

"You did!" Mary fired back. "You just got through battling on our behalf with that creep from Chicago. That's no different from my completing an experiment that may once and for all wipe out the curse and stop the chase."

"But . . ."

Mary kissed him on the cheek. "Dad, let's not get into one of our infamous fights. In that horrible jail in Chicago, I gave my life to Jesus Christ. I belong to Him. I'm ready to trust Him to take me through this cleansing process, exactly as He freed me of my past mistakes and sins."

"But Mary!" Graham protested. "What if it kills you?"

"Then I want to die in this airport rather than jeopardize the family in Israel." Mary held out her hand. "Let's do it."

Graham squeezed his eyes shut tightly and took a deep, deep breath. "Mary, I don't even know where that device is."

"In your briefcase," she answered instantly. "I saw it in there when we were loading up to leave back in Prentice."

Graham sagged. "You're sure you want to do this?"

"Absolutely."

"Well . . . I guess the time while you were gone from us taught me that I must respect your decisions more than I did in the past. This is the hardest thing I've done in my entire life." Graham walked over and took the briefcase from Jackie.

Mary beckoned for Nancy Marks to join her. "Nancy and I have talked about this problem," Mary said, reaching out for Nancy's hand. "We're both in agreement. We want to stand together when you push the green button." Mary and Nancy closed their eyes.

Graham took the small flat device out of the briefcase and held it in his hand. He stared apprehensively at the metal device. "Lord, help us," he prayed out loud, and pushed the green button.

Nothing happened.

Graham pushed the button again. "Did you feel anything?"

Mary opened her eyes. "Not a solitary thing."

Nancy rubbed her forehead. "I think they're gone!"

"We couldn't see those infinitesimal nanorobots disappear anyway," Mary said. "Don't you see? That's the most positive sign of all."

"Wait a minute," George interrupted. "I've got that palm-sized transistorized magnifier that Jeff and I play with." He dug into his backpack. "Maybe it will show something."

Graham took the magnifier and held it over Nancy's hand she had used to rub her forehead. He squinted, slowly examining every inch of her fingertips. "My gosh!" Graham exclaimed. "I can barely see them, but there's a faint line of gray color under this magnifier. The nanorobots did come off!"

The family cheered, and people around them looked up in surprise.

"We are ready to board El Al Flight 324 to Jerusalem," a voice boomed over the loudspeaker. "Please have your boarding passes out as you prepare to enter the airplane."

With their boarding passes in hand, the family quickly checked through the gate and hurried down the long hallway into the airplane. Without waiting for further instruction, they piled into their seats in the large Boeing 747 jet, and immediately buckled their seat belts.

Having taken a seat next to her father, Mary snuggled up to Graham. "We did it, Dad! Who would ever believe that we'd survive such a harrowing time?"

"It's been a real tribulation!" Graham agreed. "And it's far from over yet, but we escaped being tagged."

"I know," Mary said, "God surely had His hand on us. We're leaving this hemisphere knowing that the best is ahead."

Graham looked out the window as the airplane finished filling with passengers. Soon they would be in the air and gone from the chaos they had endured.

The stewardess made her usual announcements, and the airplane started rolling down the runway. The roar of the jet engines increased as the 747 picked up the speed needed for the takeoff. In a few moments, Graham felt the airplane lift off, and then heard the wheels retracting. They were on their way.

Looking out over the lush forests and fields of Ontario, he watched Toronto become smaller and smaller. In the months behind them, the Pecks had lived through the most harrowing demands any family could know, but they had come out together, and their lives had been dramatically touched by a grace beyond anything Graham had ever known. He was ready to live by that power, not only for the rest of his life, but for eternity.

What was ahead? Graham Peck had no idea, but whatever it was, it would happen in Israel.